Unaccustomed
Spirits

SCEPTRE

Also by Elizabeth Pewsey

Children of Chance
Divine Comedy
Unholy Harmonies
Volcanic Airs

Unaccustomed
Spirits

ELIZABETH PEWSEY

Janet

With much love

Lizzy

SCEPTRE

First published in 1997 by Hodder and Stoughton
A division of Hodder Headline PLC
A Sceptre Book

10 9 8 7 6 5 4 3 2 1

British Library Cataloguing in Publication Data

A CIP catalogue record for this title is available
from the British Library.

ISBN 0 340 68564 6

Typeset by Palimpsest Book Production Limited,
Polmont, Stirlingshire
Printed and bound in Great Britain by
Mackays of Chatham PLC, Chatham, Kent

Hodder and Stoughton
A division of Hodder Headline PLC
338 Euston Road
London NW1 3BH

For Sam and Mike

'Would the name be Byng?'

Cleo dragged her suitcase across the chilly and deserted station booking hall. She could hear train doors being slammed shut from the platform on the other side of the footbridge and then the train pulling out of the station with a shrill blast from the engine as it disappeared into the darkness.

She looked out between the stone pillars to where the taxis were waiting. A lugubrious face peered at her out of a lowered car window.

'Byng?' he said again.

'Yes.' Cleo manoeuvred her heavy bag towards the the taxi.

'For Hazard?' the man went on, making no effort to get out of his cab and help her.

'Yes, for Hazard.'

'You're going to Haphazard House?'

Oh, come on, thought Cleo, exasperated by the interrogation. Was it likely that there would be two Byngs off the London train? Each going to a different place in the same remote Eyotshire village on a bitterly cold winter's night? Hardly.

This time the driver didn't wait for an answer, but heaved himself out, took Cleo's bag from her, and opened the taxi door. Cleo sank gratefully into her seat and closed her eyes.

'Tired, eh?' said the driver with satisfaction as he pulled away.

Cleo was tired; too tired to say anything. The driver would probably take that for standoffishness, but no, her silence seemed to cheer him up. He broke into a music hall whistle and darted at hair-raising speed through the busy Eyot traffic, braking abruptly as a light turned to red.

They had stopped by a church. Not one of the stars of the city; a redbrick, morose affair this one, clearly a house of God which was designed to bring you to repentance and a sense of your general unworthiness. Maybe not, though, Cleo mused, as a rather jolly looking priest emerged, a rolled poster under his arm, which he unfurled and held up against the notice board. It was a lurid orange in colour, with bold black lettering. 'Marriage,' it proclaimed. 'Is yours in danger? Discussion group here on . . .'

And then the taxi surged forward, and the priest and his notice vanished into the distance.

'Terrible, that junction,' said the driver. 'Always a hold-up there.'

The words of the marriage service floated into Cleo's mind. Who was it that had got married according to the old order of service? She'd been to a lot of weddings over the last year or so, not surprising once you were into your twenties and your friends began to think permanence. Not a cheery start to a modern marriage, that service.

It hadn't been her cousin Justinia's wedding; her ghastly Digby had chosen the Noddy version for his nuptials. Not very surprising that the marriage hadn't survived.

Not Val and Magdalena's wedding either, that had been a hugger-mugger affair if you like; the register office and then a swift blessing in the Mountjoy chapel, with a smug bishop uttering platitudes. How cross Val had been, Cleo remembered.

And she hadn't gone to her friend Prue's wedding, which had taken place in Budapest. In the spring, Cleo reminded herself, she would be seeing Prue again. And the new baby. Something to look forward to, a trip to Hungary.

They had crossed and recrossed the river now, as you did in Eyot, and were driving past rows of grey, stone houses.

Cleo shut her eyes. It was Lydia's wedding, she remembered quite suddenly. Lydia and Alban. Alban, who had grumbled so furiously about a church wedding, and had ended up in the cathedral. 'I'll choose the music,' he had said. 'At least we can make sure that won't be crass. And the Book of Common Prayer, please; I'm not having any of that happy-clappy rubbish at my wedding.'

And there it was, suddenly crystal clear in her ears: . . .*not by any to be enterprised unadvisedly, lightly or wantonly* . . .

Wantonly, there was a good word. How did it go on? To be undertaken *reverently, discreetly, advisedly, soberly.* And the rest of it, what was it? Something about carnal lusts and appetites. Cleo yawned, and rubbed her eyes. She knew all about those. Funny, Lydia agreeing to be married with such severe words, when she was so laid-back.

Although, come to think of it, the severity would suit Perry. He did nothing unadvisedly, and as for discreetly . . . No one more discreet than Perry.

The taxi-driver spoke, startling Cleo out of her reverie.

'Years since I've been to Haphazard House,' he ventured as he drove at speed along the twisting, narrow, country roads. 'Old lady lives there all by herself, doesn't she?'

'Did,' said Cleo, sinking further into her upturned collar; the car appeared to have no heating, or none that the driver wanted to use.

'Of course, she wouldn't have been that lonely,' he went on with a braying laugh and a sharp jerk of the steering wheel to turn the car through a pair of dilapidated gateposts. 'It's haunted, you know.'

'Haunted?' She hadn't bargained on haunted, not that she believed in ghosts, of course.

'It's an old house, very old. Lots of tales to be told about it, I dare say,' the taxi-driver said obliquely as they jolted over the potholes in the drive. He scrunched to a halt in front of a square pile of house, then muttered, reversed, and drove back to an archway.

'Here you are, then. Main door's that one there. Expecting you, whoever's here, look at the lights. Music, too, maybe you're in for a party. Thank you, enjoy your stay.'

Cleo sneezed, felt for a handkerchief, and looked around her. The main door seemed to be a pointed affair of dark wood directly in front of her, and it was through the mullioned windows of that part of the house that light spilled out on to the frozen ground.

She lifted the heavy knocker and gave it a bang, then waited.

Nothing. Just faint sounds. Of what, a guitar? floating out on to the still air. Who was there? Were they listening to music, and therefore unable to hear the knocker?

Another big bang. Whoever was in there must have heard that.

Cleo was beginning to feel very cold. She gave the door an impatient shove, and to her surprise, it swung open with a grotesque squeal. Oh well, she thought, stepping inside, and lugging her bag after her.

'Hello?' she called. 'Is anybody there?'

The music stopped abruptly, but there were no answering voices, no hurrying footsteps. What on earth was going on?

Fuelled by her growing indignation, she set off to find someone. She had come into a huge hall, and was facing a wide wooden staircase with panelled walls which led up to a galleried landing. The wood was scuffed and hadn't seen polish for years, by the look of it. Bits of the banister were missing or dislodged and hanging out at odd angles.

Very Gothick, in Cleo's opinion. But what a lovely staircase. Jacobean? Anyway, she wasn't going to venture up the stairs; better try the ground floor first.

Rooms led one into the other, in a very antique way. They were all in a dreadful state, with damp blotching what must have been beautiful wallpapers, ornately plastered ceilings which looked as though they had a fungal complaint, and once-fine curtains hanging in rags and tatters at the windows.

Strangely, the rooms didn't smell fusty; they must have been kept aired. Presumably by whoever was in the house now. Cousin Henry had spoken of a Mrs Grigson, from the village, who was keeping an eye on the place.

No luck on the ground floor, so Cleo descended into the basement. Here also the lights were all on; Mrs Grigson must be down in the kitchen. Visions of a warm and cosy room and a cup of tea quickened Cleo's steps.

The kitchen was the widest door along a passage which branched off into a warren of cubby holes and sculleries. Cleo turned the large door handle and went in. It was a big, old-fashioned kitchen, complete with green dresser, well-scrubbed table, and a Belfast sink. It was also, Cleo noticed thankfully, very warm; an ancient Rayburn stood a little forlornly in a vast chimney space.

On the table was a note.

Dear Miss, read Cleo. *Have had to go as my Roy is poorly. Will come tomorrow if I can. Food in larder and tea in tin on shelf marked Bisto. Bed made up in Dragon Room, hot water bottle under the sink, you will need one. Very sorry, yours truly, Brenda Grigson.*

'Poorly, indeed,' said Giles, lounging over the banister rail.

Lambert shook his head. 'A sot, is Roy Grigson. He has no head for strong liquor.'

Giles fluttered an elegant hand. 'No head for anything, a perfect blockhead in all respects. Now, who is this? A cousin of the late Maria Hazard, did I hear Mrs Grigson say?'

Lambert liked to get things right. 'A cousin of her nephew's, I believe.'

'Ha, a Mountjoy,' said Giles. 'One of that wild and wicked family, well, we'll see about that.'

'I must say, she doesn't look wild and wicked to me.'

'Even so,' said Giles after a more concentrated look at the drooping figure in the hall below. 'Young, and beautiful, too, if it weren't for the dark rings under her eyes.'

'Leave her alone,' advised Lambert. 'What she needs is a good night's sleep.'

'Go your way, I wouldn't dream of disturbing her,' said Giles, affronted.

What with the journey and perhaps the clear, cold air, Cleo felt as tired as she had when she had first become ill. Sitting slumped in a chair by the stove, Cleo thought back to those grim weeks before she finally succumbed to illness and rest.

First there had been the feeling tired, the never being on top of her work, the days ending in red-eyed exhaustion at seven o'clock. She'd had a quick snack in a bar, and several drinks, before going home to snatch a few uneasy hours of sleep before starting again. Up early, forcing herself to appear cool and well-groomed and hungry for money-making. Into the office by eight.

Late this morning, Cleo, five past, we appreciate keenness in our people, we do notice a positive attitude.

Then had come the morning when she had woken up with the terrible sore throat and a throbbing head. She had struggled through the day, which ended, willy-nilly, at six, when her stomach finally revolted against all the aspirins she had swallowed during the day.

Cleo's thrown up in the lav.

What have you been up to, Cleo? As if we didn't know.

Cleo felt too ill to make any riposte, to scorn the innuendoes.

And, defeated, the phone call to the rarely visited doctor. *It has to be an appointment first thing in the morning, it's vital I get to work as soon as I can.*

The doctor would prescribe some vitamins, or antibiotics. She would soon be back to normal.

2

Cleo stirred, yawned, looked around the silent kitchen. Incredibly silent, not only inside the house, but outside. No traffic, no voices. Just fells and open skies and empty fields.

Then her mind drifted back to the stuffy little doctor's room. She had been completely taken aback by the verdict. It was so unexpected.

'Shingles?'

'No question about it.'

Cleo looked warily at the doctor, a motherly woman in her comfortable, baggy clothes; a motherliness belied by the set of her jaw and her steely eyes. 'Why?' she said.

The doctor drew her lips together and snapped her pen shut. 'It's a virus. You've caught a virus. It is much the same as chicken-pox.'

'I've had chicken-pox.'

'That's why it's shingles this time. It's more painful than chicken-pox.'

Cleo agreed with that. 'How long will it take to go?'

'It depends partly on how much care you take of yourself. Do you live alone?'

'I share a flat. But I can't stay at home, I have to work.'

The doctor gave a beaming smile. 'Oh, I think not. No question of that. You're quite ill, you know, and this isn't a matter of working through a cold.' She looked at Cleo's notes. 'You seem very healthy, nothing here. Are you run down? Worries? At work? Boyfriend? Family problems?'

'No,' said Cleo. 'I'm getting married on Saturday.'

'Dear me. Big affair, church, lots of guests?'

'No, Chelsea Town Hall and friends for dinner at a restaurant, actually.'

'Postpone it.' The doctor was definite. 'It's no way to start your married life, with shingles. And your husband will probably catch it from you, and he'll be very ill, men always are. Of course, it's up to you.'

She became brisk, writing out a prescription for this and that. 'Although, of course, being a virus, there's not much we can do.'

It was clearly time to go, and Cleo got up in a spasm of evil, needling pain.

'Hurts, doesn't it?' said the doctor triumphantly. 'Told you so. Put it off, dear, there'll be no delights of the marriage bed for you for a few weeks.'

Cleo closed the door carefully behind her, longing to give it a good bang. Ping! went the old-fashioned brass bell on the doctor's desk, as a sign to the receptionist to send in the next patient.

The receptionist was a thin and spiky woman with long purple nails. She hadn't been properly trained as a doctor's receptionist, that was clear, because she was kind and friendly and helpful.

'You look really dreadful,' she said sympathetically. 'You get yourself home and into bed. How did you come here? Walked?' She made a clicking sound. 'I'll call you a taxi, you'll never make it back, not in your state.'

The cab rumbled and shook in the dense London traffic. Cleo was feeling iller by the moment, and thoroughly depressed as she looked out on to the rain-sodden pavements. She could see a few dirty autumnal leaves dribbled together in soggy heaps in the gutter.

Winter in London, she thought. I hate it.

The driver said something incomprehensible, and suddenly swung out of the motionless line of traffic and darted down a side street. Cleo sighed. She knew all about these detours, which invariably ended in another, even worse jam. Then the houses, rows of redbrick Victorian terraces, began to seem familiar, and then she knew where she was.

She slid back the glass between the back and the driver. 'Stop!'

she said loudly in his ear. He made an uncouth noise, and pulled in to the kerb.

'We aren't halfway there,' he said.

'I know,' said Cleo. 'I've changed my mind.' She paid him, giving him far too large a tip in her pain and longing to be indoors and lying down, not standing here in a chill, damp wind.

Up the stairs, tread, tread, tread, every step an effort of will and muscle. Up to the top floor, a neat dark-red door. Cleo couldn't be bothered to look for her key; she just rattled the knocker.

The door opened. 'Why, Cleo,' the woman began. And then, alarmed, 'Cleo!' as her visitor gave a loud sniff and burst into tears.

With an effort, Cleo roused herself from her semi-doze and stood up. Where was the larder? The first door she opened led into a scullery, she got it right the second time. The larder wasn't overflowing with the produce of land and sea, but Cleo was grateful enough to see a loaf of bread, milk, a few bananas, half a dozen eggs and a choice of tins.

Always supposing I can find the tin opener, thought Cleo, it would be much the easiest. Heinz tomato soup, a childhood favourite, no culinary skill required, that would do fine.

Childhood, thought Cleo, as she poured the soup into a pan, and put it to heat on the stove. She yawned, saw a wooden spoon hanging on a hook above the Rayburn, and began to stir the soup.

Hard on her mother, to have Cleo turning up like that on her doorstep when she was busy working to a deadline. When Cleo drifted out of a restless sleep several hours later, she had no idea where she was. She turned her head. Slowly, because it hurt. There was the light. And there, at the door, quite suddenly, was her mother.

'Hello, Mum,' she said.

'You've got shingles,' said Gussie.

'How do you know?'

'I saw them, when I put you to bed,' said her mother. 'A band around you, like a girdle. Classic case. Painful.'

'Very,' said Cleo. She blinked, and a tear rolled fatly down one cheek. 'I feel awful.'

'Bound to,' said Gussie briskly. 'There's whatever the doctor prescribed for you beside the bed. A painkiller, I suspect, but it may help.'

'I can't be ill,' whispered Cleo. 'Not now.'

'You are. I rang Perry, told him to cancel Saturday.'

'Mum! You didn't! Oh, no, whatever will he think? What did you say?'

'I told him the truth. That you were quite ill, and covered in blistery spots.'

'Oh, help. What did he say.'

'That he remembered his mother having shingles, and how ill she was. He wanted to come and see you, but I said not. He might catch something, I told him, so he's bound to stay away.'

'Perry isn't bothered by things like that,' said Cleo with pride.

'Huh,' said Gussie.

Cleo was fretting about work.

'And Perry said, at least it wasn't your ridiculous work making you cancel again. How many times is that?'

'Three,' said Cleo, in a thread of a voice. 'Mum, I've got to get up. I've got to get to work, I've just got to.'

'Your office did ring,' said Gussie. 'The young man sounded very peeved that you were ill.'

Cleo gave a wail, and tried to raise herself to a sitting position. Her head swam, and she sank back into the pillows. 'What can I do?'

'Lie there, sleep, and get well,' said Gussie practically. She stood up, a small but formidable figure. 'I told the man from your office to bugger off, by the way. I told him you weren't likely to be back at work full time this side of Christmas.'

'Mum!'

'He said perhaps it would be best not to bother to come back at all in that case.'

'He didn't, not really, did he? Oh hell.'

'A good thing, too,' said Gussie. She had never liked Cleo's high-powered, long-houred job in the city, nor any of the people she worked with.

'And admit, it isn't really what you want to do with your life, is it?'

'It is,' said Cleo through clenched teeth. 'Mum, you had no right to say that.'

'Well, I did, and I'm glad. Don't worry, they won't take any notice of what I said. Do you think you could manage a cup of tea? I feel like one.'

'Perhaps,' said Cleo, shutting her eyes. 'Very weak, with some sugar. Like I used to have when I lived here.' Her voice sounded wistful.

'Not so long ago,' said Gussie, who was never sentimental.

Once the soup had been eaten, Cleo could cheerfully have curled up on the stone-flagged floor in front of the stove and slept exactly where she was.

Making her way back to the hall, she felt she might even have to, since Mrs Grigson hadn't thought to write down where the Dragon Room was. Upstairs, she told herself, and clutching two bananas, a glass of milk and the stone hot water bottle, she made her way up the stairs, alarming herself with the echoes of her own footsteps.

An unevenly floored passage ran from the landing, with closed, dark wooden doors leading off it. The first one Cleo tried was a broom cupboard, then came a lavatory, with the loo on a raised plinth, topped by an old-fashioned box-seat and finished off by an ancestral cistern with a long, dangling chain.

Next came a room with no working lights, which Cleo quickly gave up on, then a big bedroom containing a carved oak four-poster bed humped up with huge and ugly Victorian cushions. A bookcase ran along one wall, filled from floor to ceiling with books ranging from handsome old leatherbound volumes to garish modern paperbacks.

Great-aunt's room, thought Cleo, swiftly retreating and closing the door firmly behind her. On down the passage, a creak at every step. Not that the creaks bothered Cleo. They were friendly, gentle sounds, as though the house were settling quietly down for the night.

She opened another door. Ah, this one was different. This room had traces of fine red wallpaper, and faded but still sumptuous red velvet and brocade hangings. The remains of a fire burnt dimly in the grate, and Cleo could see that another four-poster bed – a more modest one, this time – was made up and turned down as though expecting a guest. She took in the lamps with bases in the shapes of dragons, glanced at the dragon carvings on the posts of the bed, and the dull gleam of gold-threaded dragons woven into the brocade cover on the bed. The Dragon Room, she told herself.

In a matter of minutes she was shivering between linen sheets, with total iciness kept at bay by the rapidly cooling stone hot-water bottle. She closed her eyes, and only the last conscious remnant of her brain heard the soft voices talking. They were too quiet to rouse her, and she sank into a deep and dreamless sleep.

She must have slept for several hours before she woke with a start.

Crying.

She could hear crying. A child? A wailing woman? What was it? And why from outside the window?

Shivering, she sank down under the sheets, pulling the covers up to her nose, willing herself to cut out the noise and go back to sleep.

No good.

She had to get up and investigate.

Shivering with cold, she sat up and felt for the brass switch on the wire of the light. The dim glow was reassuring, and bracing herself, she slid off the firm mattress and slunk to the window.

Two eyes gleamed at her out of the darkness, and she let out a yelp of dismay. Then the eyes blinked, Cleo concentrated, and her heart stopped beating at several times its usual pace.

It was a cat, of course. Its pink mouth opened in another wail, showing a fine set of sharp teeth. Cleo liked cats, but not, she felt, in the middle of the night. Still, if she went back to bed, the creature would presumably keep on wailing.

'Oh, bother,' she said, wrestling with the stiff catch. And then, 'Move over, you silly mog, otherwise you'll go flying.'

A blast of icy air came rushing into the room, and with teeth chattering, Cleo banged the window shut behind an enormous and sleek tabby cat. It stalked over to the bed and jumped up, curling its stripy tail round itself and looking at her with eyes of glinting contempt.

Cleo took a flying leap back into bed, huddling once more under the covers. Then a large soft shape flopped down beside her, purring loudly. Cleo put out a chilly finger and stroked its nose. Nice to have company, she thought, as she drifted back into sleep.

'That was thoughtless, I must say,' said Lambert indignantly. 'Why did you send Puss up to the window, why not to her door?'

'She might not hear him, through a heavy door like that.'

'She's probably caught a cold, now, opening the window on a winter's night.'

Giles shrugged, and took up his lute. 'Not she,' he said, and turned away to tune his strings.

3

The last time she had slept so soundly, she had been in Gussie's studio, when the drugs had done their work. She never heard the shrill ring of the phone echoing in the high-roofed room that was Gussie's studio and bedroom.

Gussie reached out for the phone with her left hand, her right hand still expertly shading the paper in front of her with fine, even movements.

'Gussie? What's all this about Cleo?' Val's deepish voice was curt. 'I bumped into Perry at the club, and he says it's off for Saturday. What the hell's going on?'

'Good evening, Val,' said Gussie, holding the receiver against her ear with her shoulder as she twitched the paper round to a different angle. 'Cleo's here.'

'What, with you? Why?'

'Ill,' said Gussie.

'She's got no business being ill,' said Val indignantly. 'I put off going up to Mountjoy on Saturday so that I could go to her wedding. It's very inconsiderate.'

'Val, most fathers do rather more than that.'

'I am,' said Valdemar triumphantly. 'I'm paying for her gathering of cronies at that restaurant after the ceremony. And I took her to dinner at Boulestin.'

'Good for you, Val, but you'll be able to go north now. She has shingles, can hardly stand up, and won't be marrying anyone at the weekend.'

A long pause.

'Gussie, do you think she really wants to marry Perry? I tried to sound him out, but he shut up like a clam.'

Gussie could imagine; Valdemar asking appalling personal questions in the brusquest way, in his normal, carrying voice, probably in the hallway of their club, friends, acquaintances and enemies coming and going, the porter with his ears dangling.

'I don't know what to think, but they have to sort it out for themselves, they are adults.'

Valdemar snorted. 'Especially Perry,' he said. 'Very adult.'

It rankled with Valdemar that his daughter had decided to marry a man of almost exactly his own age. Gussie and his wife Magdalena had tried to explain to him about father figures, and Cleo being more likely to settle with an older man, but to no purpose.

'Cradle-snatching,' he said furiously. 'It's disgusting.'

'That's what I thought,' remarked Magdalena, 'when you were carrying on with Belle.'

'I do not carry on with anyone. Carry on, indeed.' He returned to the point. 'Perry should find a wife nearer his own age.'

Gussie wouldn't let on to Valdemar how worried she was about Cleo and Perry. And why should she? A chance encounter in the fells a quarter of a century ago had resulted in Cleo. Gussie didn't regret Cleo for a moment, but she didn't feel that Val understood her or had more than a passing interest in her welfare.

Magdalena disagreed. She thought Cleo was very like her father, and perhaps, therefore, he knew her better than anyone.

Gussie neatly covered the illustration she was working on and clicked off the light clamped to her drawing board. All I know, she said to herself as she slid down from the stool, is that happy people, stress-free people, people who are desperately in love and sure about whoever they are going to marry, do not go down with shingles.

Valdemar wasn't too sure about what exactly shingles was. Or were. 'Sounds like something on a horse's leg,' he grumbled to Magdalena.

'It's a virus,' said Magdalena. 'Painful, and you don't get over it too quickly, it can pull you down.'

'That's no good in her job,' said Valdemar brutally. 'These

investment banks expect a hundred per cent from staff like Cleo. All these deals they put together, financing projects with funds in half a dozen countries. Split second timing, fast, clever work, that's what she gets paid for. She can't go wilting back in there feeling pulled down, whatever you mean by that.'

Valdemar was never ill.

'I think it's the wrong job for Cleo,' said Magdalena, scratching at a loose thread on the brocaded arm of the sofa. She slipped her feet out of her elegant town shoes and stretched her toes and legs.

'Pooh, nonsense,' said Valdemar, pouring himself a drink after handing one to Magdalena and then sitting down beside her in his vigorous way, so that all the cushions resting on the back of the sofa fell to the floor. 'Mmm, legs,' he added, his mind turning to more immediate matters as he ran an appreciative hand along Magdalena's thigh.

'No, Val,' said Magdalena. 'Concentrate. We must think how we can help Cleo.'

'Why?'

Magdalena didn't bother to mention his paternal duties or family love, neither of which would cut much ice. 'Because I like her, and I think she needs help.'

'I expect things will work out for her,' said Valdemar, with a huge yawn. 'Long day, let's go to bed and enjoy ourselves.' He rose and strolled out into the long central passage of the flat to check that the front door was locked and bolted.

Then he stopped, propping himself against a hideous marble-topped table which they kept for convenience rather than appearance. 'Bumped into Henry today,' he said. 'In Jermyn Street. At the cheese shop.'

'Paxton's,' Magdalena said, yawning widely.

'Wake up, Magdalena, this could be useful.'

'Why? How? Who to? And I don't know anyone called Henry.'

'He's a cousin,' said Valdemar. 'I'm sure you've met him.'

'At weddings and so on?'

'Um, possibly not, weddings aren't quite his style. No, no, but I'm sure you've met him somewhere.'

'Never mind,' said Magdalena. 'What about him?'

'Cleo,' Valdemar said impatiently. 'We were talking about Cleo. Well, Henry's just inherited a dilapidated house near Eyot.'

'What's it got to do with Cleo?'

'He needs someone to house-sit, can't leave the place empty, it'll go to rack and ruin.'

'Cleo? House-sit?'

'Why not? Country air, give her a chance to get back on her feet before she dives into the city again.'

'Give her pneumonia, more likely,' said Magdalena, shuddering at the thought of a northern winter.

4

'Damn this car,' said Cleo furiously. 'Idiotic Cousin Henry, imagining it would start after weeks and weeks sitting in an open barn in all the damp and frost.'

The cat, to whom these remarks were addressed, took no interest in the whining shrieks from the engine. He merely settled himself more comfortably on his perch on the broad beam of the outhouse where the car lived, and went on watching the antics below with the indifferent golden eyes of his kind.

The kitchen door opened and Mrs Grigson, a bowl of potato peel and vegetable stalks in her hand, came out. She shook her head at Cleo and sidled over to the car, her dark eyes intense.

'You have to press the accelerator three times, quickly,' she said in thrilling tones, 'and then leave it for about half a minute and then start it again.'

Cleo didn't believe a word of it, but with Mrs Grigson's troubled figure beside her, she felt she had to try.

The car roared into irritating life. 'Thank you,' said Cleo.

'That's the heater switch, there,' said Mrs Grigson helpfully. 'Now, mind you don't forget the things from the pub on your way back.'

Cleo let in the clutch. 'I won't,' she promised. How could she do anything to make Mrs Grigson's life more fraught? She'd never seen anyone with such dark and tragic looks.

It was strange to be back in Eyot; she had only paid a swift visit to these parts since she had spent an eventful summer at Midwinter. The summer before she went up to Oxford; half a lifetime ago, it seemed now.

There was a new one-way system, which flummoxed her at first, but she wound along the tortuous route to end up in the car park beside the castle. Not what she had intended, but there were spaces; it would do.

New shops, too, and old favourites had vanished. Of course, some things never changed, like the brooding hulk of the cathedral. Cleo was not a churchy person, but even she felt the power of the great stone building with its soaring twin spires.

Ah, now, unless her memory was playing tricks, this was the narrow lane where . . . yes, she was right. There was Gumbles, with the same black and gold sign swinging outside. Not that Cleo was very food-minded, particularly not just now, when the shingles had removed all traces of appetite, but Gumbles the food emporium was very Eyot; one expected it to be there, and for a friend or acquaintance to be making his or her way in or out of the elegant black door.

No sooner thought than seen.

'Lily!' cried Cleo, darting forward.

The small, alert figure started, turning to see who was calling her name. She waved and came briskly across the road to join Cleo.

'Naturally, I knew you were coming north,' she said, as they huddled in a corner out of the biting wind.

'Read it in the tea cups?'

'Nothing so crude,' said Lily.

'I'm longing to go and have coffee at Flora's, it's only round the corner from here. Do come.'

'Sylvester will be expecting me back,' said Lily.

'Pooh,' said Cleo, knowing that Lily kept Sylvester, the distinguished cellist for whom she had worked in that distant summer, exactly where she wanted him. Lily was Sylvester's housekeeper, and Lily called the tunes.

'Just a quick cup, then,' said Lily. 'In fact, Sylvester will have my guts for cello strings if I don't, he'll be thrilled to hear all the news.'

'No news,' said Cleo, sniffing the coffee-laden air as they pushed open the glass door which led into the soft-carpeted delights of Eyot's famous coffee house.

Lily chose Java; Cleo had a Kenyan blend, she couldn't take strong coffee yet.

'I've been ill,' she told Lily. 'Shingles.'

Lily made tsking noises of disapproval. 'At your age? You must have let yourself get thoroughly run down. It's that job of yours, Sylvester was telling me about it, said it sounded a complete nightmare to him.'

'I enjoy my work. It wouldn't suit Sylvester, but it suits me.'

'So why did you get shingles? I knew about the shingles, in any case, what with your cancelling the wedding yet again.'

'Oh dear,' said Cleo, stirring her black coffee.

Lily took Cleo's cup from her, and poured a slurp of cream into it.

'I can't drink that,' cried Cleo.

'Just try,' said Lily, in a voice that allowed no arguments. In her opinion, Cleo was looking shockingly thin and drawn, not at all like the vital girl who had led them all a dance that hot and merry summer.

Cleo drank it doubtfully, but found it made a refreshing change from her usual black and bracing brew.

'Now, what are you doing in Eyot? Hardly the place to convalesce, much better to go somewhere warm.'

'I'm house-sitting,' said Cleo. 'For a cousin. Henry Hazard.'

'Oh,' said Lily. 'I know Henry. He's an old friend of Sylvester's.'

Why am I surprised? thought Cleo. It was a small world, Eyot and Eyotshire; and Sylvester made a habit of knowing people.

'I've never met him,' she said. 'Is he interesting?'

'Henry? You could say that. He's different.' Lily wasn't bothered about Henry; she wanted to know what Cleo was doing. She was horrified when she heard. 'What, that ruin of a house? I hadn't realized; when you said house-sitting, I imagined . . . Cleo, you can't stay there.'

'I can, and I am. It's a bit dilapidated of course.'

Lily snorted. 'A wreck. And damp, and ghosts, too, I dare say.'

'There are some very strange sounds,' admitted Cleo. 'And I keep hearing music, I have wondered about it. However, I haven't seen any ghosts.'

'Yet,' said Lily darkly. 'You can't stay there by yourself, it's a scandal, whatever is Henry thinking of? Sylvester will be very disturbed when he hears about this.'

'I'm fine,' said Cleo. 'And tell Sylvester that when the house and its spooky noises get the better of me, I'll come over to Midwinter for some creature comforts.'

'Come anyway,' said Lily.

Cleo pottered around the shops, buying the various essentials she had forgotten to bring with her. Now the light mist which had hung about the streets had vanished, the sun had come out, and the day had a crisp and bright feel to it. Her spirits began to rise; perhaps it had been the right thing to do, to come north. Blow the cobwebs away, refresh her jaded soul, allow her to return to work in the new year invigorated and ready for battle.

She wondered what they were doing at the office right now. It would be busy, of course; it wouldn't calm down until just before the Christmas holiday. She thought of her desk, would somebody else be working there? It was strange, the idea of another person on her territory. Looking through her drawers, pushing aside her papers, dumping their own half-drunk cups of machine coffee on the ledge behind the desk, speaking to people on her phone.

Only it wasn't hers. It was just a place, with the necessary equipment for the work she did. How silly to feel possessive. Cleo caught sight of herself in a shop window, how taut and worried she looked. That's my London face, she realized with sudden insight.

All these London thoughts had driven away her feeling of freshness and good spirits; instead, she began to feel tired and slightly cross. She turned into a narrow cobbled street, out of contrariness, because it wasn't where she wanted to go.

And then she was glad she had, because there were some fascinating shops tucked away there, out of the mainstream streets and the high rents and year-round tourists. There was an establishment selling exotic fabrics: old silk velvets and new brocades from the Far East. Then there was a hand-made chocolate shop, which would have been a great temptation to Cleo in her pre-shingles days. There was a strange shoe shop of a rather ethnic kind, and a haberdashers such as Cleo hadn't seen since she was a child.

And then there was a double-fronted shop, with exquisite bow windows. The left-hand window had a single silver pyramid nestling in a heap of black lace, and encircled with a heavily chased silver chain. Next door stood a Victorian dressmaker's dummy on its stand, clad in a wisp of chiffon with peacock feathers arranged behind into an unusual bustle.

Cleo looked at the name written above the shop. Very newly written, by the look of it.

Adele.

She pushed the door, a bell jangled, and in she went. Inside, it was a single shop, not two separate ones, with a dark girl hard at work at a table on one side, a soldering iron in her hand. On the other side, a blonde girl was sitting with her head down over an old-fashioned Singer sewing machine.

She looked up. 'Can I help?' she said, in a pretty, slightly breathy voice.

Cleo stared at her, stunned by a vision with a mop of platinum curls and a pouting, glistening mouth.

'Goodness,' said the vision. 'It's Cleo, Cleo Byng. What's up with you? You look like a wraith, a creature from lands beyond.'

Cleo blinked. 'Adele,' she said in astonishment. 'You're *Adele*.'

Adele had appeared at Cleo's convent school in the sixth form. Cleo quite clearly remembered her sidling in through the door of the lower sixth Common Room, a brown streak of a girl with bad skin and dank hair.

Silence, as a dozen bright-eyed and glossy-haired girls looked at the apparition as though she had just landed.

'I don't know where my room is,' the apparition whispered in a limp voice.

'Lord,' said Gaye, a prefect, hauling herself languorously to her feet. 'Come along, Bunny, I'll show you.'

A shout of laughter followed them as they left the room. Trust Gaye to pick on the rabbity front teeth and bestow an instant and appropriate nickname on the hapless newcomer.

Bunny she had remained for a whole year, until a chance encounter with a hockey ball had broken one of the offending teeth. The dentist who did the repair job took pity on her and went on to do a mouthful of good work, and Adele returned for her final year looking very different.

She had been at Oxford at the same time as Cleo, although much more studious. She was a sleek sophisticate of an undergraduate, wearing black clothes and a cynical expression and terrifying most of the men. Her hair took on a dark-red sheen; she wore big black glasses. 'Formidable, Adele,' said her friends with a sigh.

'Good heavens,' said Cleo.

'It's rude to stare,' said Adele, with a kiss-kiss smile.

'Not when someone you've known for years has undergone a total transformation.'

'I did it before,' pointed out Adele. 'I intend to remake myself at least every five years or so.'

'And it's Marilyn Monroe for this section of your life.'

'Something like that.'

Adele was one of the friends that Cleo had more or less lost touch with since she came down from Oxford and started her busy life in the City.

'Last time I saw you,' Cleo said, 'you were going to do a postgrad course. Psychology, wasn't it?'

'Yup,' said Adele. 'I chucked that, though. Before it even started; that's for the birds, I told myself. So I went to St Martin's instead.'

'St Martin's?'

'Sharpen your wits, darling, a fashion course at St Martin's College. You know.'

'Yes, of course. That would be just the thing for you, you were always a terrific dressmaker.'

'Had to be,' said Adele. 'No money for lovely ball gowns, lots of lovely men wanting to go to balls, it was an incentive. Now, tell me all about yourself, we've got hours. What on earth are you doing in Eyot? I want to know all about you, and why you look as though you've been recently dug up.'

Reinvent yourself, thought Cleo. If only one could.

Adele jumped to her feet, and pushed a chair across for Cleo to sit on. 'Suzie,' she said to the dark girl, who pushed her protective goggles up, revealing a pair of kohl-ringed eyes with long and unreal lashes. 'This is Cleo, we go back a long way, to my schooldays.'

'Hi,' said Suzie, and pulled the goggles down again before bending over her work.

A safety-pin, thought Cleo, looking at the ornate object which was being delicately joined together. 'A decorative safety-pin,' she said out loud. 'Out of the ordinary.'

'Oh, Suzie does a roaring trade in pins and chains and locks and so on,' said Adele.

'What about you?' asked Cleo. 'Are all these yours?'

'Evening dresses and clothes for special occasions are my forte,' said Adele. 'Very busy now, coming up to Christmas, dances and parties.'

'Nice,' said Cleo, looking at a creation in taffeta with wide puffed sleeves and a tiny waist.

'Not very sophisticated,' said Adele with a little pout. 'Look at this black beaded one, it would suit you.'

'Mmm,' said Cleo appreciatively. 'If I were going to any parties, or could wear anything close to my skin, or weren't living in a desolate ruin of a house.'

Suzie snapped her goggles up again. 'Are you expecting?' she said directly.

Cleo was taken aback for a moment. 'Oh, you mean the baggy clothes,' she said. 'No, I've had shingles, so I can't wear anything fitted, like jeans.'

'Get Adele to run you up something classy,' said Suzie, returning once more to her pin. 'You look very dreary in those dungarees.'

'I must say I agree,' said Adele, looking at Cleo in a calculating way. 'I hadn't like to mention it, but if you're sore, well, there's not a lot you can do.'

'Clothes for people with sensitive skins and painful areas could be a good line,' said Suzie. 'People who've hurt themselves, got bruises and so on.'

'I wonder,' said Adele, her eyes taking on a dreamy look. Then she became brisk. 'Just in time for lunch, Cleo.'

Cleo protested. She hadn't been looking for Adele at all, had only chanced on the shop by accident, didn't want to disturb her while she was working.

'Only soup,' said Suzie. 'Don't get excited.'

'How long have you been here?' said Cleo.

'Just opened,' said Adele. 'I'm glad you came.'

Cleo followed Adele through a curtain at the back. She was taken aback to see, besides a gas ring, a bed, and several suitcases stacked to make a table. 'Is that for naps when you've been working too hard?' she asked jokingly.

'No,' said Adele, blowing out the match as the gas lit with a soft plopping sound. 'I live here.'

'No!' Cleo had seen all kinds of student and other lodgings, but this tiny slip of a room was minimal beyond the norm. 'What about heating?'

'I use the gas ring,' said Adele, pouring the contents of a tin into a pan and placing it on the ring.

'But why? Aren't there flats to rent, rooms in people's houses?'

'Every penny is needed for the shop,' said Adele. 'We rent out the upstairs, to bring in some extra cash.'

'Where does Suzie live?'

'She camps out with a friend, but there's no room for another. Besides, we see enough of each other during the day.'

Cleo looked round the cheerless little room, and was struck by a brilliant idea. 'Adele,' she said, 'why don't you come and stay with me, at my cousin's house. Have you any transport? Are there buses? It would do for a while, and anything would be better than this.'

Adele laughed. 'What would your cousin say? Would he want an uninvited and unknown guest?'

'I'm unknown, actually,' said Cleo. 'We've never met, only spoken on the phone. He told me to invite a friend,' she went on. 'I warn you, Haphazard House, which is what it's called, is in a dreadful state, don't go imagining anything fancy. But there are some habitable rooms; better than this, anyway, and a warm kitchen. I'd like your company, I have to say, because although it didn't seem lonely to me, I've only spent one night there, and I was too exhausted to notice what it's really like in the dark hours. Oh, and there's a resident cat.'

'I've got a motor-bike,' said Adele. 'And I like cats. I'll come. I must say, washing in the swimming pool showers and managing with just a tiny basin in the loo doesn't make for an easy life.'

Suzie swished the curtain back, rattling the rings on the pole.

'Good idea,' she said. 'It's a bit sordid, your being here, Adele. And we can do with the extra storage. And there's a customer come for a fitting.'

'Help yourself to soup,' said Adele to Cleo, vanishing into the shop.

5

Henry had said she would need company, after all. And there was plenty of room at Haphazard, and if Adele was a stranger, so, in a way, was she. It was odd, really, being a guest of someone you'd never met, but had only spoken to on the phone. Henry had never suggested they meet for a drink or a meal, or for a proper briefing.

She had been wary when he first rang.

'Is that Cleo?'

A pause at her end. Was this some ex-flame ringing her? It was a pleasing voice, and unfamiliar, but then he had addressed her as Cleo.

'Cleo Byng? I'm Henry Hazard.'

'Ah,' said Cleo, relieved.

'We're cousins, I gather. We must be, Valdemar tells me you're his daughter.'

'So my mother assures me,' said Cleo gravely.

'Good. Val says you're off work, had the measles.'

'Shingles, actually.'

'Ah, shingles. Just so. I need someone to keep an eye on a house for me. And make sure the builders turn up.'

'You're redecorating?'

'Didn't Val tell you? The house is in a bit of a state; needs some work doing to it.'

'Oh?'

'A ruin, you might say.'

So much for any hopes she might have had of thick towels and ravishing gardens, thought Cleo. 'It's kind of Val to suggest it,' she said. 'Unfortunately, I have to go back to work as soon as possible.'

'Fine,' he said, quite unconcerned. 'Let me know by Thursday if you're coming or not. Goodbye.'

Cleo put the phone down. Go? she thought. What were her options?

One, stay here, and drive her mother mad. Hardly fair; Gussie had a living to earn.

Two, go back to her flat. Plenty going on there; her flatmate, Charlotte, had dozens of friends and relations who descended on the flat in waves of exuberance and noise. How exhausting, and what would she do with herself all day? Read? Look out of the window at dreary, drizzly London? Go for grey walks to get her strength up, or genteel swims at pools full of women fighting to keep themselves trim; about as relaxing as running a marathon, in Cleo's opinion.

'Do make up your mind and go,' said Gussie with affectionate exasperation. 'Take a chance, opt for something new, it's always the best thing.'

Henry sounded very incisive, if not at all grateful, when Wednesday night came, and Cleo dialled his number to say she'd come. For a short time, only.

Henry had been surprised that she didn't have a car.

'What's the point of having a car in London?' she had said reasonably. 'I go everywhere by taxi, no problem.'

'I don't think you can survive at Haphazard without a car.'

Find yourself someone else to watch over your house, then, Cleo thought with irritation. 'What did your great-aunt do? Didn't Val say she was terribly ancient?'

'Eighty-six,' said Henry. 'Drove a sports car at great speed until the week before she died.'

'Ah,' said Cleo.

'Her car's still there, but if you can't drive . . .'

'I can drive. I have a licence. I just don't own a car.'

'That's solved that,' said Henry. 'How old are you?'

'Why do you want to know?' said Cleo.

The voice at the other end sounded amused at the suspicion in Cleo's voice. 'Insurance.'

'Oh. Twenty-two. Clean licence, no accidents or claims.'

'Well done.'

'It's because I don't drive much,' said Cleo, always one for honesty.

'I'm sure you'll get used to it. I'll arrange for a taxi to meet you at the station and take you to the house, if you let me know what train you'll be on.'

'Won't you be there?' Cleo had been looking forward to meeting this cousin with a wild-sounding great-aunt.

'No,' said Henry. 'I'm very busy now. I'll get over when I can. Mrs Grigson will be around, she'll tell you what you need to know. I expect the builder will be there before me if he hasn't already been.'

'Builder?'

'You don't have to worry about him, he knows what he's got to do.

'Oh.'

'Are you going to be lonely?'

'It sounds like it.'

There was a pause. 'Look, if you've got a friend, or a relation, after all, the place is crawling with Mountjoys, then do ask them to join you.'

'Thank you,' said Cleo.

'We're only nine miles from Eyot,' he added. 'For the cinema and so on.'

'Yes,' said Cleo.

Although even now, thought Cleo as she carried Adele's suitcase into the hall, she wasn't sure why she had found herself in the ticket queue at King's Cross.

It had something to do with her getting herself ready to go into work for just a few hours and being unable to get further than the entrance to the tube station. Or something to do with the look of absorbed passion on her mother's face as she bent over her work.

Funny, she'd watched her mother working for years, why had she never noticed that before?

And then there was Perry, back from America.

Concerned.

'Not the north, Cleo, darling,' he'd said. 'Such a long way, and so cold. I'm very busy, I'll hardly see you at all.'

Cleo didn't like being at a disadvantage with Perry. And with shingles, she was, and would be if she stayed in London. She looked ghastly, for one thing, and then she didn't feel inclined to stand up to him with her usual spirit.

A nudge here, a nudge there, and then there she was at King's Cross.

'Return?'

'I'm not sure when I'll be coming back.'

'Single, then. Much more expensive.'

Don't care, thought Cleo, rattling the handle of her luggage trolley to make it shift. Cousin Henry was paying.

'Suitcases,' said Mrs Grigson, seemingly cast into despair by their appearance. 'Where have they come from?'

'They aren't mine,' said Cleo. 'They belong to an old friend of mine, who's coming to stay. To keep me company. Cousin Henry suggested it.'

Mrs Grigson's face took on a tormented look as she considered possibilities. 'The linen's a bit damp, you see,' she said. 'Mouldy. And as for a room, oh dear, I'm not sure. I could put her in old Miss Hazard's room, that might be best.'

That was the book-lined bedroom which Cleo had dipped into. It would hold no fears for Adele, indeed, Cleo couldn't think why she hadn't liked the look of it. As she trailed into the room after Mrs Grigson, her arms full of pillows, she remembered. It was all those carvings on the bed. Very grotesque. She mentioned this to Mrs Grigson.

'Miss Hazard said they kept evil spirits away.'

'Why should there be evil spirits?'

'There have always been spirits at Haphazard House, and among so many, some are bound to be evil.'

Mrs Grigson cheered up at this grim thought, and tackled the bed with surprising energy and efficiency, refusing Cleo's feeble offers of help. 'I know this bed, and it knows me, and it'll be done in a trice. Then it's down to the kitchen with you, for a nice cup of tea. Wish it could be coffee,' she went on, sounding wistful. 'Miss Hazard liked a good cup of coffee, but we've run out since she died.'

Cleo had noticed, and she told Mrs Grigson that she'd bought some in Eyot. Together with several other goodies which she considered necessary, and which seemed to be lacking in the Haphazard household which boasted an austere and uninteresting larderful of staples that she, Cleo, would never want to eat.

'I remembered the eggs from the pub,' she said, laying the tray down on the kitchen table.

'You can't go wrong with eggs,' said Mrs Grigson. 'And I'll need to show you how to stoke the furnace, in case it goes out. It's a cursed contraption, but you'll freeze to death if it starts playing up and you don't know what to do.'

Cleo didn't like the sound of that, although the reality proved less fearsome than Mrs Grigson had suggested. And the room in which the antiquated boiler lived was blessedly warm and dry.

'The washing machine's in here,' said Mrs Grigson, opening the door into a scullery. 'The hanging rail's in the boiler room, as you saw, and there's the deep freeze, should you want it. It's empty now, but you can switch it on any time.'

'I'll hardly need it,' said Cleo. 'Just for me and Adele, who won't be here in the daytime.'

'Mrs Hazard used to have a houseful, come Christmas,' said Mrs Grigson. 'Ah, difficult days those were. Hard work, very hard work, but it was still a happy time. As Christmas should be,' she added in her mournful way.

Giles, floating through the boiler room and up the back stairs after Mrs Grigson and Cleo, was not impressed. He found Lambert brooding in the library. 'Happy days, upon my word! Endless quarrels from what I remember, frayed tempers all round.'

Lambert sighed. 'Christmas is a pagan time, when the enemies of the Lord find their way easily into people's hearts.'

'Much you know about it,' said Giles. 'You forbade the keeping of Christmas.'

More sighs.

'Oh, desolation; we tried, we tried. For a few years the spirit of misrule and excess and fleshly delights were banned from this country, and people's minds turned to God. They were good days, good days.'

'No, they weren't, you old misery,' said Giles, flicking a cobweb from his velvet sleeve. 'This house was desolate and dull and the saddest it's ever been in those years. No yule log, no games, no eating and drinking and enjoyment. Plain clothes, plain food and plain dull, that's what Christmas was like then.'

Lambert's attention was distracted from the wickedness of Christmas by the distant sound of a telephone bell. With one accord they left the library and reappeared in their own special chamber on the first floor. On the window seat was an old field telephone, brought back from the war by a fighting Hazard. Lambert, who was of a mechanical turn of mind, had discovered it, and been fascinated by how it worked. He had explained it, as a scientist would, to Giles.

Subtle Giles had at once seen its practical potential. 'How useful such a listening device would have been at court,' he had remarked more than once.

Lambert lifted the lid and picked up the receiver.

'This is a terrible line,' said Cleo. 'Crackle, crackle, hiss.'

'Perhaps it's tapped,' said the deep voice at the other end.

'Lines eaten by rats, more like,' said Cleo. 'Sylvester, you can't come and spend the evening here, it isn't your style at all.'

Sylvester's affronted voice boomed back down the echoing line. 'Nonsense, I can't tell you how good I am at coping with adverse surroundings. I shall drive Lily over, with food, and you can tell me all your news, and I can meet this friend of yours. I can't trust you not to have picked up someone very strange for company.'

'Sylvester, she's an old friend.'

'They're the worst.'

Giles and Lambert looked at each other. 'Visitors,' said Giles, brightening at the prospect. Life had been very tedious of late.

'He sounds a sensible man, whoever he is,' said Lambert.

'He could be a lover.'

'No,' said Lambert. 'No lover, mark my word. And besides, he's bringing Lily.'

'Who,' said Giles, 'is Lily?'

'Lily who?' said Adele, making a dramatic figure in the hall in her black leather gear. 'And Sylvester? Who's he? Are they local?'

She pulled off her helmet and shook out her platinum curls. 'Eek,' she said, looking around her in awe. 'Are you sure you've got room for me here? However big is this place?'

'About twelve bedrooms, as far as I can tell,' said Cleo. 'Mostly uninhabitable.'

'I hope the lights don't go. Do you know where the fuse box is?'

'Haven't a clue,' said Cleo. 'There are some candles in the pantry, though, I noticed them earlier. Leave your things here, I'll take you up to your room later. We're all in the kitchen. Sylvester is Sylvester Tate, the cellist, and I know him because I worked for him one summer when I came up north with Prue Pagan. Before I went to Oxford.'

'What did you work *as*? You never could cook, and you know nothing about music.'

'Secretary,' said Cleo. 'I was a whizz at the typewriter. Lily is Sylvester's housekeeper and guardian. Sylvester lives in Midwinter with Gabriel, who is a violinist. Gabriel's seldom at home, since he tours a lot and teaches in the States.'

'Downstairs?' said Adele, peering doubtfully into the gloom. 'Are you sure?'

A door opened at the bottom of the stairs and light flooded out. 'Come along, come along,' said Sylvester in a welcoming way, but casting an enormous shadow across the bottom steps.

'Creepy,' said Adele. 'Definitely creepy.' She sidled into the kitchen and looked around the huge old kitchen. 'Wow, look at that range.' She eyed the vast black construction, with its sundry ovens, hooks and a large black pipe which vanished into the ceiling. 'Wonder when that was last used.'

'Still in working order,' said Lily. 'But not tonight. The Rayburn is easier.'

'You've left a radio on upstairs,' said Sylvester, coming away from the door and shutting it behind him. 'Good idea, keep the hobgoblins away.'

'I haven't got a radio,' said Cleo. 'And Mrs Grigson says there's only the one in the main bedroom, and it's unplugged. But it's funny you should say that, because I'm sure I heard music last night. I think Mrs Grigson's forgotten there's another one, and it's playing away to itself in some neglected corner.

Guitar music, that's what it was. And voices, too, so definitely a radio.'

'Guitar!' said Giles crossly. 'What an ignorant girl.'

'Better for her not to love music,' said Lambert. 'It frets the soul, and awakens the senses.'

'Cleo looks to me as though she knows much about the senses,' said Giles. 'And her friend . . . well!'

Lambert shook his head. 'Sin,' he said. 'I smell sin.'

'Then you'll be happy,' said Giles impatiently. 'I never knew anyone who spent so much time thinking about sin. For centuries, now; what unwholesome zeal.'

'Sin is eternal.'

'Poof,' said Giles, taking up his lute once more.

'That's no guitar, ignorant and misguided girl,' said Sylvester. 'That's a lute. Strange tuning; it must be one of these authentic renderings.'

'I can't hear anything,' said Adele.

'Of course, the house is haunted,' said Lily in matter-of-fact tones, as she darted to and fro.

'Rumour and country stories,' said Sylvester scornfully.

'No,' said Lily. 'This place is full of spirits, I felt it as soon as I came through the door.'

'Henry's great-aunt?' said Cleo, thinking of the room upstairs.

'I shouldn't think so. Older than that. Much older.'

6

Adele moved in on Sylvester with a skilled relentlessness which took Cleo by surprise.

'Look at the size of you, you can take my bags upstairs for me; all in one go, I should think.'

Sylvester was very tall and bulky.

'Yes,' agreed Lily. 'An excellent idea. Off you go, all of you, leave me a bit of space to get on. You can do with the exercise, Sylvester, far too much sitting around at this time of the year.'

Sylvester got to his feet with a terrible groan. 'I do hours of practice, as you know. Very exhausting and strenuous for the muscles. And human beings were not designed to run about the fells in the middle of winter. Not with those easterly winds blowing over from Siberia and even the sheep looking for shelter. All it does is make work for the mountain rescue; in these months, thoughtful people stay at home.'

'And make themselves useful,' said Lily, brandishing a wooden spoon. 'Come on, Cleo, make the effort, I'm sure you can do the trip up to Adele's bedroom.'

Cleo wasn't at all sure her legs hadn't turned to cotton wool after her day in Eyot, but she couldn't leave Sylvester and Adele to wander about the house; they might vanish through the floorboards.

'Why has this Henry guy let the house get into such a state?' asked Adele, as they toiled upwards. 'Does anyone know? Cleo, I can't understand you coming here and not finding out anything beforehand, what a lack of curiosity.'

'*I* know why,' said Sylvester.

'Right,' said Adele. 'Out with it, then. Why has he neglected this place? Is he dreadfully poor?'

'He hardly knows the house,' said Sylvester, pausing for a quick breather on the galleried landing. 'His great-aunt quarrelled with his father, years ago, so Henry only came here once while she was alive, as far as I know. When he was very little.'

'Isn't it a family house?' asked Cleo, rather breathless after a too rapid ascent. 'There's the name, he's called Hazard, after all. Why did it belong to a great-aunt?'

'There was a tontine,' said Sylvester. 'Henry's great-aunt outlived all her brothers and sisters and scooped the pool, including the family home. Only it wasn't a very big pool even then, and this is a costly house to run. No money left at all, I gather, by the time she popped off. She must have been living on the capital for years.'

'How do you know all these details, Sylvester?' asked Cleo, leading the way along the corridor.

'One hears this and that,' said Sylvester airily. 'I hope we're nearly there, my arms are dropping off, very bad for a cellist, you do appreciate this.'

'Nonsense,' said Cleo. 'You're as strong as an ox. In here.' She felt for the light switch, and the room was filled with strange shadows from the single forty-watt light bulb which dangled down from the ceiling, suspended on an old brown plaited wire.

'Surely we can do better than that,' said Sylvester, craning down to look at the light beside the bed. 'Does this work?'

'I don't feel too happy about the electrics,' said Cleo, as Sylvester turned the smaller light on and flipped the centre light off. 'Cousin Henry said the electricity was checked not long ago, and pronounced safe, but I'm not too sure.'

'Don't fuss,' said Sylvester. 'Just think what a privilege it is to stay in a house like this, what a stunner it is. I'd forgotten, it's been years since I was here.'

'Bet it was in better order then,' said Cleo.

Adele was examining the carvings on the four-poster bed with stunned awe. 'These are really something,' she said. 'Hey, do I really get to sleep in here? Don't you want this room, Cleo?'

'No, I don't,' said Cleo. 'Gives me the creeps.'

'I have no problems with that,' said Adele. 'I'm not in the least bit sensitive. I don't believe in creepy atmospheres or ghosts or poltergeists or any of that crew, because I've never felt or seen anything, even in places which everyone says are haunted. Was this the great-aunt's room?'

Cleo nodded.

'Well, she's safely six feet under, and she isn't going to bother me.'

Up on the canopy, an invisible Giles and Lambert watched and listened. As the little group trooped out of the room, they slid down to the floor and followed.

'I wish to hear more about Henry myself,' whispered Giles.

'Curiosity is a tool of the devil,' said Lambert, who was eaten up with nosiness about the new owner, but would never admit it.

'You stay here, then,' said Giles. He snapped his fingers. 'I don't care that for sin, but I must know what manner of man this Henry is.'

'You need a protector,' said Lambert, moving quickly to keep up.

'Glass of wine for Cleo,' said Lily, after a swift look at her. She whisked a pan from the Rayburn to the sink and drained its contents with an expert flourish.

'Glass of wine for all of us,' said Sylvester, pouring as he spoke. 'Except for Lily, it's her turn to drive.'

'Okay, Sylvester,' said Adele, wrapping her hands round the bowl of her wine glass and fixing him with a ruthless gaze. Her long nails were almost the colour of the wine; Cleo wondered how she managed to do her dressmaking with such extraordinary talons.

'False,' said Adele, without looking at Cleo. 'Now, Sylvester, spit it out; Cleo and I want to know more about Henry. How old is he? Where does he live? What's he going to do with this wonderful house? What does he do for a living?'

Sylvester took a good sip of wine, and waved a large hand in the air. 'You,' he said amiably, 'are very nosy.' Then he leant forward on his elbows. 'Henry's younger than I am. So, thirty-nine, forty, forty-one, about that.'

Younger than Perry, thought Cleo inconsequentially. 'I thought he was old, Sylvester, sixties or something.'

'No. He lives in a flat in Eyot. Had a wife, an American, but she buzzed off a while ago. Back to America.'

'Why?' said Adele.

'Never you mind,' said Sylvester. 'No loss, in my opinion. Grasping little thing, and no wife for an artist; she didn't understand him at all.'

'Artist?' said Cleo, much surprised.

'Why not? People are.'

'I know, Sylvester, but he sounded like, oh, a lawyer or someone like that. What kind of an artist?'

'Cartoonist.'

Cleo shook her head. 'Never heard of him. Political cartoons, or what?'

'More of an illustrator,' said Sylvester.

'Children's books, then?'

'No, very adult, although teenagers like them, if their tastes run to the grotesque. Highly detailed, extremely strange and sinister houses and castles, all a bit Transylvanian. Very, very big in America and on the continent, but not here. A prophet in his own land . . .' He shook his head, and gave himself another glass of wine.

'Lots of money, then,' said Adele shrewdly. 'If he's big in the States. Plenty to do this house up with.'

Sylvester shook his head. 'It's not so simple. His ex, Mathilda, is one very expensive lady, and I think he's chosen the wrong lawyer. The more he makes, the more she takes. Bit of a treadmill, actually.'

'How feeble,' said Cleo contemptuously. 'Why doesn't he just tell her to get stuffed? I would.'

'He's far too much the gent, and her lawyers are too smart,' said Sylvester. 'What a sad institution marriage is when it goes wrong.'

'Pretty sad when it's going okay,' said Adele, with a toss of her blonde curls. 'Hey, Lily, that smells wonderful. Shall I lay the table, or what?'

That had Giles and Lambert puzzled. 'Cartoonist?' said Lambert.

'Those picture jokes in the newspapers,' said Giles. 'They're called cartoons.'

'Not work for a proper man.'

'He may be a satirist,' said Giles, remembering Hogarth.

Lambert let out a huff of breath. 'Dangerous work, if so. Very dangerous.'

'Not these days,' said Giles. 'Times have changed, Lambert. You may say what you like nowadays; indeed, do what you like. Everything is permitted.'

Lambert groaned. 'The world is full of sin.'

'Yes,' said Giles appreciatively. 'And some of it very delectable, such a cornucopia of temptations and delights. We didn't have nearly such a lively time; we had to be discreet.'

'Wicked days, wicked days,' said Lambert with gloomy relish.

'It's the nights you need to worry about,' said Giles, with an elegant and derisive flourish.

7

'What are you going to do today?' Adele asked Cleo as she strapped herself into her helmet.

'This and that,' said Cleo guardedly. 'Ring London, find out what I'm missing. Explore; there's a lot of the house I haven't seen. And I expect Mrs Grigson will appear.'

'Does she drive a little van?' asked Adele.

'No, she comes on an aged black bike,' said Cleo.

'Only there's a van just drawn up by the door. Looks as though you've got visitors. Don't tire yourself out, ring and tell me what you want me to bring from Eyot, if anything. I'll be back about six.'

Snort, roar, purr, and Adele was gone in a crackle of ice and a flurry of frozen leaves.

Cleo went to see what the van was for. It was parked by the door, with a lugubrious-looking man, short and stout, surveying the house.

'Look at those chimneys, oh dear, oh dear, what a disaster. That's what I always say when I come to Haphazard.'

Cleo looked at the chimneys. 'What's wrong with them? I like chimneys like that. Jacobean, aren't they?'

'They may be, they may be. But they're old, they're inefficient, they're ugly, and they don't meet the regs.'

'Regs?'

'Regs,' the man said, as though it were a new name for rats or cockroaches. 'You've got to comply with the regs. And you can tell at a glance that this house and regs are strangers to each other.'

Cleo was still in the dark about the regs, but she was beginning to feel very cold out in the open without a coat.

'Are you delivering something?' she asked, hopping from foot to foot.

'Cold, are you? Best go in. No, I'm not delivering anything. I've been sent by Mr Hazard to see what needs to be done here. I'm Arthur Nugent, from Nugent and Sons. My card.'

Cleo read that Nugent & Sons had been established for more than a hundred years, were based in Eyot and undertook all types of building works. 'You'd better come in,' she said. 'I'm Henry Hazard's cousin, and I'm looking after the house for him.'

'He did mention that,' admitted Arthur Nugent, scrunching along behind her. 'Only I thought it was a man, this cousin.'

'Well, it isn't. It's me.'

'All alone in this great house?'

'No, I have a friend staying with me,' said Cleo. Arthur Nugent looked thoroughly respectable, but Cleo was a Londoner, and not given to easy trust. She'd better give Henry a ring and check that he really had sent this little round man along.

'You do that,' said Arthur approvingly. 'You aren't local, so you don't know me. And you won't know any of the people my firm does work for.'

'No, not being local, I wouldn't,' said Cleo, heading for the fire which she had managed to get going in the hall that morning.

Mr Nugent looked at her appraisingly. 'You wouldn't be a Mountjoy yourself, would you?'

'Why do you ask that?'

'You've got a look of them, old family from these parts.'

'I'm related to Valdemar Mountjoy.'

Arthur gave a foxy smile. 'You could phone him up, if you can't get hold of Mr Hazard. Our firm has done all the work up at Mountjoy Castle for nearly a century.'

There was nothing to say to that, and Cleo was spared a reply by the arrival of Mrs Grigson, who greeted Arthur with surprising enthusiasm, urging him to descend into the kitchen for a warming cup of something.

'I will by and by,' he said. 'But business first, and I'd like to have a look round, get my bearings as it were. We did the roof some years back, you'll remember that, Mrs Grigson, in the old lady's time, that was. But we never came into the house, she was very strict about that.'

'She had her ways,' said Mrs Grigson in dark tones.

'I'll come with you,' said Cleo. 'Only, if we're going round the whole house, then I'll put a jacket on.'

'Not used to our winters,' said Mr Nugent. 'It's quite mild, really, for the time of year.'

Cleo, shivering despite the jacket, opened the door off the hall and led the way into the depths of the house.

Cleo had only made the most cursory inspection of the house, but now she went round every inch of it with Arthur, enraptured by its character and the sudden, unexpected delights revealed as the builder led her along the warren of passages. One passage led to another passage which would end, as like as not, in a panelled little room with mullioned windows looking out to the fells or a bay overlooking what must once have been a vegetable garden.

'Knot garden they had out there, centuries ago,' said Arthur, with a jerk of his head towards the window as he scribbled down some measurements. 'Fine house it was then.'

'It still is,' said Cleo, shivering despite her coat.

There were changes of level everywhere, two steps up here, three twisting ones down there. There was another staircase, this one with narrow wooden treads, which Arthur said was far too dangerous to use.

On the first floor there was the wing where Cleo was installed in the Dragon Room, where rooms led off a corridor; not so in the main part of the house, where the rooms led one into another.

'No passages in those days,' said Arthur. 'And there'd have been another staircase down there. This house has changed a lot over the years, a room moved round here, a passage put in there, doors shifted around like nobody's business. Not to mention lavatories and bathrooms. Could tell quite a story this house, if it wanted to.'

'Think of all the people who've lived here,' said Cleo, padding along a worn piece of carpet behind Arthur.

'Best not,' said Arthur. 'Make you go potty, that would. Now, this gallery here, this is what you could call exceptional. They had pictures up here in the last century; all gone now, of course. But originally, they'd have used this for indoor exercise, did you know that?'

'No,' said Cleo, who had already fallen in love with the long, narrow room and its row of tiny-paned windows.

'Yes,' said Arthur. 'Kids running up and down, Mum strolling round yakking to her friends. Very useful kind of room, all things considered, but not the sort to fit into a modern house.' He looked up at the ceiling and tut-tutted. 'Dear, oh dear. more damaged plasterwork. Nothing to be done about that, I'm afraid, not unless you've got a very deep pocket, and I shall have to tell Mr Hazard so.'

'Honestly, Mum,' Cleo said, snuggled into a rickety old armchair by the kitchen stove, with her legs and feet swatched in a rug. 'He's so depressing. He stood in the middle of this wonderful long gallery at the top of the house, "Oh, that'll have to go, there's nothing that can be done about this, that's in such a terrible state it'll all have to come down." I despair.'

'Cleo,' said Gussie suspiciously, 'you sound thoroughly worked up about this house. Why?'

'I'm not,' said Cleo hotly. 'Well, perhaps I am. It's an amazing house, or the shell of a wonderful house. It could be restored, I know it could. Only horrible cousin Henry says everything costs too much, and Arthur's going to tell him about hundreds of man hours to just restore the plaster and woodwork, let alone the rest of the work, oh, the stupidity of it.'

'It is Henry's house,' said Gussie, surprised at Cleo's vehemence. She herself never took much notice of her surroundings, providing the light was right, and her work was at hand.

'It shouldn't be.' Cleo was definite. 'There should be a law saying that philistines aren't allowed to own lovely, decrepit old houses.'

'What about the National Trust? If it's so lovely.'

'Mum, you're impossible. It's not grand, and it shouldn't be a museum kind of place, it needs to be lived in. It feels as though it's lived in, even though it's been unoccupied for a while, and just one old lady before that.'

Gussie changed tack. 'Has Adele settled in? I must say, I'm glad you've got a friend there with you.'

Cleo's mind was set in its single-track furious mode. 'Adele is hopeless. She thinks the house is smashing, but she likes it just as it is, tatty and faded and rotting away.'

Cleo twined a strand of rug fringe round her little finger. It was four o'clock in the afternoon, and already well and truly dark, in that peculiarly intense way that winter days had in Eyotshire. She shouldn't be phoning her mother now, even though it was after one; evening calls were much more economical, especially if one wanted to fume at length.

'What?' she said. 'What was that? This is a bad line, all echoes and clicks; I'm sure it's tapped. Did you say Perry? Oh, no, surely he doesn't want to come all this way? He does. No, of course not, I'd love to see him, but he'll hate it here, he'll think it's all terribly uncivilised. No, I don't do him an injustice; he hates to be uncomfortable. Yes, I expect I'll feel the same when I'm his age, what a dispiriting thought, but just the same . . . Oh hell.'

Do I want to see him? Cleo pondered the point as she made herself some toast and Marmite, funny what a taste for Marmite she had at the moment.

He wouldn't like her wan looks, but then, that was what commitment meant. That was why Perry would marry but not cohabit, so he said.

Cohabit. Such a disagreeable word. An accurate and chilling word, why not living together? Nothing wrong with a euphemism, now and then.

'You have to accept both the rough and the smooth,' Perry had said. 'So there's no taking a temper and walking away. There are no guarantees, I know that perfectly well, and people do walk away, just as my wife did.'

More like run, thought Cleo rebelliously, and then winced at her disloyalty.

'But at least not on a whim, not easily. That's why it has to be marriage. Nothing casual about it.'

'She was talking to her mother,' said Giles, putting back the receiver on the field telephone. 'In London.'

'London,' said Giles with longing. It was a centuries-long grievance that he had breathed his last in Haphazard Hall, so many miles from the court and his friends and all the mischief of London. 'Just think how many acquaintances we'd have in London.'

'I expect it's as licentious and lascivious as ever, no place for a man to consider his soul.'

'Bother the soul,' said Giles. Then, sensing a sermon brewing, he hastily brought the conversation back to Cleo and her mother. 'Another visitor, by the sound of it. One Perry.'

'Peregrine, do you think?' asked Lambert, duly distracted. 'I knew a Peregrine once, a rascally fellow, he stole my second-best hose.'

'These days,' said Giles, 'it could just as well be a girl. We shall have to wait and see.'

'That's all we ever do,' said Lambert. 'Waiting and seeing.'

'Let's have a song,' said Giles, taking up his lute. 'To cheer your spirits.' He struck a chord, pursed his lips, and set about the serious business of lute-tuning.

'I'm sure this Perry is a man,' said Lambert, who had been thinking things over. 'And not a relative. I sense a lover.'

Giles tightened a string too tightly in his excitement, and winced when he heard its sharpness.

'A lover,' he said. 'What pleasure if you're right. It's a long while since there were any lovers in this house. Oh, for a little liveliness!'

'I shall go and read my Bible,' said Lambert and stretched so vigorously that his jacket rose above his waist. He gave it a firm tug to pull it back into place. 'I can tell that you're going to play love songs, idle ditties. Tunes summon the devil,' he added, causing Giles to strike a most insolent chord.

'Okay,' said Adele. 'This Perry bloke is on his way, right? Who is he?'

It wasn't easy to make out what she was saying, since her mouth was full of clothes pegs for the flimsies which she had just washed out. She and Cleo were down in the little room with the washing machine.

Cleo had put some of her washing into the machine, but this

had been summarily tossed out by Adele. 'You can do yours later, you're here all day.'

Cleo wasn't too pleased about this, but she recognized self-ishness of a high order when she saw it, and it wouldn't do to be fighting over every little thing. No doubt there would, in due course, be plenty of big things which they would disagree over. Meanwhile, Adele was excellent company, and look at the lovely food she'd brought back for their supper.

'I thought you were hard up.'

'I am, but we can't starve. And you're in no state to be slaving over a stove all day. Besides, I sold a very expensive dress today, to one Belinda Purley. She'll pay a fortune for something different and flattering, so I'm in the money.'

'Oh, good,' said Cleo, turning off the light as she left the washing machine to its solitary rumbles and shudders. 'I hope that washing machine works,' she added, as they went up the stairs.

'What, haven't you tried it?'

'No,' said Cleo. 'I was going to, only you removed all my things.'

'Disaster! Suppose it rips all my clothes to shreds, oh, Cleo, how dire.'

'Stop fussing,' said Cleo. 'It's on now.'

'Well, let's stop it, and put in your washing instead.'

'No way,' said Cleo, pushing her friend up the chilly stone steps.

Adele flew about the kitchen, opening a bottle of wine and putting it to warm, tossing a salad, whipping up a dressing, and deftly setting out the goodies which she had brought from Eyot. 'You never said any more about Perry. Is he a relation?'

'Not yet. He will be, sort of, because I'm going to marry him.'

That stopped Adele in her tracks. Why should she look so astonished? thought Cleo, am I the sort who looks destined for the single life?

'You never said a word, how sly of you.' Adele pulled a chair up on the other side of the stove. 'Tell me all about him. When's the wedding, that's the first thing, and who's doing your dress?'

'Three weeks ago, and only the Register Office, nothing fancy.'

'Three weeks ago?'

'I had to postpone it. Because of the shingles.'

'Oh, I see. Oh, what a shame, you could have had a lovely domestic Christmas. Where are you going to live?'

'In London. He has a flat.'

'Is he an artist?'

'An artist? Why should he be an artist?'

'I always thought of you as being essentially that way inclined, but of course, you're a money person now, aren't you? Is he in the City as well?'

'No,' said Cleo. At least I've been spared that, she thought with an unexpected surge of relief. How terrible to be married to one of those driven men she worked with. Or to one of those suave and deeply boring, smoothly groomed merchant bankers that she saw thronging the city streets as they patrolled in their navy blue overcoats.

'So, is he on the dole?'

'No, he isn't,' said Cleo, much amused at the thought of Perry in the job centre. 'He's an art historian. He writes books, advises on pictures, collections and so on. Gives lectures, that kind of thing.'

'An established art historian, then,' said Adele perceptively. 'Not a mere youth, one may say.'

'Not exactly.'

'Fifties?'

'No, no. He's in his forties.'

'Father figure,' said Adele wisely. 'Not necessarily a good move in your case, but time will tell.'

'Don't talk nonsense,' said Cleo, beginning to feel ruffled. 'He's not a father figure at all, he's a great companion, not paternal in the least.'

Adele gave a pretty shrug of her shoulders. 'Now you're het up about it. Well, if he's coming for the weekend I can look him over, let you know what I think of him.

'Thank you.'

'He'll share your room, which is lucky, with the room situation as it is.'

No, he won't, Cleo said to herself. I couldn't bear to share a bed with a teddy bear, let alone a man, with my skin the way it is; the agony.

8

Valdemar was haranguing Gussie, and she didn't like it.

'Look, Val, it's lovely to be taken out to lunch like this, but you're spoiling the food.'

'What? Don't you like it here?'

'Yes, but if you hammer away at me, I get nervous, and then I won't enjoy my food any more. Lay off while I'm eating, please. Then you can buy me a large brandy, and I'll hear you out without giving myself indigestion.'

'I don't know what you're talking about,' said Valdemar. 'I ask one or two questions about my daughter; perfectly simple, straightforward questions, and you get into a lather.'

'Val, if you don't stop it, I'm leaving. Now, calm down and tell me about Hugh and Helena. Are they enjoying school?'

'They are, their teachers aren't, apparently,' said Valdemar who was both a doting and a cynical father. 'Of course, all this child-centred learning is so much rubbish, they'll have nothing but trouble with the twins if they carry on like that.'

'It encourages self-expression.'

'Time enough for that when they've got some self to express. Meanwhile, they need keeping under control, and I don't see any signs of that happening. Nor much going on in the reading line, that seems to be left to Magdalena to do. "They'll read when they're ready to," is what their idiotic teacher says. God, they'll still be at school and completely illiterate come pension time, if they wait for them to be ready.'

Gussie tried a less aggravating subject. 'Work going well? Busy; careering off abroad and so on?'

Valdemar had grudgingly to admit that his firm of structural engineers were not doing too badly, given the appalling state the country was in. 'Of course, it's the foreign work that keeps us alive.'

'Good,' said Gussie, who had little interest in the large banks, museums and corporate headquarters which Valdemar worked on in most of the capital cities of the world. 'I'm so glad.'

'What a liar you are,' said Valdemar, with his sudden and charming smile. 'You couldn't give a bugger about my work. Now, you don't want a pudding, do you? I'll order you that brandy, and you can tell me what Cleo thinks she's doing.'

Gussie beckoned to the waiter. 'I'll have some of that trifle, please,' she said. 'With lots of cream.'

'Got to watch your figure, you aren't getting any younger,' said Valdemar agreeably.

'I can still get into the same size jeans as I could twenty years ago,' said Gussie. 'Bet you aren't wearing the same size in suits.'

'It's different for a man. And of course you can't afford to buy new jeans, so you have to stay slim.'

Gussie laughed and dug her spoon into the trifle. 'Cleo, then. I don't think she really wants to marry Perry.'

'I'm bloody sure she doesn't,' said Valdemar furiously. 'In which case, she must tell him so, and not keep him dangling about at her beck and call.'

'Perry wants to be at her beck and call, he's in love with her.'

'In love? Nonsense, he's a grown man, far too old for all that Romeo and Juliet lark. No, no, he's a sensible enough chap, he'll understand.'

'Cleo's too kind to give him the push. And she was very keen on him at one time, I just think it's gone off the boil, rather. Maybe if she'd married him straight away, they would have got to know each other better, and it would have been all right.'

'I never heard such balls. Much better for her to wait a bit and then realize he's not the man for her.'

'Who is the man for her?'

'How the hell should I know? I'm not a soothsayer. She's attractive enough, lots of men friends, she should pick someone her own age.'

'I think most of her men friends bore her.'

'Perry must bore her.'

'Val, what a thing to say.'

'Don't pretend, Gussie, hardly your style. Perry's bored me for years.'

'You're old friends.'

'We were on the same staircase at Cambridge. In fact, I shared a set with him in my first year. Doesn't mean he isn't boring.'

'I find him extremely good company.'

Valdemar gave Gussie a mocking look. 'Perhaps you should marry him.'

Gussie pushed back her chair and got to her feet. 'Val, there's no talking to you when you're in this kind of mood. Perry's going up to Hazard this weekend, and I expect he'll be in touch when he gets back.'

'You won't get the truth out of him,' said Valdemar, looming over Gussie in his tall way. 'Or out of Cleo. Better go yourself, then you can see how things really are. I'll stand you the train fare, if you're broke. Or, I know, beg a lift from Perry.'

Cleo was sitting in what had become her favourite chair in the kitchen, warmed by the stove. Mrs Grigson had been and gone, leaving the kitchen sparkling, and all Cleo's washing done and hanging on the drier. 'Leave it to me,' she'd said, with a harrowing glance.

Porthos stalked into the kitchen and jumped on her lap. 'Silly name for a cat,' Mrs Grigson had said when asked if he had a name. 'Foreign, and he's a real Eyotshire mog, that one.'

'It's from a book,' Cleo said. 'Porthos was one of the three musketeers, the big and beefy one. From a French novel,' she added, not seeing any response in Mrs Grigson's deep, dark eyes.

'French!' she said. 'Foreign! I told you so. Poor cat.'

'Only you aren't a poor cat at all, are you?' said Cleo, stroking his thick fur. She had open on her lap a copy of the *Guide to the Buildings of Eyotshire*, which she had found abandoned in a distant chamber. Perry will be interested, she thought. On the other hand, he probably had his own copy. She shrugged herself further into the fat cushion on the chair, causing Porthos to run his claws into her leg.

Perry.

No, she wouldn't think about him coming. It wasn't that she didn't want to see him, exactly; of course not, she missed him, naturally she did. But she was still feeling rather feeble, and not in good looks. Yes, she knew that when lovers turned into husbands, they got used to their wives having colds and scruffy hair and so on. Just as she wouldn't notice or mind about his wrinkles or saggy bum.

Saggy bum?

What was she thinking of? Perry wasn't in the least bit saggy; he was a thin, trim man, no spare flesh anywhere. No lovejugs on Perry. In fact, as time went on, they'd look like Jack Sprat and Mrs S, Cleo reckoned. She had always been curvy, and curves grew with age. Except when you'd been ill, and took on a temporary skeletal look.

Perry wasn't too keen on the plumpness, now she came to think about it. There were touches of austerity to Perry, and he liked to be careful about what Cleo ate. And drank. Perry was a great man for moderation.

Cleo could see Perry's flat in her mind's eye. Cool and elegant, full of creams and beiges. Full of light, flickering in from the river on fine days, shining up and down and across from artfully placed lights on dark ones. Pictures everywhere; they were the heart and soul of the flat, and Perry had some very good ones.

I sometimes think I'm not so very keen on pictures, thought Cleo. Not those pictures, anyway. Perry's period was the nineteenth century. Cleo didn't feel any great affinity for the nineteenth century. Gussie, when she dined the flat, had been loud in her appreciation of Perry's collection. They had chatted enthusiastically and knowledgeably about this artist and that technique, while Cleo gazed out at the river, rather envying the people out there on boats.

Cleo shook herself, earning a look of fury from Porthos's great golden eyes. He yawned, showing his fine, rat-crunching teeth, and stretched out his large paws.

'No moderation for you,' said Cleo, tickling his nose. 'You're an all-or-nothing cat, I can tell. Wish I could find that radio we keep on hearing the voices from. I do wonder where it is, I seem to have looked everywhere. If I had a radio, I could listen to the weather forecast. Perhaps it's going to snow, extremely heavily, and the roads will be blocked. Or there might be one of those great fogs I've seen on the television. Perry wouldn't be able to get through one of those.'

She decided to ring up Adele and ask her if she had a radio in the shop. If not, she could nip out and buy a cheap one, they needed some contact with the outside world.

Adele did better than that. 'Here,' she said, staggering in with a box. 'I thought it would fall off the back of the bike, but no, all is well.'

'Adele, what is it? It's heavy, is it a giant saucepan?'

'A saucepan?' Adele looked at Cleo with huge and indignant eyes. 'A *saucepan*? Why ever would I buy a saucepan? No, it's a TV set.'

'You bought a television?'

'For twenty quid,' said Adele with pride. 'The people Suzie's staying with were given it as a present last year. They've got a whacking big set, and don't like portables, the screen's too small. So I made an offer, and they were glad to see the back of it. Where shall we plug it in?'

'Pictures? It must be a film, Giles. They watched films in the drawing-room, after dinner, in the forties and fifties, do you remember that? Popeye. Charlie Chaplin.' Lambert gave a happy sigh, and then pulled himself together. 'They should have been prohibited. The stage and all its works are a sure path to destruction.'

'The destruction was yours,' said Giles, 'closing down all the playhouses. Poor Will must be fretting still, wherever he is.'

'He can't complain,' said Lambert. 'From what I heard Miss Hazard say, one of his works is playing somewhere every day of the year.'

'Never mind that,' said Giles. 'This isn't a film, although it's not unlike one. There's no reel, no projection. And no member of the Hazard family uttering terrible oaths when it jams. This is completely different. Just a box, with a moving picture on the screen. A colour picture,' he added temptingly.

Lambert, although he denied it vehemently to beyond the grave, loved colour.

'I will see for myself,' said Lambert. 'In the kitchen, no doubt, what a come-down, spending all this time in the kitchen.'

'The kitchen is where the action is,' said Giles, leading the way.

Lambert, technically-minded from boyhood, circled the set. 'Plugs in,' he said. 'And that's an aerial wire.' He gave a tweak to the trailing wire which it had taken Adele a good half hour to run up through a grate to enable the set to work in the bowels of the earth, as she put it. 'No mystery here, it's a wireless.'

'Radio,' said Giles. 'Keep up, Lambert, no one says wireless any more.'

'Miss Hazard did.'

'Miss Hazard was of another age. And this isn't a radio; I told you, it has pictures, which move.'

Lambert and Giles had much enjoyed the radio in Miss Hazard's day, although they could never listen in for as long as they would have liked. Miss Hazard kept the radio in her room. She had spent many hours of the day in there, but reading rather than listening to the radio, which was tiresome of her.

'Turn it on, then,' said Lambert. 'Let's have a listen.'

'Look,' said Giles, peering at the set. He found a likely looking knob and gave it a twirl. The screen buzzed for a moment, and then a balding man appeared, standing in front of a gaudy map festooned with little clouds and stars.

'The penetrating frost currently dominating the weather across the whole of the north of England will continue.'

The words vanished, as Giles tried another knob or two.

'Turn it on again,' said Lambert in a high state of excitement. 'I fear this is undoubtedly the Devil's work.'

'Nonsense. God's work,' Giles said firmly. He had changed channels, and they found themselves in the middle of a police thriller. Cars rocketed across the screen, there were close-ups of actors expressing violent emotions, and the music pinged and crashed in the background.

'Well!' said Lambert, floating over to Cleo's chair. 'Well, the Lord be praised.'

Two floors up, Cleo stirred and turned in a restless sleep. Her fading blisters were painful tonight, and she had taken a sleeping pill to help her sleep.

'Only it's not working,' she said crossly, sitting bolt upright and looking out into the chilly room. It was light, now why? Oh, the moon, shining in a clear sky, bringing ever deeper layers of frost. Cleo shivered. Why aren't I in London? she thought. What am I doing here?

Then as her eyes became less sleepy, all thoughts of chilliness and London left her. This wasn't the room she had gone to sleep in. This was different. There were hangings round the bed, and it was a different bed, squarer and higher and more ornate.

The window was in the same place as her room, but further away from her. The room was bigger, and the door was definitely not where it should be. Cleo shook herself. This was one of those uneasy, disturbing dreams, where everything was just slightly and menacingly out of place; the familiar distorted.

She got out of bed and went to the door. There was no passage outside, just another room, with shadowy shapes of unfamiliar furniture, and then another one. No worn dregs of carpet underfoot, either, but polished boards. Polished, what a joke, when had this house last seen polish? What an army of Mrs Grigsons it would take to polish this expanse of floor.

Here was the landing, not so strange, but the stairs were in the centre, not running up against the wall. And the hall below had a huge fireplace, not at all like the neat Georgian one she was used to.

Why am I tip-toeing? Cleo asked herself, certain that there was no one to hear her, and that she could go through every room in the house and not find Adele. You don't find your friends in your dreams, she thought, fascinated by the patterns of light made by the moon shining through the tiny faceted window panes.

Back through the rooms, now not so strange. Back to her bed, which wasn't hers. Then she was suddenly wide awake, and in bed in her room which was exactly as it had always been. Cleo sat bolt upright in bed, putting out a hand to stroke Porthos as though to be sure she wasn't still dreaming.

'Only it wasn't a dream,' she said to the cat, who wasn't

pleased to be disturbed. 'I'm sure that was the way the house used to be. Do you know what, I think there's something very strange indeed about this house? And I think Lily's quite right, and that it's haunted. And what's more, it doesn't bother me at all, because whoever or whatever is doing the haunting isn't at all threatening.'

Porthos yawned, and tucked his nose under a large striped paw before sinking back into his slumbers.

Giles and Lambert, going back to their quarters after watching every minute of viewing until the last beeps after the epilogue, had been alarmed to see Cleo wandering about like that.

'She'll catch her death of cold, in that flimsy nightgown,' said Lambert. 'Good flannel is what you need here. I made all the womenfolk wear flannel in my time. It was pretty, though, she has a very shapely form.'

Giles had never been interested in the female form. He was worrying about something else.

'Do you suppose she noticed where she was and what she was seeing?'

'Sleep-walking, I expect. No recollection at all the next day.'

'Let's hope so,' said Giles. 'If she remembers, she may begin to wonder, and want to find out more. By and by, she'll talk about it to this friend or that, and then we'll have those perfidious rogues in, hot after hauntings.'

Lambert shivered. 'Surely not?'

'I don't like it,' said Giles with foreboding. 'I don't like it at all.'

9

Cleo felt the warmth of efficient central-heating waft over her as Sylvester opened his front door and greeted her with glad cries.

Midwinter Hall brought back a flood of memories. That idyllically and unbelievably hot summer she had spent up here when she was eighteen. Impossible to think of endless, lust-filled sunny days now, with an east wind howling through the chimneys.

'Of course, the house is really much smarter now,' she told Sylvester as they headed for the kitchen to find Lily.

'Courtesy of the insurance company, but I'd still rather not have had those burst pipes,' said Sylvester. 'And it involved me in a lot of extra expense, I may tell you. It's all very well revealing old fireplaces and so forth, but then the floor has to be re-done, and grates and slabs and suchlike.'

'You can afford it.'

'I had to do an extra series of concerts,' said Sylvester. 'Very wearing, although I have to say my agent was very pleased.'

'Do you good, getting about a bit more,' said Lily, who miraculously had coffee just ready. 'Knew you'd be over,' she said to Cleo. 'Been having odd dreams?'

Cleo dropped into her old place at the the kitchen table. 'Lily, you witch, how do you know?'

'Because a lot of people have strange dreams at Haphazard House. Rooms changing round? Staircases in different places, doors where they shouldn't be?'

'Something like that,' said Cleo. 'I thought when I woke up this morning that it might be the sleeping pills I've been having.'

'No, no,' said Lily, putting a piece of freshly made cake in front of her.

'Lily, lemon cake, how delicious, but I don't know if I can manage it.'

'And what did you have for breakfast? A slice of toast and a scraping of marmalade, I dare say.'

'Marmite, actually.'

'You eat that up.'

'I'll have a piece,' said Sylvester cunningly.

'You will not,' said Lily. 'It's the thin end of the wedge, you eating cake at this time of the day. It's Cleo needs fattening up, not you.'

Sylvester, well used to Lily's excellent work on keeping his bulk within reasonable limits sighed, and drank his coffee black. 'You never told me all this about Haphazard House, Lily,' he said accusingly. 'Is it really haunted?'

'So people say,' said Lily. 'Voices, music, weird dreams . . .'

'The lute music that you heard, Sylvester,' said Cleo, fascinated. 'Maybe that was a ghostly musician.'

'No peace for us artists even when we're dead,' said Sylvester gloomily. 'No doubt he still has an agent, goading him on. One thing I can tell you: there's no one alive in Hazard today who plays the lute. And precious few anywhere in the world who could play it the way I heard it played at Haphazard the other evening.'

'Goodness,' said Cleo, licking the crumbs off her plate with her finger.

'Cleo, if it worries you being in that great rambling place with only Adele for company, then you come and stay here. Your old room is always ready, isn't it, Lily? And you can go back and forth to keep an eye on the workmen, if that's what Henry wants you to do.'

'I'm not sure what Henry wants,' said Cleo gloomily. 'His builder came and went, saying it was all too expensive, and better to let the place fall down. Since then, not a word from Cousin H. I rang in the evening but only got an answering machine, and he hasn't rung back yet.'

'Oh, he'll be in touch soon,' said Lily. 'He's spoken to Arthur, that I do know; I heard them talking about it in the village shop. Arthur's going up to the house this afternoon.'

'Arthur?' said Sylvester.

'Arthur Nugent,' said Lily.

'Ah, the builder,' said Sylvester. 'A merry fellow.'

'He's to put the staircase and decayed floorboards to rights,' said Lily. 'So that the young ladies don't go tumbling to their doom, is what he said.'

'He isn't related to Mrs Grigson, is he?' said Cleo. 'She seems heavily doom-laden.'

'Funny you should say that,' said Sylvester, pouring himself and the others more coffee, and gazing into the depths of the mug he was holding in his huge hand. 'Arthur is Mrs Grigson's nephew.'

'Oh, help.'

'Still, if you're having visitors, it'll be for the best if they don't all disappear through the floorboards,' said Lily from the depths of the fridge. She stood up and shut the door. 'I've a few bits and pieces here, Cleo, that you can take back with you.'

'Visitors?' said Sylvester, interested. 'Who?'

'Perry,' said Cleo.

'Perry,' said Sylvester. 'Not quite his cup of tea, Haphazard House. Not unless he's changed a good deal.'

'And your mum's coming too,' said Lily, shaking open a carrier bag.

Cleo shook her head. 'Just Perry. He's not staying at Haphazard, though. He's going to stay at the Hazardous Head.'

'There are two rooms booked,' said Lily in her definite way. 'One for Gussie, and one for Perry.'

'No point in arguing with Lily,' said Sylvester. 'She's always right. It isn't very friendly, though. Why not at Haphazard?'

Cleo laughed. 'It's because I told Mum that Perry would have to stay in a room with no proper lighting, and wainscoting chewed by rats.'

'Sounds as though you were trying to discourage him,' said Sylvester, giving Cleo a knowing look.

'Very keen on style and a certain level of comfort, is Perry,' said Cleo with some pride.

Perry's style was what had first attracted Cleo. She had been bowled over by his sense of style and his beautiful manners and his certainty that his behaviour on every occasion and in all circumstances would be perfect. And his arranging of

circumstances to suit him. Poor Perry, what a mess she'd made
of his superbly organized plans for their wedding.

'Haven't seen Perry for years,' said Sylvester. 'Of course, I
would have bumped into him at your wedding, if it had ever
happened. One supposes he would have been there, unless he'd
got confused about the date.'

'Sylvester, that's hitting below the belt.'

'Not at all. I shall look forward to seeing him again.'

'You must have known him at Cambridge, too; you were there
at the same time.'

'Only slightly,' said Sylvester. 'We were at different colleges,
but I knew him through Val. Perry is, by the way, completely
unmusical. I do hope you realize that.'

'Art's his thing,' said Cleo.

I should have taken Sylvester up on his invitation, thought
Cleo, slamming the car door shut, and heading into the wind
tunnel of icy air which streamed between the barn and the
house. No warm air and soft rugs here when she pushed open
the front door. Just the chill of ages, and the gloom of a
midwinter day.

Cleo had only just shut the door behind her when she heard
a tapping. It was someone knocking on the door, and she edged
it open again, peering cautiously round to see who it was.

'Ah,' said Arthur standing there. 'Come to do a bit about the
house.'

'Come in.'

Rotund Arthur wasn't a tall man, but he had an impressive way with him, and the hall seemed much smaller with
him in it.

'A coincidence,' said Cleo. 'Both of us arriving at the same
moment.'

'I've been waiting out there for,' and he consulted his watch,
'thirty-five minutes.'

'I'm sorry,' said Cleo. 'You see, I haven't been able to get
in touch with Cousin Henry; I had no idea when you were
coming back.'

'Ah, an oversight on the part of Mr Henry Hazard. He'll pay
for it, because I charge my time out by the hour, and if I spend

that time waiting to start a job, then down on the worksheet it must go. Regs, you understand. Nothing personal.'

'No, I'm sure not,' said Cleo.

Arthur's eyes, which had very much the same brooding quality as his aunt's, were fixed on the staircase. 'Dear me, dear oh dear, just look at that, I'd forgotten how bad it is, although I wrote it all down. Fancy letting it get into such a state. Wicked neglect, that is, wicked.'

'I agree,' said Cleo. 'Are you going to repair it?'

'Repair it? That's not my brief, no, I gather Mr Hazard's working to a limited budget. I'm to make things as safe as I can, which is quite a different proposition. Now, that staircase could be taken down in a trice, put up a nice, plain new one, no rot, no woodworm, nothing bouncy, and the job is done. Safe as houses. You'd have destroyed part of history, mind you, and I don't happen to believe that our history belongs to any man, however much property he owns, but then that's just my way of thinking.'

Cleo frowned. 'Can you tear down bits of old houses? Aren't they protected or something?'

'Some of them are, yes. Listed, they started that after the war. But it's a strange fact that not a single house in Hazard or the neighbouring villages is listed. And yet I know for certain that there are at least half a dozen that should have a high rating, maybe Grade I even.'

'Oh?'

'The listing people never came here. Missed out this area entirely.'

'Skulduggery?' said Cleo, much interested.

Arthur pursed his lips, considering, and then let out his breath in a thin whistle. 'I should like to say yes, because that's what capitalist landowners are like. However, I am an honest man, and I think it had more to do with the foot of snow lying hereabouts and the fifteen-foot snowdrifts at the very time when they should have been here. They passed it by, went on to the next place, and never came back.'

'So Henry Hazard could pull the house down tomorrow.'

'And may well do so,' said Arthur.

'He couldn't,' said Cleo, paling at the thought. 'He wouldn't.'

'Who's to say what a rich man may choose to do on a whim? He can't sell it, not in this condition, that's for sure. The land's worth a bit, but more without an old ruin sitting on it. And he could sell the lead off the roof and the tiles and timbers for a few quid. Yes, I think Henry Hazard might well think of pulling it down. In his place, who knows if I'd do any different?'

He bent down and picked up his bag. 'Now, I'd be obliged if you could let me have some light here, I need light to do the job.'

'Yes,' said Cleo, flicking the wobbly brass switch by the passage door, and casting a dim and shadowy light over the hall.

'Is that the best you can do?'

'I daren't put a brighter bulb in there, it smells funny as it is.'

Arthur sniffed. 'Bakelite burning,' he said. 'Trouble with your light fitments. I'll tell Mr Hazard that the electrics need attention.'

Cousin Henry won't pay for rewiring, thought Cleo as she went away to the kitchen to brew a strong cup of tea for Arthur. Not if he's planning to knock the house down. All these negative reports coming back, he'd hardly be able to resist the easy way out.

If he's going to knock it down, why bring me up to live in the house while it's empty? she thought angrily, as she heaped tea into the pot. There was nothing worth stealing, after all.

Giles and Lambert sat on the top stair, watching Arthur at work.

Lambert still lamented the change of ways. 'No leather apron,' he moaned. 'None of the signs of his trade.'

'Stop whingeing,' said Giles impatiently. 'He's doing the job in a proper fashion, see, he's measuring, feeling the wood, testing the strength of each tread, like any carpenter these last six hundred years . . . Oh, Lord save us!'

That was Arthur with one leg through a stair. Cursing and grumbling, he restored himself to a more or less upright position, made a squiggly note in his little books, and continued, albeit more gingerly than before.

'Terrible state, that wood's in,' said Lambert, shaking his head. 'Such a fine staircase, allowed to crumble like that. It is a symbol of the folly of man, where . . .'

Giles wasn't in the mood for Lambert on the folly of man. He had co-existed with Lambert for about three centuries now, and had been glad of the company. However, in the silent watches of the night he still wondered why fate had twinned him with a Parliamentary officer, who had lived by such a gloomy and joyless set of untenable beliefs.

'Sanctimonious,' he said.

'Calipers,' said Lambert. 'He's taking measurements of the banisters.'

'You don't do that if you're working for a master who's planning to pull the house down. That's what you do when your thoughts are on repairs. Repairs and renewal.'

'Pull the house down!' Lambert shuddered. No house meant an eternity of external flitting; what a terrible thought. No cosy nooks, no phone tapping, no people to take an interest in. And no more television, just when they had discovered its joys. He blanched at the prospect of such deprivation.

'We can't let it happen.'

'You tell me what we can do to stop it.'

10

Adele thought Cleo was becoming obsessive. 'It's a crummy old house, right? Picturesque, okay, but not practical. No good to live in, no good to rent out, no use as a B & B. It's a heap of stones.'

'There's a perfectly good roof.'

'Oh?'

'Yes, it was repaired a few years ago. Mrs Grigson told me.'

'What idiot spent good money on that?'

'Old Mrs Hazard.'

'Who then popped off.'

'At least it means that the house won't get any worse.'

'You mean it'll stay a half-ruined shell. Great.'

'This house has a heart. It has a history. It's begging to be looked after.'

'Cleo, sweetie, has this disease affected your wits? Are you heading for the funny farm? This is a house we're talking about. Not Auntie Flo or even your old and decrepit horse. A house. A thing. An inanimate object. I grant you that it was once a terribly beautiful house, but time passes, houses which nobody wants to live in fall into ruins and vanish.' Her hands fluttered downwards. 'Kaput, finish, end of story.'

'A week ago, I'd have said that, too. But there's something about this house. It isn't a thing, it's almost alive.'

'Plenty of wild-life, I quite see that. Did you notice that one of the bedrooms has ivy growing through the window frame? Tendrils wrapping themselves round the post of the bed. Before you know where you are, there'll be squirrels in residence on the bed, and badgers in the fireplace. Come on, Cleo, reality time.'

'This house is real enough.'

'No, I mean *real* real. Sex, friendship, food, fun.'

'Done that,' said Cleo morosely.

'Do it again. It never tires.'

'No?'

'Then there's work, making money, creating beautiful things.'

'This house could be a beautiful thing.'

'I give up,' said Adele. 'Any crisps left? And who's the commie on the stairs?'

It was early closing in Eyot, and Adele had come back after lunch, ready to settle herself at the kitchen table for some serious design work. She laid her portfolio down on the scrubbed surface, and tugged at the ribbons.

'Arthur,' said Cleo. 'The builder. Making the stairs safe.'

'More likely sawing floorboards in two so that the nobs can fall through.'

'You had a chat, then.'

'A quick exchange of views, yes.'

Adele settled herself down at the table. Cleo realized with sudden, irrational irritation that she had exactly the same look of concentration on her face that Gussie did when she was working.

Did she, Cleo, look like that when doing swift calculations in dollars and yen? She thought not.

Mrs Grigson appeared at the kitchen door, duster in hand, cast a desperate look at Adele and announced in her dark way that Arthur had a question to ask.

'Okay,' said Cleo, wondering what in the heap of dust and disorder Mrs Grigson could be applying her dainty yellow duster to.

'Can I help?' she said, addressing Arthur's rear.

He leant back on his heels, his mouth full of nails, which he spat genteelly out into the palm of his hand.

'Been having a look round,' he said. 'Good plasterwork here, did you know that?'

'There was once,' said Cleo. 'It's in the book about the house, it was famous for its ceilings. It's all gone now; I looked. Just lumpy bits left.'

'Wrong,' said Arthur. 'You come with me, and I'll show you something. Got a bucket of water?'

'Not about me, but I could fetch one,' said Cleo. 'What for?'

'You bring a bucket of warm water and a scrubbing brush into the little parlour through there.'

Clearly, he wasn't going to say any more until the water was provided, so Cleo went down to the scullery and toiled back up the stairs with an old galvanised bucket two-thirds full of water and a rather toothless scrubbing brush.

'Best you can manage?' asked Arthur, looking at the scrubbing brush as though it was about to lose its head under the guillotine. 'It'll have to do, I suppose.' He pulled a mothy chair out from where it was propped against the wall and gave it a shake. A leg fell off, and rolled across the floor to a resting place in front of the fireplace.

'I'll be back,' said Arthur.

And he was, in a very short time, carrying a small aluminium stepladder from his van under his arm. He snapped it open and hopped nimbly up it. 'Pass that bucket and the brush,' he said.

Cleo handed them up, and watched amazed as he ran water on to a patch of thick plaster where the cornice must once have been, and began tapping it gently with the back of the scrubbing brush.

'What are you doing?' said Cleo, peering upwards.

'Watch,' said Arthur, as a strip of the shapeless white stuff detached itself and fell to the floor.

'You've knocked it off,' cried Cleo. 'Vandal!'

'Vandal? For taking off layers and layers of distemper and old covering plaster? I'll have to report that; you can't stand there and call a certificated craftsman names, even if you are paying my wages.'

'I'm not paying you anything,' said Cleo. 'Do stop it, this ceiling is in bad enough condition without you having a go at it.' She looked up at the bubbling, cracked ceiling with something like despair. 'Hopeless,' she said to herself.

'There,' said Arthur, rattling down the steps, and pointing upwards with the dripping brush. 'Told you there was plasterwork.'

Visible now, in the patch where the lump of plaster had fallen off, were the imprecise but quite recognizable lines of the original plaster.

Cleo was too surprised to speak for a moment. She blinked. 'Do you mean it's all here? Under that gunk?'

'I do,' said Arthur with great satisfaction. 'Of course, it's impossible work. I don't know where you'd find workmen with the patience to restore that. It all needs to be eased off, all the overlays. Underneath, I bet you it's mostly good as new. In this room, and probably in most of the others. Now, I'm ready for that cup of tea, if Auntie hasn't forgotten.'

'Good to see that again,' said Giles. 'I well remember when they did this ceiling.'

'Decoration,' said Lambert in pained tones. 'Frivolous.'

'A feast for the eyes,' said Giles. 'What time is it?'

'Five o'clock.'

'Let's go and see if Cleo's got the television on. There's a quiz programme about this time.'

'As on the radio?'

'Better,' said Giles with certainty. 'Faces are much more interesting than disembodied voices.'

Lambert wasn't too happy about disembodied, but he wasn't going to miss anything new. He closed the field telephone carefully to keep the dust out, straightened his jerkin, smoothed back his grizzled, wavy hair and followed Giles to the cellarage.

No more troublesome dreams, but Cleo woke to a chilly room and an icy hot water bottle clamped to her toes. She hustled herself into all the clothes she could manage to fit on, still avoiding anything that pressed on her girdle of little scars. Then, wrapping her arms round herself and banging her sides to ward off the cold, she went downstairs.

The fire in the hall was a dull glimmer, and Cleo stirred it into some kind of life before easing open the front door and venturing out into a fairytale of spun ice and shimmering crystal.

What a frost, she thought, blinking in the grey-pink light of a still and frozen morning. A hoar frost, that had left the trees fixed in time, and cobwebs glistening with icy threads, and grass which cracked and crunched underfoot.

Cleo went to the gate, to peer down the white path of the road, and then to look back at the house, silhouetted against the lightening sky. It had an extraordinary presence, and she felt dismay in her heart and stomach at the thought of that regard being tumbled into dust and rubble.

A window on the second floor was flung open with a violent squeak, and Adele, all tousled curls and face cream, screamed at her to come in, was she mad, she'd catch pneumonia.

Cleo obeyed, although she could have stood outside and gazed and gazed. But she pushed open the front door and went across the hall and down the stairs to the kitchen, her teeth chattering,

'It's so heartbreakingly beautiful,' she said, still shivering as she clutched a mug of steaming tea.

'And you're so heartbreakingly stupid,' hissed Adele. 'If you get ill again, I'll have to look after you, and I can tell you, I don't have time. Or the inclination.' She crunched her way through a second piece of toast, rescued her portfolio from beneath Porthos, and made ready to start her morning wrap-up, fit for the journey to Eyot.

'I sometimes think,' she said as she wound a long woolly scarf several times round her neck, 'that it would be a break to get hitched to some rich man who could keep me in luxury and a good studio. I could cope with that.'

'You always had hordes of boyfriends,' pointed out Cleo.

'Uh huh, but you know how it is, as you get older, you get picky. You know what you want out of a guy, and you have to hook up with one who's sympathetic to your needs.'

'Needs?'

'Needs. We all have needs, and some of us have more outré ones than others.'

Cleo didn't attend to that, because a naughty thought had entered her head and distracted her.

'Bye, Adele, no I won't go out and mooch round in the freezing cold. Have a lucky day, sell lots of frocks.'

Cleo poured out another cup of tea, now very stewed, and sat down to work on her scheme. Adele and Perry. They'd be a perfect couple; all style and interest in arty things. Perry loved women to be absolutely in fashion; it was one of the many ways in which Cleo felt she let him down.

'Yes, Perry, I know that a tight, lean look is in for spring, but

I am not tight and lean. Those dresses only come in size 8s, and I haven't been a size 8 since *I* was eight. Yes, I know my mother is very trim, and very chic in her way, fine, but I'm not her, and I'm not wasting my money on clothes I'd never, ever wear.'

'Planning, are you?' said Mrs Grigson, coming into the kitchen and giving Cleo a particularly soulful look. 'Up to something, I can tell from the expression on your face.'

'Just thinking.'

'About a man,' said Mrs Grigson. 'As you should be, at your age. When you've been through what I've had to endure, then your expression is very different.'

Cleo could have sworn that Mrs Grigson signed off with a muffled 'Aye me,' and she had to struggle to look serious.

'Visitors this weekend,' she said brightly. 'My mother's coming up, and a friend.'

Mrs Grigson looked alarmed. 'There's nowhere for them to stay at Haphazard House,' she said. 'Nor the linen for their beds.'

'No problem, they're staying at the pub.'

'Best,' said Mrs Grigson. 'But you'll be glad to have company.'

'I've got Adele.'

Mrs Grigson sniffed. 'Flighty,' was all she said before diving under the sink for supplies and heading for the scullery.

Flighty describes me, thought Cleo, settling back into her chair, with her legs dangling over the arm. Look at me. In love with Perry practically from the moment I met him, quite sure that this was quite different from all my other amours. And now, here I am, six months later, idly wondering if he and Adele might suit.

Cleo stretched out first one leg and then the other, and looked at her feet, absurd in thick woolly socks. As if she wouldn't be beside herself with jealousy if he cast an eye in that direction. Not that Perry had a wandering eye. Look at his faithfulness to his wayward wife, which had amazed all his friends, so they had told Cleo.

Mrs Grigson returned and stood by the table in a vaguely menacing way, a mop in one hand and a bucket in the other. 'I don't want to bother you, but there's this floor to do.'

'That's all right,' said Cleo. 'I'm going upstairs for a spot of handiwork. Is there a stepladder anywhere?'

Mrs Grigson stared at her. 'Stepladder?'

'Yes, you know. Steps, for standing on. To reach things.'

'Reach what?'

'Oh, this and that,' said Cleo airily.

'There's one outside the boiler room,' said Mrs Grigson. 'Rickety, mind.'

'I'm sure it'll be fine,' said Cleo.

A few minutes later, she was opening the wooden steps in the little parlour. Several dead spiders fell out, but the steps seemed stout enough to bear her weight. Cleo pulled on the yellow gloves she had found by the sink, seized the bucket of water and the old scrubbing brush which she had brought up from the kitchen, and climbed gingerly up the ladder.

To work.

Perry drove fast. Gussie enjoyed the speed, the comfort of the car, and also Perry's company.

I must be grateful, she thought, that Cleo has picked a husband who is so easy to get on with.

She watched the countryside flash by, hillier now, with few houses; an occasional farmhouse with light from one or two windows shining out in the dusk, a pub, a deserted barn.

When I was Cleo's age, I would never have fallen for a Perry, so adult and composed. I like it now, but then?

What had she liked then? Life was different all those years ago. There was Valdemar, of course. She would never forget the pleasures of rolling in the bracken with a wild and wicked young Valdemar. In the fells near where she was going now, on hot summer days. All caution thrown to the wind, with the result that Cleo . . .

Cleo had had her share of wild flings, Gussie knew that. So now it was probably time to stop her relentless search for more exciting lovers, more fascinating men. One grew out of that. With the job and responsibility came a more sober and long-lasting approach to her men friends.

Not that she believed for a moment that Perry was dull in bed. Cleo wouldn't put up with that, not for all his poise and man of the world ways. Gussie had the feeling that Perry was probably delightful in bed, but that was definitely Cleo's business.

Perry would make Cleo very happy, just as he had made his first wife happy until she had run away with a Persian student who had the darkest and most fervent eyes anyone had ever seen.

Would Cleo make Perry a good wife? Was Cleo the wifely sort? Gussie suspected she was more than half Mountjoy, ready to toss aside what no longer pleased or interested her; a dangerous trait. Always supposing, thought Gussie with wry amusement, that they ever actually make it to the registrar.

'Are you asleep?' Perry asked out of the darkness. 'We're nearly there.'

'No. Just thinking,' said Gussie, noticing absently what attractive hands Perry had. He drove without gloves, thank goodness, she hated men's gloved hands on a steering wheel, not that she drove with so many men. Not these days.

Twisty roads, icy and treacherous. And then a swinging inn sign, and an opening door, and light spilling on to the frozen ground. Cloudy breath on the freezing air; goodness, the cold! Then indoors, and a wonderful log fire with flames leaping in the huge old fireplace, and polished wood, and the smell of good food.

12

'Mum? Oh, good. I'll come right over. No, you can see the house in the morning, it's freezing here, even the cat has frozen fur and whiskers. No, not literally, he's curled up in the only warm spot, he's very snug if truth be told. I'm bringing Adele, we'll be there in ten minutes.'

Gussie remembered Adele, or thought she did, although this pretty blonde creature with her huge blue eyes and luscious mouth didn't look at all familiar; was this really the same person?

'Yes,' said Adele, throwing pecks to right and left of Gussie's face. 'The same Adele, just done over differently.'

'This is Perry,' said Cleo, watching her affianced with bright, calculating eyes as she introduced the sparkling Adele.

What is she up to? thought Gussie, alarmed. She knew that look of old, and it boded mischief. Not Perry, she thought. Don't tease Perry, he doesn't like it.

Perry laughed at Adele, easy and relaxed, but his eyes were on Cleo. He took her hand and raised it to his lips before using his other arm to draw her closer to him.

'Ouch,' said Cleo. 'Do be careful, Perry, I'm ringed with blistery remains, and they hurt.'

'Of course,' he said, releasing her at once. 'Now, a drink before we go into dinner.'

'Dinner,' said Cleo. 'How civilized, it makes a change from the kitchen table or pasta on trays, doesn't it. Adele?'

'I'm grateful for a room and a roof over my head. And especially for the kitchen, which is warm,' said Adele primly. 'Although one can live, after all, with very little.'

'How much better if one doesn't have to,' said Perry. 'Cleo, have you a bad case of dandruff?'

Cleo brushed at her shoulders. 'Sawdust and plaster,' she said. 'It's everywhere. Horrible Henry has asked Arthur Nugent, who is the builder, to get some part of the house fit for habitation, such as the staircase and landings which are presently perilous places. I think he must be planning to spend Christmas there; thank goodness we shan't be here to share it.'

'It isn't long till Christmas,' said Perry.

'I'd like to spend Christmas abroad,' said Cleo. 'On a warm and fragrant island, bathing in a jewelled sea.'

'I never go abroad for Christmas,' said Perry, eating a handful of nuts. 'It's the only thing the English still do well.'

'Abroad!' said Gussie, taking her appreciative eyes away from the dark polished sideboard, the generous fire, the copper pans and scuttle. She was enjoying the warmth and comfort for which the inn was famous. 'I nearly forgot. Cleo, your visa is through. For Hungary.'

'Hungary?' said Perry. 'I didn't hear anything about Hungary.'

'Calm down, my pet,' said Cleo. 'I told you ages ago, one of my oldest friends lives in Budapest. She's married to a Hungarian musician, and I promised to visit her early next year. Prue. Adele, do you remember Prue?'

'Pale Prudence with the wonderfully weird aunt? I heard she'd gone to live abroad.'

'I'll come with you,' said Perry.

'No,' said Cleo, rather too quickly. 'She's only got a tiny place to live, and the hotels aren't safe, phones tapped and so on. Besides, aren't you persona non grata behind the Iron Curtain?'

'I can't go to Czechoslovakia, no, but Hungary's different.'

'Can't risk it,' said Cleo. 'You'd be whisked off to some Moscow jail and never be seen again, I couldn't bear it.'

'Hmm,' said Perry, hardly mollified. 'Well, we'll see when the time comes.'

'Better not,' said Cleo, stretching out her hand to take his. She flushed as she saw her mother giving her a very foxy look. 'Food,' she said brightly, easing herself out of her chair. 'I'm extremely hungry.'

'I've asked Sylvester to come over tonight,' Cleo told her mother as they made their way across the frost-whitened grass behind Haphazard House.

'I must get a proper look at it,' said Gussie, taking in the house and the deepening greys of the woods and hills behind with an admiring eye. 'What wonderful chimneys, and what a palimpsest of a house. Fifteenth century on, did you say?'

'According to the *Buildings of Eyotshire* it is.'

'Lovely to see Sylvester again,' said Gussie. 'And Gabriel?'

'Gabriel's away.'

'And what are you planning to feed your guests on? Sardines on toast make a good meal for a working artist, as you know, but I suspect that Sylvester and Perry may expect more.'

'Oh, Perry,' said Cleo. 'Do him good to rough it for a bit.'

'I'm sure he did plenty of roughing it in his student days,' said Gussie, quite sharply. 'He's grown out of all that.'

'I haven't,' said Cleo. 'And don't fuss, we've got it all planned. Adele's making a huge hot-pot affair, which simmers on the range. She's says it'll be delicious. I'll toss up a salad, you can treat us to a pud, and there you are. Perry can see to the wines,' she added.

'You make very free with Perry's purse.'

'Perry's purse is good and deep,' said Cleo. 'No big bonus for me this Christmas, so I've got to be careful or I won't be able to manage the fare to Budapest.'

'You aren't really going alone, are you?' asked Gussie.

'Why ever not?' Funny old mum, thought Cleo. She's been all over the place on her own, including some very dangerous nooks of the wood, and here she is, fussing about a little trip to Hungary.

'I got the impression that Perry would like to go with you.'

'Not really,' said Cleo, her mind on plasterwork. 'I think Hungary would be a bit bleak for him. Come on, let's go in, you've seen what there is to see out here.'

Gussie cast a final look up at the façade as they went round to the front of the house again.

'No back door?' Gussie asked.

'There is, but I can't open it; Mrs Grigson said no one has used it for years.'

'Strange, in the country,' said Gussie, as Cleo pushed open the big oak door. 'Brooding, this house,' she added, with a quick shiver as the chill reached her bones. And then she was inside, blowing on her hands, the whiff of a presence which seemed to hang about the house forgotten in her longing for coffee.

Perry was in the kitchen, chatting to Adele. He was installed in the warmest part of the kitchen, but rose to his feet as the others clattered in. 'Good morning, Cleo,' he said. 'Should you be out on such a cold morning?'

'I can hardly hibernate,' said Cleo, for a moment hating his concern. How mean of her; it was just his thoughtful way. 'Adele's the one who's up really early, I thought you were going to sleep in.'

'Being Saturday and so on, I was. But being so blinking cold, I couldn't,' said Adele.

'No shop on Saturday?' asked Perry. Adele had told him and Gussie about her fledgling dressmaking business over dinner the night before.

'Suzie's looking after things for me,' said Adele. 'You don't get serious shoppers on Saturdays, just browsers and nosy-parkers. If they're serious, and that's the only day they can come, then Suzie will make an appointment for them. I've got some design work to do, and I'm going to cook for everyone, so here I am. What's for breakfast, Cleo? Have you had yours?'

'Yes,' said Cleo, waiting for Adele's sharp eyes and ears to detect the lie.

'Don't tell fibs,' said Adele mildly. 'Eggs for you, then, to build you up. Shift,' she added unceremoniously to Perry, who had offered Gussie the warm spot and was now leaning against a cupboard door.

Perry shifted.

'And after breakfast,' said Cleo, 'I'm going to show you both over the house. I hope you've come prepared, because it's mostly arctic.'

'Must we?' said Perry.

'Yes,' said Cleo. 'I'm longing for Mum to see it.'

'Arctic?' said Giles, sitting on his favourite perch at the top of the stairs.

'She means extremely cold,' said Lambert.

'I know that's what she means,' said Giles. 'It's discourteous for guests to complain of the cold. Besides, it isn't.'

'We wouldn't know,' said Lambert. 'Of course, cold is bracing. I always made sure the servants' rooms and the bedrooms weren't warm. Much healthier.'

'Fires in winter,' said Giles. 'Always fires in winter, in my time. And plenty of jostling together and dancing and hot wine to keep the body warm and the spirits up.'

'Disgraceful,' said Lambert, wondering, as he so often did, whether his purer life had been as much fun as Giles's.

Giles did an elegant swoop down the banister rails. 'Where are they off to?'

'Through the little parlour to the great parlour, into the library, then the dining-room, the old great hall, upstairs, and along the west gallery,' chanted Lambert.

'Into any bedchambers that have floors they won't vanish through and then they'll dive back into the cellarage in their chilly way,' continued Giles, keeping an eye on the little party as they went into the little parlour.

'Like black beetles, this generation,' said Lambert.

'It was worse during this last war,' pointed out Giles. 'Miss Hazard even made her bed down there, do you remember?'

'Dark days, dark days,' said Lambert. 'Although it was exciting, listening to the news on the radio.'

'Much better now that we can *see* what it all looks like in the world beyond Haphazard,' said Giles. 'So many of the young women and girls in short skirts, like Adele.'

'Strumpets,' said Lambert. 'Depraved.'

'Delightful,' said Giles.

'Funny, that,' said Gussie, as they came back into the hall.

'What's funny?' asked Cleo. 'The house? Mum, you can't think that.'

'No, of course not. It's stunning, or must have been in its days of glory. No, I'll tell you what it is, I'm sure this house is bigger on the outside than it is inside. Come out and I'll show you.'

'Thick walls,' a freezing Perry said quickly.

'It's too cold to go out,' said Cleo. 'What we need is hot coffee.

And you've been all round the house now, Mum, you've seen it all, no hidey-holes.'

'What about the locked doors?'

'At the end of the passages? Downstairs, it's a jammed door to the outside world, upstairs an old cupboard. How do I know this? I asked Mrs Grigson. She locked the cupboard because the floor in there has rotted away.'

'I can believe that,' said Perry with feeling.

There was an obstinate set to Gussie's jaw, but the prospect of coffee had too strong an appeal. After all, there was no great hurry; she had the rest of the weekend for another prowl round the outside of the house to see why she felt there was a disparity between within and without.

'While you were doing the Cook's tour,' said Adele, 'Sylvester rang.' She had thoughtfully foreseen the need for coffee and was busily pouring it out. 'He says he has a friend staying with him, could he bring him tonight? I told him yes, plenty of grub, and that I'd tell you. Okay?'

'Fine,' said Cleo. 'Did he say who the friend was? It might be someone I know.'

'From Eyot, was all he told me. One Will, and they'll be here early so that this friend can see around the house before we get too sociable. He is, apparently, mad about old houses and their ghostly inhabitants.'

Giles didn't like what he'd heard. Not one bit. He clicked the receiver back in place with an irritable whistle through his teeth. 'One of those ghost hunters; how irksome, I thought we'd done with those.'

'Do you remember the bunch of braggarts who came to flush us out in the thirties?'

'The Victorians were worse. All those whiskers, most off-putting.'

'We gave them a good run for their money.'

Pause.

'Of course, they're very scientific these days. All kinds of equipment to measure temperature and air disturbance. They had a programme about it on the radio.'

'I heard it too. Veritable nincompoops.'

'Quite. Not a sensible idea between them.'

A few thoughtful chords on the lute. Then a sequence of brisk flourishes in the major key. 'We'll make the best of it. We will give them something to think about, and still come out ahead. By my troth, there's not much they can do about us.'

'Exorcism,' said Lambert gloomily.

'Keep your spirits up. They've tried that twice, and we're still here.'

'It's very uncomfortable, and what if it's third time lucky?'

'Most unlikely, considering what a bunch of lily-livered unbelievers these clerics are today,' said Giles. 'No, no, we've nothing to fear from them, and I doubt it will come to that. These are heathens, I don't suppose they'd even know where to find a priest willing to attempt an exorcism. Look on the bright side; life's been very dull, and we may be able to have some merriment here.'

'Merriment!' said Lambert. 'Folly. Besides, we aren't here to be merry.'

'How do you know? Nobody's ever come to say what we are here for, so I say, let enjoyment prevail.'

'A dangerous game,' said Lambert.

'Excellent to see you again,' said Sylvester, wrapping Gussie in a bear hug. 'Ah, Perry. It's been a long time. How are you?' He patted Perry on the arm, and then noticed Cleo's rapt expression. His face lit up with amusement. 'Hello, Cleo!'

Cleo's eyes were not on Sylvester. Cleo's eyes were on his companion, as were Adele's, and even Gussie was riveted.

'Ah,' Sylvester said again, much pleased. 'Cat among the pigeons, is it? I see. Let me introduce you. This is Will, Will Wrackham.'

'Hi, Will,' said Cleo. 'I'm glad Sylvester brought you. I'm Cleo, this is my mother, Gussie, and that's Adele.'

'Yes,' said Adele, with a wild flutter of her exaggerated lashes.

'And Perry, of course.'

Will's flashing eyes took in the company and he smiled courteously; it was obvious to all, however, that his thoughts were elsewhere.

'Ghosts,' he said expectantly, raising a hand as though to quieten the throng. 'I can sense presences. Sylvester said there might be ghosts, and there are. I can feel them all around us. How truly wonderful.'

13

'What an extraordinary man,' Gussie said.

Cleo was slumped in the kitchen chair with her eyes closed, but she wasn't asleep. 'Wow,' she said.

'Cleo, be careful.'

'Careful about what?'

'About falling for a young man on a passing whim. However stunning he is.'

'I've had a lot of fun with passing whims.'

'Yes, but that was before you met Perry.'

'Who doesn't want to be a passing whim,' said Cleo.

'Certainly not,' said Gussie, giving the glass in her hand an extra stern rub with the tea towel.

'I'm not sure, you know,' Cleo went on in a dreamy way, 'that I really do want to get married.'

'I'm not sure that wanting comes into it very much,' said Gussie, rejecting a fork from the washed pile and flinging it back into the suds. 'I think marriage creeps up on you. Inexorable, it seems to me.'

'What about undying love and wanting to be with someone all the time?'

'Is that how you feel about Perry?'

'Who knows?'

Gussie gave her a sharp look, which Cleo noticed from under her drooping lids. She yawned and stretched into a more comfortable position. 'Are you sure you don't want help with that?'

'No, and don't change the subject.'

'I don't want to talk about marriage at all. I find it a depressing subject. There's something very final about a husband. About someone you sign up with and then have to sign lots more if you want to say goodbye.'

'Live with Perry then. I never married, it's never bothered me.'

'I suggested it. I go on suggesting it. It's fine me spending time at his flat, he has no qualms about that. But setting up together, in any kind of permanent arrangement, is only possible with a wedding ring.'

'Commitment,' said Gussie.

'Wonderful hair,' said Cleo, her mind sliding back to more pleasurable thoughts. 'And crackling with vitality; I do like a vigorous man. And I love his enthusiasm about the ghosts. He doesn't have any doubts, does he? Astonishing to have that kind of belief.'

'I wish Sylvester had never brought him here,' said Gussie crossly. 'And he seems to me to be batty as hell.' She thrust the dishcloth under the sink and banged the cupboard door shut.

'It'll smell if you leave it there,' said Cleo helpfully. She slid out of her chair and retrieved the dishcloth, hanging it over the tap. 'There.'

'I can see domesticity is going to suit you.'

'And those eyes,' said Cleo, snuggling down into her chair again.

'Manic, if you ask me,' said Gussie briskly. 'I wouldn't say Will is at all well balanced.'

'Who cares? He's very sexy and altogether desirable, what has balance to do with it?'

'Oh, go to bed. I wonder where Perry and Adele are? It's time Perry and I went back to the pub.'

'They're playing cards in the little parlour,' said Cleo. 'Perry is an inveterate gambler, did you know? Probably lost his shirt to Adele. You'd better go and rescue him quickly.'

'I think it's a very good thing that Will Wrackham lives in Eyot and not locally.'

'Mum, here in the country, Eyot is local. And he has a bike. But he won't need it tomorrow; he's staying with Sylvester, so he's going to pop over in the afternoon, see if he can sniff out a few more ghosts.' Cleo felt quite warmly towards the strange sounds and drifting voices; anything that brought Will back had to be a benefit.

'Ghosts,' said Gussie with feeling. 'I never heard such nonsense.'

'Hussy,' said Giles, in a forgiving voice.

'Wanton words,' said Lambert. 'Women in my day . . .'

'. . . felt and thought just as Cleo does, but rarely spoke of it. Although some did,' said Giles, remembering.

'And her future husband sitting there, while she eyed another man across the dinner table.'

'What a flirt,' said Giles. 'What wonderful blue eyes she has. All the Mountjoys have those eyes, I remember them well.'

'Yes, she's a flirtigig, a lightskirt, no better than she should be.'

'A modern young woman who's chosen the wrong husband for herself. Not an uncommon situation, and not irredeemable, there's time for her to realize her folly.'

'Folly! In marrying a steady man.'

'Old enough to be her father.'

'And none the worse for that,' said Lambert, who had been married at thirty-eight to a girl of fifteen.

'Not up to her weight,' said Giles.

'This Will is a bold fellow.'

'Yes, and too much interested in ghosts. We'll have to be careful of him.'

'I swear you think he would make a better husband for Cleo.'

'A livelier one, certainly, but he doesn't look like a husband to me.'

'A lover, then. Disgraceful,' lamented Lambert.

'A lover on the wild side,' said Giles definitely. 'Too strong meat for Cleo.'

Cleo took herself off to bed in a contented mood, looking forward to seeing Will again the next day, relishing the first stirrings of lust since she had been ill. A girdle against folly, she told herself as her faded blisters prickled an uneasy warning. Still, they couldn't last for ever. And meanwhile, Perry got a chaste and sleepy kiss which left Cleo's nerves untingled, and she went upstairs and Gussie and Perry went off into the night.

Gussie was much troubled by the disapproving look on Perry's face, but she was too wise to say anything. This was something they would have to sort out for themselves.

What a good thing I'm past the worst agonies of love and lust, she thought, as she climbed into the comfortable if solitary hotel bed. She was glad to have escaped matrimony. Yes, she granted the companionship and, if you were lucky, years of happy sex, but look at how most marriages turned out. Look at Magdalena with her chequered history, now on her third husband, having lost two through no fault of her own. One bastard, one sweetie, and now Val, Gussie thought as she twiddled the dial on the radio. What a fate.

There was Sylvester, a happy man if she knew one, and no marriage in his past or future, although his relationship with Gabriel had lasted for years, it was true. There was Perry himself; he must remember some pleasures from his first marriage to be planning a second. Or was he just hopelessly in love with Cleo, and inclined to forget the darker days which had plagued his nuptial home?

To hell with them all, thought Gussie, putting her hands behind her head and settling down to enjoy a mellifluous voice reading aloud from *The Semi-detached Couple*.

14

No way was Adele going to glance out of mullioned windows to see if any young men might be cycling up to the house. And Cleo, when challenged by a restless Gussie, denied that her drifting towards the windows at the front of the house had anything to do with Will.

'You're making an exhibition of yourself,' said Gussie crossly. 'Perry won't like it.'

'Perry isn't here,' pointed out Cleo. 'And why are you making such a fuss about me looking out of the windows? What else is there to do?'

'You could carry on with your plaster disembowelling,' said Gussie.

'Rude, when there's company,' said Cleo. 'Listen, I hear voices.'

'Those ghosts again, I expect,' said Adele, who was painting her nails with utmost precision. She waved the wickedly scarlet nails to and fro to dry, surveying her handiwork.

'They sound earthy enough to me,' said Cleo, running out of the room. 'Hello? Is anyone there?'

They had been sitting upstairs in the long gallery, and Cleo hung over the banister to see who was below. There was Will, as expected, looking very dramatic with his icy eyes glinting up at her and his hair flowing back from his forehead . . . But who was that with him? A strange man, of medium height, built on elegant lines with one of those witty, creased faces and a line of receding dark, crinkled hair.

Cleo bounded down the stairs. 'Come ghost hunting, Will?' she said. 'And your friend? Another ghost hunter?'

Perry appeared from nowhere, looking not altogether delighted to see Will. 'I hope not,' he said shortly, looking at the stranger. 'I personally do not believe in ghosts,' he added with a tight smile.

'No ghosts at all?' said the stranger politely.

'Not ever,' Perry said coolly. 'It's always a hoax, or a mentally deranged person living in the house.'

'There are no mentally deranged people here,' said Cleo.

'That's as may be, but equally, I can assure you, there are no ghosts.'

Will made a snorting and dismissive noise and his dramatic eyes sparkled. 'Just you wait.'

The stranger was looking at the other two men in an amused way.

'Do you work with Will?' enquired Cleo.

Will stared at the stranger. 'No, he doesn't,' he said. 'He was at the front door when we arrived. Nothing to do with me. I've never seen him before. I expect he's another one who doesn't believe in ghosts, God knows the world's full of fools, and this is probably another of them.'

'Who are you, then?' asked Cleo.

'Your cousin Henry, actually,' he said. 'That is, if you're Cleo, and you have to be, with that hair and those astonishing Mountjoy eyes. Henry Hazard,' he went on, holding his hand out to the other two. 'Owner of this house. To which you are very welcome.' He turned his attention back to Cleo. 'Would there be such a thing as a cup of tea?'

'Sneaky,' said Cleo, banging around the kitchen and unearthing a horrible little tin teapot. 'Just arriving like that, when he's never bothered to answer any of the messages I left when I rang.'

'You can't use that,' said Gussie, whipping the horrid tin teapot away from Cleo. 'There's a perfectly good china one on the shelf, with roses on it.'

'Henry Hazard is not a rosy man,' said Cleo.

'How do you know?' said a male voice, as Henry himself came into the kitchen. He looked in astonishment at the battered teapot on the table and reached up for the more seemly one. 'There. I remember this pot when I was little, the only time I came here. It's a miracle it survived; my great-aunt was a great thrower of china.'

'Was she?' said Cleo, diverted by this unexpected sidelight on Miss Hazard's character. 'I thought she would have been very po-faced and conventional at that sort of age. Belonging to another time, you know, when people knew how to behave and so forth.'

'Not at all, in fact, quite the contrary,' said Henry. 'Very uninterested in what other people thought of her behaviour or character, my great-aunt, like many others of her generation.'

Cleo frowned; she didn't like to feel corrected, if that was what Henry had intended. It was difficult to tell; his face, although full of life, gave nothing away.

'Um, if I can ask,' said Henry, 'how many friends of yours are there here? Very welcome, of course, I'd just like to be clear in my mind. Your mother, of course, and I'm delighted to meet an artist whose work I much admire. But the others . . .'

'Only Adele is staying here with me,' said Cleo. 'You said I might ask a friend, for company, and Adele is a very old friend. The others are visitors. They couldn't stay, there aren't the rooms. Gussie's staying at the pub. And Perry is as well.'

'Perry?'

'Another friend,' said Cleo quickly, before Gussie could say anything. 'You met him in the hall just now. Have some sugar,' she added, pushing the bowl across the table.

'Thank you,' said Henry, scooping a large spoonful into his cup and stirring vigorously. 'You know, there are plenty of rooms here.' He investigated the contents of a jar and politely offered a biscuit to Gussie and Cleo before taking one for himself.

'I suppose there are, if you don't mind ivy growing through the window and rats in the wainscoting,' said Cleo.

'Mmm,' said Henry. 'Which room are you in?'

'The Dragon Room.'

Henry dropped his biscuit, which exploded in a crumby heap on the kitchen table. 'Bother,' he said, sweeping the crumbs into his hand. 'The Dragon Room? Why? Do you have a yearning for decayed grandeur? What about your blonde friend?'

'Adele is in the room which was your great-aunt's,' said Cleo.

'Extraordinary,' said Henry. 'Still, each to her own, I suppose.'

Cleo's temper flared. 'Since there aren't any other rooms which are remotely habitable, there's no point in making sarky comments.'

'Nonsense. There's the whole of the new wing. Four good bedrooms there, five if you don't mind one with a very sloping ceiling.'

'New wing?'

'I knew it,' said Gussie, pleased. 'This house is bigger than we thought.'

'Come with me,' said Henry, helping himself to another biscuit and holding the door open for them to go through. 'I have my set of keys here,' and he jangled his hand in his pocket. 'I wonder just what Mrs Grigson has been up to.'

He led them, as Cleo had a suspicion he would, to the locked door at the end of the passage. 'This leads to the outside,' she said weakly. 'So Mrs Grigson said.'

'Mrs Grigson is pulling a fast one,' said Henry, opening the door with a turn of the key and a hefty shove with his shoulder. 'A trifle stiff, but then it shouldn't be kept shut and locked like this. Hold on, there's a light switch here somewhere, it's a bit gloomy, that woman must have drawn all the curtains. And the ivy hasn't been cut back at all; very remiss.'

'Oh,' said Cleo, looking about her. 'A sitting-room. Pretty dim, though.'

'There's another room through there, and a kind of pantry affair, to save you having to trudge up and down to the cellars if you want a cup of coffee. Loo,' he went on, opening and shutting a door on to a large cloakroom with many serviceable pegs along one wall and a large white basin.

'Stairs,' said Cleo.

'To go up,' Henry said helpfully, and earned himself a tart look from Cleo. He raised an eyebrow at her in acknowledgement.

Gussie led the way up to a first and then a second floor.

'Three bedrooms here, and then two on the next floor,' said Henry. 'Bathroom, linen cupboard . . . and there's a little shower room on the top floor.'

'All very modern,' said Cleo.

'Not modern, exactly, but perfectly comfortable,' said Henry. 'You see why I was surprised when you said there were no rooms. Mrs Grigson is a wretch. Of course, she hoped you wouldn't have people to stay if there were no rooms. Much less trouble for her.'

'And the threadbare sheets and fraying towels,' said Cleo, opening the linen cupboard and staring at neat piles of towels and bed linen. 'Very off-putting, I do see.'

'It's all very clean,' said Gussie, running a finger over a table set against the wall on the landing.

'That's why she scoots off with the duster,' said Cleo. 'I did wonder.'

'I'd move in here if I were you,' said Henry. 'At least you won't wake up in the morning and find the house has fallen down about your head. As will inevitably happen with the older part.'

'Inevitably?' said Cleo. *'Inevitably?'*

'Past saving,' said Henry in laconic tones.

Cleo gave him a blazing look of dislike. Philistine, she thought. Vandal. Destructive idiot.

Henry was talking to Gussie as they went back towards the kitchen. Cleo slopped moodily along behind them, listening with a discontented ear to the gossip and expert chat about the art world. She didn't know whether to be pleased or sorry when, as they crossed the Little Parlour, a lump of plaster detached itself and landed in a soft, floury heap on Henry's shoulder.

He brushed it off in an unconcerned way, and went on talking.

No soul, Cleo said to herself. A cold man; she hated cold men. She peeled off in the hall; quite unnoticed, she thought huffily, and went to find Will. Lively, wicked-looking Will, with his passion for ghosts. Now there was a man who definitely had a soul.

And there was Adele, making pretty little moues at him with her luscious mouth as he ran some kind of meter over the floor and round the doors.

'All very scientific,' Adele said as Cleo joined them.

'All very unscientific and pointless,' said Perry, who was watching the proceedings with a very cynical look on his face. 'Hocus pocus.'

He means it, thought Cleo. And two weeks ago – a week, even – I would have agreed with him. Now I don't. I don't know that I share Will's enthusiasm and certainty, but I do know that there's something going on in this house which is beyond anything Perry can understand.

'And likewise, mumbo jumbo,' said Will, straightening up and flashing a brilliant smile at Perry. 'Much you know about it. You should be a clergyman; they never believe in the supernatural.'

'There is no place in the modern world for the supernatural,' said Perry. 'Belief in the supernatural is a refuge for the inadequate.'

Will shrugged, and gave up on such a hopeless specimen. He twirled a long piece of wire around his hand and stuffed it in his pocket; Cleo watched, fascinated. 'How do you set about finding these ghosts?' she asked.

'The secret,' he said with authority, 'is to let the ghosts find you.'

'What does that mean?' asked Adele, who was going round the panelled walls and knocking them with the back of her hand.

'You get to know the terrain,' said Will, 'and their haunting habits, and then you work from there.'

'Haunting habits,' said Giles furiously. 'What a nerve.'

'Calm down,' said Lambert. 'This Will is no problem, we can easily keep an eye on him. It's the other one we have to watch.'

'He doesn't believe in us, no trouble from him.'

'That's what he says,' said Lambert with a shake of his head, 'but it's not what he means. He'll ferret about, his sort always do. He'll watch and listen, just to prove Will wrong, and he's bound to notice something.'

'Oh, that for the silly fellow,' said Giles airily, with a swish of his gloved hand.

'Records,' Will was saying. 'We need to check any records, diaries, letters, that kind of thing, which describe hauntings over the years. And witnesses. Who lived here before you came, Cleo?'

'Henry's defunct great-aunt,' said Cleo. 'You can't question her.'

'Did she live alone? No companion?'

'Mrs Grigson,' said Cleo. 'I doubt if you'll get anything out of her. She's the daily, and a complete tragedy-queen. Practically a ghost herself.'

'Oh, excellent,' said Will. 'Come along then, we'll go into the main parlour and have a snoop around there.'

'Waste of time,' said Perry, following them in what Cleo felt was an oppressive way. 'Except for the light it throws on the psychology of people who believe in ghosts.'

'Coming?' Cleo said to Adele.

'No,' said Adele, inspecting a tiny flaw on the polished perfection of her nail. She frowned and clicked her tongue. 'I shall have to start all over again; what a nuisance.' She shot Cleo a very sharp look. 'No point in trailing round after Will, his head's full of nothing but ghosts at the moment.'

'Trail, indeed,' said Cleo indignantly. 'I'm not trailing. Just admiring and lusting.'

'Isn't Perry enough for you?'

'Perry?' Cleo pondered. 'No, actually he isn't. I like Perry well enough, but he doesn't make my blood run hot like Will does.'

'Will's speciality is likely to make your blood run cold, not hot,' said Adele in a gnomic way.

'Speciality?'

'You've been around, Cleo. Doesn't anything strike you about Will?'

'He's very attractive. Very sexy, very vital.'

'Nothing else?'

'No. Why should it?'

Adele sighed, flexed her fingers once more and turned to head for her room and the nail polish remover. She paused on the threshold. 'If I were you, I'd steer clear of Will, that's all. If you want an interesting man, what about that cousin of yours?'

'Henry?' Cleo was almost offended. 'Rather Perry, given that choice.'

'Good,' said Adele. 'Stick to the status quo, which is Perry. That's what I'd do.'

'You wouldn't,' said Cleo, switching out the light and pulling the door shut behind her. 'Not if you were me, you wouldn't.'

15

The house was quiet; Cleo had the place to herself. Completely, today. Mrs Grigson was off on a melancholy trip to the dentist; from her tragic expression when she had imparted this information to Cleo, you would have thought that she was surrendering herself into the hands of the Spanish Inquisition.

Strange, thought Cleo, because from what she remembered, the Eyot dentists were an agreeable lot, strong on painkillers, and swift and efficient in their work.

'I won't come in at all, Monday,' Mrs Grigson had said. 'You never know with these dentists how long it'll take. And then I'll need to recover, I always feel weak after the dentist.'

'Are you having a tooth out?' asked Cleo, full of sympathy.

Mrs Grigson was shocked. 'Oh, no. Nothing like that. A check-up, but you never know what they'll find.'

No Arthur, either.

'Won't be in Monday, got to go and shore up a wall over Unthrang way,' he had remarked cheerfully on Friday afternoon. 'You get on with that plasterwork, that'll keep you occupied.'

But what's the point, Cleo thought as she wandered into the Little Parlour. She had had quite a spat with an exasperated Henry before he'd driven off the afternoon before.

'No point being sentimental about a house. Fine if you're extremely rich, a monstrous parasite if you aren't.'

'Then why don't you sell it to someone rich?'

'Believe me, I've tried. Too remote, not famous enough, just too much work needed.'

'I didn't think you were allowed to let old houses just crumble away.'

'Very true, mostly you aren't, and what a nightmare that must be for the owners; you'd have to flee the country to get away from officials slapping orders on you about necessary works. Thank God, by some oversight, this house has never been listed.'

'It should be.'

'Not now,' said Henry. 'It's too far gone. Past saving.' He gave a gentle pull at a loose flap of wallpaper, as though to prove his point, the whole strip came away from the wall in a soft cloud of flaking plaster. 'You see?'

'I'm surprised he's letting you stay,' said Perry, as he tucked himself into his coat for the long drive back to London. 'Are you sure you want to stay? You can come back with us, now.' He paused, and looked directly at her. 'Come and stay at my flat for a few days.'

That was not an offer he had ever made before. A night, yes. Anything more, no. Perry didn't want there to be any doubt about commitment. Meaning marriage. Up until now, more than a single night in the flat would have ranked as the thin edge of the wedge.

'What for?' said Cleo. 'I might as well be convalescent and wintry up here. The air's better, and it's far more beautiful.'

'Lonely, though,' said Perry, taking her hand.

'Lonely is as lonely does,' said Cleo, giving Perry a quick, blue look from under her thick lashes, and wondering what she meant. Fortunately, Perry wasn't given to analysing what Cleo meant; the subject was dropped.

Only to be taken up again two minutes later, by Gussie.

'No, Mum,' said Cleo, feeling strangely out of sympathy with her mother. 'I am not lonely, it isn't a lonely house. Yes, I will wear rubber gloves if I tackle the plaster; I hate having eczema. Yes, I will ring you at any time, don't worry, horrible Henry's paying, and he has no soul. No, I won't get cold; yes, I will get plenty of sleep.'

'Thank goodness they've gone,' she said, sinking dramatically into the kitchen armchair. 'Fuss, fuss; I think Mum's far worse than she used to be.' She sat up and looked at Adele, who was perched on a stool at the table, reading a fat Sunday paper. 'What about Will?'

'He's in the loft,' replied Adele, deep in the lurid story of a pop star's nuptial disappointment. 'Tapping. Now, just listen to this: "Singer discovers wife is man on wedding night."'

'Pretty thick singer,' said Cleo. 'Not to notice sooner.'

'I wonder if the wedding's valid,' said Adele, blowing at the pages to separate them. 'It says they were married in church.'

'Shouldn't think they'd mind,' said Cleo. 'When you think what they get up to . . . Clergymen, I mean.'

Now, wandering around the empty house, looking at the marks in the dust which showed where Will had been carrying out his investigations, Cleo reflected on Perry's antipathy to ghosts.

'He did become very keen on the idea of hidey-holes, though,' she said to Porthos, who had chosen to accompany Cleo on her rounds. 'Knock-knock on all the panels, convinced there must be a priest hole.'

And Henry laughing, saying that his family had been hunting for a priest hole for decades. 'The family were famous recusants, so my grandfather and others before him felt there had to be a secret place. Still, if there is one, we'll finally find it now.'

'Why?' Cleo had asked.

'When it's demolished.'

'You aren't even going to let it fall down? Gracefully?'

'No. People pay money for bricks and roof tiles and so on.'

'So what's Arthur doing?'

'Not a lot. He's reported back to me, given me quotes for what would need to be done; I put them in the bin. I can't pull it down until the estate is settled, there are some queries still.'

Queries, thought Cleo, touching a tattered fragment of brocade curtain which shivered into dust between her fingers. Estates. Estranged wives, whooping it up on money which should come into the house. What a waste. And what about the ghosts?

No problem, Perry had declared. Since there were no ghosts, you didn't have to worry about them.

Will, who hadn't taken any interest in quotes, came to life at this point, to speak with authority. He wasn't having any of that from Perry. Wasn't he aware that ghosts whose home was destroyed were in a bad way? It could never be the same for them; hanging round the overgrown shrubbery or nestling in some cellar ruin was bound to be unsatisfactory. Of course, if a new house were built, they could move in there. It happened all the time, those housing estates where people bought so much more than they had expected. But nobody would build here, in the middle of nowhere.

'Can't they do a flit?' Cleo had asked. 'Take up residence somewhere close by? The inn, perhaps, or Mrs Grigson's house.'

'They never do,' said Will, eyes flashing.

Cleo watched him appreciatively. Untidy he might be, but who needed neat or natty clothes when you looked like that and breathed such passion and energy?

'You really care about these ghosts, do you?'

He swung round, intense and dazzling, far too virile to be hand in hand with a ghostly past, thought Cleo for an irreverent moment. Then she reflected that it didn't matter in the end what he felt so strongly about, it would have just the same effect.

'I do care,' he said intently. 'It's the answer to so many questions, don't you see?' He didn't wait for an answer, but gave an impatient toss of his head. 'It doesn't matter, ultimately, whether you care or believe in them or not. If they're there, they're there. And in this case, they are; I can sense them everywhere. They inhabit this house in a way that none of the living do. And that's why it's so important to save them, make sure they aren't lost in eternity when the house comes crashing down.'

'Much he knows about it,' said Giles furiously. 'We had that young poet visiting here for a hundred and fifty years. You remember? There were no means by which we could persuade him to leave, until he went into Lincolnshire to find his brother. He was free to roam, because his house had burnt down. It was completely destroyed; a nasty affair, and they never built another one in its place. If Haphazard House falls down, we could go and stay, oh, anywhere. On a long visit.'

Lambert shook his head. 'Tricky,' he said. 'I doubt if it could be done. Not while there were any buildings still here. And there could be, for a few centuries.'

'Very uncivilized, having to haunt a pile of rubble,' said Giles with a dramatic shudder.

'If it's the Lord's will,' began Lambert.

The field telephone gave a tinkle. 'Quick,' said Giles, relieved to be spared Lambert on the Lord's will. 'Pick it up, see who it is.'

Lambert picked up the receiver and listened.

'Well?' hissed Giles.

'Don't interrupt,' said Lambert. 'It's Gussie.'

'What's she saying?'

'I can't *hear* what she's saying if you talk in my other ear.'

Giles leant closer to Lambert, who drew the earpiece away from his head so that they could both hear.

'. . . very late,' Gussie was saying.

'It's an expensive time to ring,' said Cleo. 'And the line's very bad again. I did mention it to Henry, but I don't think he took any notice.'

'I do feel uneasy about you,' said Gussie. 'I wish you'd come back to London. I don't like your being up there in that great empty house.'

'Not empty, Mum, remember the ghosts.'

Long pause.

'I agree with Perry about ghosts,' said Gussie finally. 'I find spirits hard to take.'

Cleo said nothing.

'Cleo, you're obviously feeling much better. Why don't you come back now? Perhaps you could go into the office just one or two days a week.'

'It's not that kind of job,' said Cleo impatiently.

'Whatever's going to get you back on your feet again,' said Gussie. 'And then there's Perry, and your wedding.'

'Don't start on that again, Mum, please. Look, I'm fine, get stronger every day, the air up here agrees with me. I'm not feeling lonely, Adele's here at night.' There was a pause before Cleo went on. 'And Will's planning to come back again.'

'Hmm,' said Gussie. 'Will. And I'm not at all sure about Adele. I like her, but . . . There's something not quite right.'

'Mum, what is all this? You've never interfered with my life or my friends. Why now? Why these friends?'

'I think you're treating Perry very badly.'

'Honestly, Mum, that is my business.'

'Of course it is. I'm sorry. Maternal fussing, which as you say, has never been my style. See lots of Sylvester, Cleo, that'll keep you sane.'

'Good idea,' said Cleo.

'And Charlotte brought round a clutch of letters. One from Hungary; from Prue, I expect. I've sent them on.'

'Oh, good,' said Cleo.

'Ho,' said Lambert as he replaced the receiver.

'Why ho?' asked Giles, flipping the faded ribbons on his lute with his elegant fingers.

'Girls should do as their mothers bid them.'

'If girls did that, the world would end.'

Lambert shook his head. 'Family is family. Marriage is not to be entered into lightly, nor cast aside on a whim. Cleo has given her word to this man, and her mother approves of the match. She should marry him, not yearn after Will or any other fine young man who comes into the house. She'll smart for it, if she follows an idle lust.'

'Will would make any woman's eyes widen,' said Giles. 'And Perry is a dull dog, no use to Cleo. He wants to change and guide her.'

'So a husband should.'

'So he shouldn't, if he wants a wife there when he wakes up in the morning. Perry's too old for Cleo, too set in his ways, too unimaginative.'

'Imagination,' said Lambert in a deeply solemn voice, 'is bad for the young. This Perry has many virtues.'

'Oh, fiddlesticks,' said Giles.

16

'Who was that?' asked Adele, biting her toast in a series of mouselike crunches, so as not to blur her lipstick.

'Postman,' said Cleo. 'Something for me.'

'A fat package. Anything interesting?'

'Mmm,' said Cleo. 'It's my post sent on from the flat in London.' She manoeuvred the bin towards her with her foot and pressed it open. She flicked quickly through the pile, sending special offers, tempting prize draws and charitable appeals flying into the plastic bag.

'Doesn't leave much,' observed Adele.

'Mostly junk mail; I don't write many letters, so I don't get many,' said Cleo, wiping her marmalady knife and inserting it underneath the flap of a dull-coloured envelope with a foreign stamp.

'Where's that from?' asked Adele, spreading out yesterday's paper on the table.

'Budapest,' said Cleo, holding it up. 'It's from Prue, though you wouldn't know it from the scrawly writing; what a mess. However, it has her address on the envelope, look.'

'Great,' said Adele, returning to her tabloid. 'Let me read it after you, if it isn't private.'

Silence reigned, broken only by a few crunches from Adele as she absentmindedly chewed a crust of toast. Then they both spoke together.

'There's a piece about Hungary in here.'

'I think something's up with Prue.'

They swapped, Cleo handing Adele the letter as Adele pushed the paper across the table to Cleo.

Further silence.

'Awful rubbish, this paper,' said Cleo, much dissatisfied. 'It doesn't actually tell you anything.'

'Nor does Prue,' said Adele, finishing Prue's letter and handing it back to Cleo.

Cleo looked at it again, seeing in her mind's eye Prue's interesting and attractive face, the sudden flash of a triangular smile, that distinctive Botticelli fair hair. She felt as though those intent green-blue eyes were watching her, that Prue was there, urging her to pay attention. Cleo shook herself back into the present and the steamy kitchen.

'Is she unhappy, do you think?' she asked Adele. 'Husband trouble, perhaps?'

'No.' Adele was definite. 'But for some reason she's worried about her husband, that's for sure. Geza *is* her husband, isn't he?'

'Yes, Geza.'

Cleo's thoughts were back once more in that hot summer when she and Prue had worked together up here, in Eyotshire. Delightful Geza, loved by everyone. Geza who had whipped Prue away from Valdemar's clutches or the alternative prospect of marriage to the dullest man in the county. He had taken her off to Hungary where she was, apparently, blissfully happy, with her attention divided more or less equally between her husband and her beloved ancient bones.

'Some kind of a fiddler, isn't he?'

'A violinist, yes.' Cleo contemplated the headline, which announced a crackdown in Hungary, with the secret police flushing out enemies of the state, on orders from Moscow. 'Geza wouldn't be involved in politics, he's too busy with his concert and recording schedule, moves in a different world.'

Adele wasn't so sure. 'I think you're involved in politics in that part of the world from the moment you can walk,' she said. 'And you said Prue was having a baby.'

'She is.'

'No mention of it in this letter. Just bibble-babble, and that bit about Geza's concert, and then droning on about your forthcoming holiday – by which I assume she means your trip to Budapest – and how you must be looking forward to it, and have you done all your packing.' A thought struck her and she held out her hand for the letter. 'Let me check. I thought so. Cleo, when are you going?'

'Oh, in the spring. March, April. The baby's due around Christmas. I remember that, because Prue said it was perfect timing for the University vacation.'

'Yet it sounds as though she was expecting you to be off any minute.'

Cleo read the letter again. Adele was right; it was mostly full of banalities: the weather, a concert, a book she had read, a professor at the university awarded a prize. And yes, Adele was right. *Such a good time to travel, now*, Prue had written. *Likely to be very cold, but of course you will be staying with old friends and will receive a very warm welcome, I feel sure.*

Now she came to think about it, it was a very strangely phrased letter indeed. Not like Prue's usual chatty and lively style. Hormones? Had pregnancy affected Prue's wits? Hardly.

Adele tapped the headline in the paper. 'It's to do with this, I'm sure it is. Prue reckoned this letter was going to be read. That's why it's so boring, Prue was never boring. And why she doesn't mention the point of your trip is actually to see her.'

'She must know I'm not going anywhere in December.'

'Sharpen your wits, she's asking you to go in December. She needs help, that's what I'd say.'

'Oh, nonsense.'

'Ring her up.'

'If what you say is true, her phone might be tapped.'

'You needn't say anything in particular, you could just ring up to ask how she is and say happy Christmas. Have you got her number?'

'Yes,' said Cleo. 'I'll ring her. Find out what's going on.'

Giles and Lambert adored the tabloid papers. Giles was quite open about it; Lambert wouldn't admit it, but couldn't take his eyes off the saucy pictures and extraordinary stories.

Worldly-wise Giles knew to take the articles with a pinch of salt. 'Tall tales,' he said. 'To amuse and frighten.'

'There were never these kind of tales in *The Times* and the *Telegraph*,' said Lambert, eyes as round with awful but delighted shock as he caught sight of the photo of a spectacularly well-endowed blonde. 'Or pictures.'

'So much the better for you,' said Giles, twitching it away from him. 'Let's be grateful to Adele for livening things up at Haphazard. Look, this is what they were talking about.'

'Secret police,' said Lambert with a sigh. 'Nothing changes.'

'Hungary,' said Giles, in a longing voice. 'Just get on one of the planes we saw on television, and you're there. I never went to Hungary. A heathen country, ruled by Turks, no place for a good Englishman except to fight.'

'I never left this land,' said Lambert with pride. 'There's no need to roam abroad, England is enough for any man to live a life of duty.'

'I used to dream of the East, of the islands of spice, of countries full of strange people and animals . . .' Giles played a few plangent notes.

'Are there strange animals in Hungary?'

Giles took no notice. 'I went to the Low Countries, once. And to Italy; oh Italy was a wondrous place. Italian poetry is the finest in the world, such perfection.'

'Nothing wrong with English poetry,' grunted Lambert, deep in an advertisement for curing piles. Lambert was fascinated by modern medicine.

'Phone,' said Giles as the warbling sounds came through which indicated that somewhere quite else in the house, someone was making a phone call.

'Must be Cleo,' said Lambert, lifting it up. 'Mrs Grigson wouldn't dare to use it now, Cleo's much too sharp for her, she'd be bound to notice.'

'Cleo and Adele's conversations are far more lively than Mrs Grigson and her problems,' said Giles. 'Isn't she through yet?'

'Long number, and then a lot of strange pips and clunks,' said Lambert, holding the receiver away from his ear.

'Perhaps someone's listening in.'

Lambert thought for a moment. 'Yes, we are.'

'No, at the other end.'

'Phone tapping's illegal,' said Lambert knowledgeably. 'I read an article about it in the paper.'

'That's what they say,' said Giles, even more knowledgeable.

'But what government has ever not read any privy writings which it can? And listened to any conversations that may be overheard.'

'Now, this is a strange language,' said Lambert. 'Greek, perhaps.'

'She's phoning abroad,' said Giles, excited but not losing his cool.

A voice quacked at the other end, an unfamiliar voice spoke briefly in light, nervous tones, and then the connection was broken.

'Ho,' said Lambert, putting the phone down with neat precision.

'Tell,' said Giles. 'What's up?'

No Arthur that day either. Presumably the wall had taken more time than he had planned, thought Cleo, as she sat on the window seat that was becoming a favourite spot. A warm jacket was draped over her shoulders to keep the all-pervasive draughts away, and she had drawn her feet up and out of the currents of chill air which blew about at ankle level.

The view was of distant, cloud and snow-capped fells, with grey on grey piling above them. Nearer were the still outlines of trees and hedgerows in the grip of an icy winter's day. And even closer, was a huge holly tree, aggressive in its shiny, unfrosted green, and ebullient with red berries.

Cleo had never seen such berries. No hollies to speak of in London, she thought, not of this wild and majestic kind. At least, none that she had ever noticed. There had been holly bushes at school, but they were neat and tidy affairs, trimmed and controlled; the nuns would have nothing unruly about the place. They must have had berries; she dimly remembered actual sprigs of holly figuring in some long afternoon lesson on symbols of death and resurrection.

This holly tree, she told herself, was symbolic of nothing except life. Surging, powerful and indomitable life.

Like the house, a survivor. Unlike the house, probably going to go on being a survivor, Cleo reflected. Unless when the bulldozers came they casually hacked down the superb tree. Men employed by Henry Hazard would no doubt commit such murder without a second thought. Cold and unfeeling, that was Cousin Henry.

The day was fading, in the slow creeping way of wintry northern afternoons. Inside, with no lights shining, it was darker than the gathering gloom without. And then, for a moment, there seemed to be a glimmer of light beyond the door. The sound of quick feet, a flurry of laughter, ending in a giggle and a whisper.

Cleo blinked, and rubbed her eyes, feeling suddenly very tired and chill. Bother these shingles, all her vitality sapped by a coil of pink blisters. Vitamins, that would stop the ringing in her ears.

When she opened her eyes again, she blinked even harder. The room was not so dark, although still shadowy. A candle flickered on a warm coloured but plain wooden table, and reflections of light bounced off mellow panelling. Which isn't there, Cleo told herself. Nor were there wide, darkly polished floorboards underfoot, nor plasterwork perfect and unmarred, if a trifle smoky.

Dreams, idle dreams, that was what came of shutting yourself up in a northern fastness with only a cat for company.

Strange, that she could hear a dog barking in the distance. Two dogs, by the sound of it. And more voices, one raised in mock anger, then more laughter.

The room grew darker, returning to the sombre dullness of a December twilight.

Goodness, Cleo said aloud. I must have fallen asleep. Downstairs, and a cup of coffee. She slid down from the window seat.

Such a strange phone conversation with Prue, she thought, remembering it. Prue had promised to ring back later, maybe she would make more sense then. Such a strange life Prue must be leading. Such a relief that she herself lived safe and sound in staid old England. 'Come along, Porthos,' she said, as the tabby cat stalked towards her. 'Time for your tea.'

Adele arrived back from Eyot quite pink with the cold, and longing, so she said, for a hot bath.

'There's the bathroom in the civilized part which Henry opened for us,' said Cleo. 'I had a shower this morning, no problem with hot water. Mrs Grigson was here, just for an hour about tea time, lots of opportunity for a cup of tea and chat, and not much work.'

'Was she full of remorse about locking up the only truly habitable part of the house?'

'She was not. She says she did it because the haunting is so bad there. Keep us awake all night, it would.'

'Oh, really! I suppose these ghosts, which I've never seen or heard a whisker of, like their creature comforts.'

'Mrs Grigson doesn't. She says it's a newfangled boiler in there, instant hot water. She disapproves. Mrs Grigson doesn't like life to be too easy.'

'Mrs Grigson should be on the stage, starring in Victorian melodramas,' said Adele, shivering as she held her frozen fingers out towards the kitchen stove. 'She'd make a fortune. The hot water is a strong temptation, but can I face the miles of utterly cold passages to get there? And then, once I've thawed out and feel human again, the long trek back.'

'Run,' advised Cleo. 'I'll get some food ready while you're wallowing. Of course, you could always move into the better wing. Since the ghosts don't bother you.'

'Are you going to?'

'No,' said Cleo. 'I like the Dragon Room. More in keeping with the house, I feel.'

'I wouldn't give up my four poster for anything. Once in a lifetime, a chance to use a bed like that.'

'Henry will think we're mad.'

'His problem,' said Adele, blowing into her hands and holding them against her cheeks to warm them. Did you get through to Prue today?'

'Yes. She sounded strange. She's going to ring me back tomorrow morning, she said. There's clearly something wrong, I wish I could help.'

'Better not,' said Adele, breaking out into an enormous yawn. 'Other people's lives are always so complicated if you don't keep your distance.'

'Prue's a friend.'

17

'Cleo? Oh, thank goodness. Cleo, what bliss to talk to you. I must be quick, I can't make a long call.'

'Why not? Is it very expensive?'

'No, but I'm not at home. I can't speak to you from the flat, they listen in.'

'Who does?'

'Secret police.

'Adele said they would.'

'Adele?'

'Don't you remember Adele? From school? She's staying here with me.'

'You're in Eyotshire, I recognized the code. I thought you must be with Sylvester.'

'No, in a cousin's house. Prue, how are you? What's up?'

A pause. Howlings and hissings down the line, and then a few vigorous crackling sounds as the line cleared.

'I'm okay. Being pregnant and so on. But, Cleo, we're in trouble. Or rather Geza is. Big trouble.'

'Oh, hell,' said Cleo. 'I knew it.'

'So,' said Adele. 'I didn't know you were coming into Eyot today.'

'Neither did I,' said Cleo. She looked across to where Suzie, masked and gloved, was wielding a soldering iron with great verve. 'Is Suzie reliable?' she asked in a lowered voice.

Adele looked at her friend in complete astonishment. 'Reliable? What are you talking about?'

'She's isn't, you know, incredibly left-wing, in with neo-Stalinists or anything like that?'

Adele gave a shout of laughter. 'No, no, I can tell you that for sure. Suzie is definitely, but definitely, nothing to do with any of that. Strictly far to the right, our Suzie. Chilling, in many ways, but a fine artist, so all is forgiven.' She gave Cleo a penetrating look. 'Are you feeling all right?'

'Come and have a coffee,' said Cleo mysteriously, 'and I'll explain.'

Adele liked to get things straight. 'First,' she said, tossing several pieces of crystalline sugar into her coffee and stirring vigorously, 'first, how come she could say all this if the phones are bugged?'

'I asked her that.' Cleo glanced round before she went into details. The table next to theirs was unoccupied; beyond that two solemn types from the University were discussing the state of the college accounts, and at the bar what looked like a pair of ballet dancers were drinking mineral water with polite expressions as they rubbed their ankles and feet.

'Nobody's listening,' said Adele. 'Come on, spit it out.'

'Prue rang me on the K system,' said Cleo. 'Her phone's tapped, and if you ring from the main post office which is what you have to do if it's abroad, they take your name and everything. Too risky, Prue says. But big cheeses use this K system because it isn't tapped. Prue's got a friend who's an Olympic official, he organizes team trips and so on. He rings abroad all the time. Says his calls aren't monitored, and the tappers would die of boredom if they did listen in, because it's all hotel bookings and flights.'

'So Prue used his phone?'

'Yes. Listen, things are really bad there. They've put the black spot or whatever it is they do on Geza, and he's gone into hiding.'

'Where?'

'She didn't tell me, that would be stupid. Somewhere in Hungary.'

'Why? What's he been up to?'

'I'm coming to that. It seems he gave a series of concerts in Russia about six months ago, and he brought out some letters and papers which he took to Switzerland.'

'Bit stupid.'

'Geza wouldn't see it like that, not if it was for fellow artists, or dissidents or Jews or those samizdat people. Geza isn't very keen on the Party. Apparently he's had a run in or two with them.'

'Unfortunate,' said Adele, taking several sips of her syrupy coffee.

'I don't know how you can drink that,' said Cleo, momentarily distracted.

'I like it, don't be so priggish,' said Adele robustly. 'Carry on. Geza's been up to mischief, and they're after him.'

'Yes.'

'Is Prue safe?'

'She's English, and I don't suppose they'd have a go at her. However, and this is why there were all those heavy clues about coming over now, she and Geza think it's terribly important that she gets out of Hungary fast, and comes back to England before the baby's born.'

'Why? Do they take the children of wrong-doers away at birth?'

'No, of course not. It's just that once she's had the baby, she's a hostage to fortune. Those were her words, not mine. And she and Geza think that if she's safely in England, then he can come out of wherever he's lying low and slip across the border. It can be done, it seems, through Yugoslavia. If he's on his own, and if he knows that Prue isn't there for them to pick up.'

'Tricky,' said Adele. 'She'd better book herself a flight and get the hell out of there, then. I hope you told her that. Is she short of cash? Can we send her some?'

'She'd have to pay for a flight in pounds, which might be difficult, but that isn't the point. She can't fly.'

'Can't fly?' Adele was puzzled for a moment. 'They have an airport, planes fly in and out . . . Oh, I see. Because of expecting a baby.'

'Yup. They won't let you on the plane at that stage, Prue says, you can't risk it; a slight change of pressure, and whoosh.'

'Train, then.'

'Yes, exactly, but it's a tricky and tiring journey when you're eight and a half months pregnant, and you're being watched. It means going to Vienna, and then across everywhere to France and then the Channel and home. She can't do it alone.'

Adele rose, picked up their coffee cups, and headed towards the bar. A remote-looking girl with her hair piled up in a French roll gave her a cool look.

'Yeah?'

'Two more coffees, please.'

The girl stretched a swan-like arm towards the machine and shook out the drum of grounds. 'Espresso, cappuccino?' she said, hardly moving her lips.

'One of each,' said Adele, plonking money down on the counter. 'I'll come back for them when they're ready.'

'Yeah,' said French roll, tipping the ground coffee into the machine in a desultory way. 'Pay now.'

'Right,' said Adele, going back to her seat.

'So,' went on Cleo, who had been gazing into the middle distance while Adele saw to the coffee, 'I said I'd go.'

Adele was surprised. 'I didn't know Prue and you were that close.'

'We were, but then we went our separate ways. Me to Oxford, Prue to Hungary, and university there and marrying Geza.'

'How ever did she manage to go to university in Hungary?' asked Adele, distracted. 'Isn't that one of the languages that no one can learn?'

'Prue's good at languages. And if you live there and your husband's Hungarian, I suppose you just pick it up. And she's terribly clever, don't you remember?'

'Yes, I suppose so. Intellectually, that is. Doesn't seem to be very practical, though.'

Cleo had to agree. Prue had never had her fair share of common sense. And she used to be a bit panicky, not surprising when you'd been orphaned and brought up by a terrible aunt. Who then expired, leaving you homeless and penniless while you were still at school. Perhaps she was panicking unnecessarily now, perhaps she was imagining these secret police and the danger to Geza.

Cleo didn't think so. She had bought *The Times* and the *FT* before going to Adele's shop, and it was clear that there was a clampdown under way in Hungary. All too likely that Geza would be caught up in it.

The laconic girl dumped their coffee on the table in front of them and lounged back to the bar. Adele pushed her cup to one side and became businesslike, taking a sturdy notebook out of her dinky handbag and uncapping an elegant fountain pen. 'Right, she said. 'First things first. Passport, in order?'

'Yes,' said Cleo. 'Complete with Hungarian visa, which is very lucky, because they don't do those in a hurry.'

'Good,' said Adele. 'Now, how are you going to get there?'

'Fly, I suppose,' said Cleo. 'If it's to be quick.'

'Travel agent, then, book ticket as soon as poss.' Adele was jotting down points as she spoke. 'Money? A one-way flight won't be cheap. And then there's the train journey back. If Prue's expecting, she can't sit up all night in a crowded compartment. That'll cost, and you might have to pay for her ticket as well as yours.'

'No problem about money, fortunately,' said Cleo, swirling her coffee into a black whirlpool. 'I got a bonus from my office, there was a letter about it in the lot that came yesterday.'

Not much of a bonus, compared to what it would have been if she hadn't fallen ill. But then if she hadn't been ill, she would now be married to Perry, she wouldn't have come to Eyotshire, wouldn't have bumped into Adele again, and wouldn't be in a position to whisk herself off to Budapest.

'Will your cousin mind if I stay in the house while you're away?' Adele ran her beautifully manicured hands through her artfully arranged blonde curls and tossed them back from her forehead.

Cleo had to admire the way Adele managed to keep her hands so immaculate. All of her immaculate, in fact. Cleo was feeling dumpy today; loose clothes were very, very unflattering, she had decided. When the prickling, stabbing pains turned to itching, as she had been assured they would, she would go out and buy herself a wardrobe of new clothes.

Always supposing she had any money to pay for them. Always supposing she had a job to go back to. Perhaps she could become a professional house-sitter, flit from empty mansion to plush flat . . .

'Cleo! You aren't listening to a word I'm saying. Look, I'm trying to help here. Concentrate.'

'Sorry,' said Cleo. 'What did you say?'

'About Haphazard House.'

'Oh, yes.' Cleo waxed indignant. 'Cousin Henry? Mind? He's got no business to mind, he should be grateful that anyone's prepared to put up with the house and Mrs Grigson, not to mention him popping in and talking about pulling it all down. Won't you mind being there by yourself?' she added.

Adele doodled the outline of a swirling dress, and then, becoming interested, started to block in the sleeves in more detail. 'Set in like that, do you think?' she said, twisting the page so that Cleo could see the drawing.

'Don't ask me,' said Cleo. 'I'm hopeless about clothes until I've got them on. Could Suzie come and stay?'

'Suzie?' Adele thought for a moment. 'I think not.' Inspiration struck. 'I know, I'll ask Will. Scientific investigation, nothing there to set the old dinks of Eyot aflame with gossip and rumour. He can ghost-hunt to his heart's delight, and have one of the bedrooms in that other wing.'

Cleo wasn't at all keen on that. Adele would have Will at her disposal, as it were, while she, Cleo . . . On the other hand, Will had shown no particular interest in anything except the ghosts. And she wouldn't be away long, surely. A day to Budapest, pick up Prue, two days back, could it take any longer? Will might like to stay on, once he was ensconced among the spirits.

'I'll ask him,' said Adele. 'I've got his number here somewhere.'

'Doesn't he have to stay in school?' asked Cleo. 'If it's a boarding school, and he teaches music there?'

'Nope,' said Adele. 'He has a grace and favour flat, in the Close. He'll be glad to get away, think about it; all those clergymen, and some very fierce women live there, too, let me tell you.'

'Wives?'

'Relicts, mostly.'

The girl in the travel agent was very keen and completely incompetent. Hours I've been here, thought Cleo wearily, and we haven't even got as far as Paris.

The girl trotted back from some distant region where she had gone – for the third time – to ask the manager about a nice detail of routing.

Cleo sighed. 'It would be quicker if I could just speak to the manager,' she suggested.

The girl bridled. 'Mr Rowlandson doesn't do trains,' she said. 'Planes, yes, trains, no.'

'I want to book a flight,' said Cleo, very slowly and clearly.

That didn't go down at all well. 'You asked about trains. You asked about trains to Vienna. Now you want to *fly* to Vienna, do you?'

'No, I want to fly to Budapest. And I asked about trains *from* Vienna, not to.'

The girl very deliberately tore up all the figures and timings she had written down on the sheet in front of her. 'Perhaps you'd like to start again,' she said, in an voice like an icicle.

Outside the travel agent, Cleo paused, ignoring the bitter east wind which was blowing with renewed ferocity, and examined her ticket. That girl could have booked her anywhere. Get to Heathrow and find herself on a plane to Outer Mongolia, like as not. And that pompous manager, telling her in a drawly way that all flights to Eastern Europe were fully booked until well into the New Year. One way? Impossible. Cancellations? Not a hope.

Well, he was wrong, thought Cleo, tired but triumphant after her skirmish. She had given up the unequal struggle to get information about train times from the experts, and with those in mind, she headed for Droggs, the bookshop.

It was warm in there, and quiet. She'd need something to read on her travels, now she thought about it, and Prue might like a book or two, to take her mind off spies and secret policemen.

An obliging young man with a beard produced an up-to-date Cook's timetable for the whole of Europe, and recommended some good new reads. With these tucked into a carrier bag, she wandered downstairs to the secondhand section; you never knew what you might find.

And, rather to her surprise, she found treasure, in the shape of a small, no-nonsense volume entitled *Haphazard House from its Building to the Present Day*, by Tobias Wortle. True, the present day wasn't exactly present, being about 1820, but Wortle, on inspection, proved to have a snappy way with words. This, thought Cleo, handing over more money than she had intended to spend, I am going to enjoy.

'You're going tomorrow?' said Adele, impressed, as she laid some packages on the kitchen table. 'Quick work.'

'It was tomorrow or January,' said Cleo, opening what turned out to be a tub of garlicky olives. 'Mmm, you've been to Gumbles.'

'I have.'

'Extravagant.'

'You need feeding up before you set off for the ends of the earth, and I sold three dresses today. At least, sold one off the peg, and took orders for two more.'

'I thought you had all the work you could handle for Christmas.'

'These angelic customers don't want them for Christmas. One is going off on some posh cruise, just hope she isn't seasick in my best silk, what a waste, and the other has a London do in February. Now, you'll have to pack. There's a paper in there, look and see what the weather is like in Budapest.'

Cleo obediently found the paper. 'Help,' she said. 'Minus ten. I didn't realize it was so cold.'

'Wind from the steppes, I should imagine,' said Adele. 'I'll lend you my thermal gloves, and have you got a hat?'

'A hat? I never wear hats.'

'If it's minus ten, you wear a hat.'

18

Cleo hadn't for a moment imagined that she would be retracing her steps south so soon. She lay half-asleep in her bunk; running backwards, she thought idly as the train rattled through stations. We must have crossed the Trent by now, and out in the darkness the scene would be changing from rolling hills to industrial heartlands, and soon suburbia would begin.

Of course, she had planned to go to Hungary before she got Prue's letter. But as a tourist, in the spring, when she would have been celebrating three months or so of marriage. A week's holiday taken from work, a normal trip, taken in an orderly way.

Booking a flight at a moment's notice and sweeping off to Budapest to escort an old friend out of the clutches of the secret police was quite different, and not orderly at all.

At the last minute in the bookshop, Cleo had added a guide to Hungary to her other purchases. 'Not a lot of choice,' the assistant had said regretfully. 'Not a lot of people go to Eastern Europe just at present. Except on business, and they don't use guidebooks much.'

This guidebook had clearly been compiled by a writer who had covered a good deal of Marxist dialectics at university. It sang the praises of state housing, of universal medical care, of happy, singing pensioners, retired after a lifetime of devoted service to the mines, or to agriculture.

Cleo was not misled. She knew something about East European economies and life under socialist regimes from her own time at university. True, many of the more humourless lecturers and professors spoke passionately about the perfection of life under the new czars and their cohorts; Cleo wasn't convinced.

It was noticeable that they didn't actually choose to live in Eastern Europe. Trips were taken, generally at some organisation's expense, so that they could come back with glowing accounts of socialist paradises, before continuing their comfortable existences in a wicked capitalist state. Cleo knew perfectly well that, when it came to holidays for which they had to pay, they bundled wife and children into the car and headed for France or Italy.

No, Budapest sounded as though it must have been sensational once, but depressed and depressing now. On the other hand, she thought, cheering up, if it was full of people like Geza, the company would be good.

'Send him my love,' a concerned Sylvester had said, very alarmed when Cleo rang to tell him the news. 'When are you going?'

'Tomorrow.'

'Mercy dash to foreign city, eh?' he said. 'I don't like the sound of this; Geza shouldn't be involved with smuggled documents and secret police.'

'For his friends,' said Cleo. 'Wouldn't you, in his shoes?'

Sylvester roared. 'No chance I'd fit into Geza's shoes, we're hardly the same size.'

'Be serious,' said Cleo. 'You can't criticize him.'

'I certainly can, very stupid and dangerous to bring papers out of Russia, the way things are at present. I dare say I'd have done the same. Dear, dear, I suppose I'd better ring a few people here and there, see if anyone's heard anything about this on the grapevine. Meanwhile, young Cleo, look after yourself. They carry guns there – no, I'm quite serious – and moreover, they're quite capable of using them. So you just keep your head down, be a bona-fide tourist and get Prue out in one piece.'

'Literally in one piece,' said Cleo. 'No good Prue going into labour while she's in my hands, I wouldn't have a clue what to do, and I could hardly spirit two of them away.'

'Eight and a half months, you said?' Sylvester made disapproving clicking noises. 'Risky, very risky. Babies have a habit of arriving at the most inconvenient times. And I know what you're thinking Cleo, I'm not in the running for the baby stakes, but you'd be surprised how many cases one comes across. Why, I remember the second oboe, when we were in Nicaragua. Of course, we had no idea, but . . . Anyway, enough of that. Bon voyage. Ring me any time, day or night. If I'm not here, which I will be, I've got a lot of work on, then Lily will know where I am.'

'Thank you, Sylvester,' said Cleo, touched.

'What are you doing with Prue once you get back to England?'

'Ah.' Cleo thought hard. Dover was as far as her plans had got; once on English soil, she had imagined that all would magically be well. 'London?' she said doubtfully. 'Mum? Should Prue go straight into hospital?'

'Probably not,' said Sylvester. 'Bring her up here, Cleo. If it's quicker and more comfortable, hire a car on me. A big one, mind, nothing worse than bumping up the A1 in some ghastly little tin can. I'll talk to Lily, she can have a word with the doctor here, and he can see to a bed if need be.'

'Lily will cope,' said Cleo thankfully, knowing just how limited her own experience of mothers and babies was.

King's Cross. Cleo considered the tube for a few brief seconds, sighed at the thought of a bus, and headed for the taxi rank.

'Cromwell Road,' she said as she climbed in, shoving her bag in front of her. 'The Air Terminal, please.'

The driver whistled tunelessly through his teeth as he headed off down the Euston Road. 'Going on holiday, then? Somewhere hot? Or is it business?'

'Going to see a friend,' said Cleo. 'In Hungary.'

'Hungary. Well now, I've never been there, but I've got a friend who has. Born there, in fact, him being Hungarian. Came over in fifty-six, when the Russkies brought the tanks in. A bad job that was, very bad.'

'Mm,' said Cleo. 'I don't remember it exactly, because I was very small, but I know it was a grim affair.'

'Terrible,' said the man with relish. 'Terrible. Mowing them down in the street, squashing people under the tanks like they were flies. Inhuman. I handed in my party card then, I wasn't having anything to do with them any more.'

'I think a lot of people did that,' said Cleo, feeling in her bag for her passport as she was seized with the awful conviction that she'd left it in Haphazard House. No, there it was, complete with visa and her air ticket.

'Not the intellectuals,' said the taxi-driver, swinging his taxi in a brisk arc round a stationary bus. 'Not many of them handed in their cards. They all made excuses, pretended it hadn't happened, or said the Hungarians wanted the Russians in like that.'

'Really?'

'They should have spoken to my friend. He knew what the Hungarians wanted, and it wasn't the Russians, neither. Freedom was what they wanted. Their democratic rights. Same as we take for granted. That's what my Hungarian friend says. "You English take it all for granted." He'd seen his dad and his brother killed right in front of him, changes your attitude, something like that.'

'Yes, it would,' agreed Cleo.

'Course, they say it's all starting up again,' the driver went on with relish. 'Troops moving out of Warsaw, crackdowns on dissidents as they call their democratically minded citizens, tanks rolling in again any day now.'

'I hope not,' said Cleo.

'Let's put it like this,' he said as he turned smartly into the terminal at Cromwell Road. 'If I could take a trip, right now, Hungary would be a long way down the list. Thank you, miss, have a good holiday. Hope you make it back all right.'

'I'm sure I will,' murmured Cleo, shouldering her bag and heading for the escalator.

Cleo had been surprised to be questioned at passport control about her proposed visit to Hungary.

Purpose of visit?

'I'm going to see a friend.' She nearly added, although it's none of your business, but she bit her tongue. True, it wasn't their business, and she felt aggrieved at being asked questions like that in her own country. On the other hand, she needed to get on the plane, and she knew how tricky officials could be, and how much within their power it was to delay you. Legally, but inconveniently.

And wrongly, she thought indignantly, as she made for the

departure lounge. I'm supposed to be going to a police state, not coming from one.

At least, she thought some three hours later as she looked around the cramped, bleak arrival hall at Ferihegy airport, at least at Heathrow they didn't have men in uniform standing by the passport control with machine guns at the ready.

19 ∫

Budapest, decided Cleo, looking out from the bus window as she tried to blow some heat on to her frozen fingers, is like a battered aristocrat who's facing the world on slender means; poor, tired, but undaunted.

The blue Ikarus bus rumbled relentlessly along the concrete road towards the centre, p'dum, p'dum as it went over the joins. Cleo felt jolted, disoriented and very foreign.

An aristocrat who's been forced to marry a yoick, was her next thought, as she stared incredulously at a huge item of social-realist sculpture posed ridiculously outside a rococo building. What a contrast, such elegance and style and so many hideous buildings and municipal artworks jostling next to each other.

It was a relief when the bus pulled up in Vorosmarty Square. The passengers clustered at the door, eager to be first off the bus. The young woman standing beside Cleo gave her a friendly nudge and pointed to a stately building with a Union Jack flying above it. 'British Embassy,' she said.

'Do you speak English?' asked Cleo, quick to seize the opportunity.

'A little. Can I help?'

'I want to catch a tram to Buda,' she said, holding out the address which she written down.

'I show you. It is not far.'

Cleo stole a quick look at the woman next sitting next to her in the yellow tram. She looked as grey and grim as the sculptures. A mother, thought Cleo fancifully. Husband off working in the mines, three poor children to bring up in a tiny cheerless flat and an ailing grandmother in the corner, possibly dying of TB.

Then she looked again, and decided she couldn't be a mother, because no man would ever have married her; any man would, in fact, prefer to be down the mines to spending more than twenty-four hours with such a threatening personality. Cleo was quite glad when the tram reached her stop.

'You'll know it, you go up a slight hill, and there's a strange garage on the corner, and then a café. It all gets quite green and leafy, no pavements or anything. Buy a map when you get to the terminus, then you'll know where you are.' Prue's voice had echoed hollowly down the line, but her directions were clear enough.

Luckily, there was a detailed fold-out street map in the guide Cleo had bought, with index. Cleo was an intrepid traveller, not fazed by strange cities and alien ways, and used to wrestling with strange public transport systems. She was even alive to the habit of having your ticket punched on the tram.

'Very sensible,' she had remarked to a fellow English traveller she had met on a tram in Amsterdam on a visit during her student days.

'Nothing of the kind,' he had replied with spirit. 'And they don't *tell* you before you get on.'

A pleasing encounter, remembered Cleo with a stab of nostalgia as she swung off the tram. Which had led to dinner and a delightful few days in and out of bed. Not so long ago, but it seemed like another life.

A roly-poly figure in a fake fur coat stepped out from the side of the road and accosted her. 'Cleo, oh Cleo, it's you.'

Cleo returned the hug, with difficulty. 'It's not twins, is it?' she asked with alarm. 'Or triplets, even?'

'No, no, just the one,' said Prue, laughing.

'That biddy who got off the tram after me,' said Cleo, looking round. 'Do you think she's a downtrodden mother, trudging home to her fatherless children?'

'Not she,' said Prue, with one scornful look at Cleo's grim neighbour. 'Look at those boots, a member of the secret police if ever I saw one, and look, she's been shopping in one of the hard currency shops.'

'Something special about that?' asked Cleo, as she walked slowly up the hill beside Prue.

'Party members and foreigners only,' said Prue. 'Here we are.' She pushed open the gate of a large old villa and led Cleo up a short flight of steps. 'Luckily, we've got the ground floor flat, because otherwise it'd be exhausting, heaving the bump up and down stairs all day. Although lots of women do it, of course, and the exercise is probably good for you.'

Inside the flat it was stiflingly hot, and Cleo felt her skin tingle with the change from the chill air outside. 'Pouf,' she said.

'It is hot,' said Prue. 'Municipal heating, piped through to all the houses and flats. We have no control over the temperature; all we can do is open and shut windows.'

'Goodness,' said Cleo.

'Yes, didn't you see the works as you came into Budapest? Great furnaces burning up cheap brown coal and belching foul fumes into the air. Unwrap yourself, I'll make some coffee.'

Prue hung up Cleo's bulky jacket, and pushed her into a largish room overlooking an area of garden. Cleo looked around her with interest, and went straight over to a very fine piece of painted furniture.

'Lovely,' she said.

'It belonged to Geza's grandmother, she gave it to us when we got married. They paint them like that in the villages, each region has its own style.'

'This is very comfortable,' said Cleo, looking at the wide sofa piled with cushions, the big table with a bench set into the corner on two sides, and carved chairs on the others; the shelves full of books, and everywhere photos: of Geza playing his violin, of Prue, of Geza and Prue together.

'You've been very happy, haven't you?' Cleo said abruptly. 'With Geza.'

'Blissfully,' said Prue. 'Not to say we don't fight. All Hungarians fight, but really we get on terribly well. He doesn't mind my university and my old bones, I love his music and life's good. Until now.'

'Until now,' echoed Cleo, following Prue into a tiny kitchen. There was a basic gas cooker, an aluminium sink set in a scratched imitation formica surround and several cheap-looking

wall cupboards, all lit by a dim light bulb. This spartan approach
was alleviated by the gaily decorated plates ranged on the walls,
and the bright cloths, covered in a similar style of embroidery,
which were pinned up and draped over the tiny table.

'Poky,' said Cleo, looking around. 'The kitchen at Haphazard
House is fairly basic, but nothing like this. On the other hand,
I like the array of bottles, and look at that enormous ham. Are
these paprikas?'

'Yes, also from Geza's family in the country,' said Prue, lighting the ring under an Italian coffee pot and shaking out the
match quickly before it burnt her fingers. 'There. Now, come
into the other room, tell me everything. It's ages since I've
seen you.'

Cleo dropped on to the sofa and leant back against the
cushions.

'You look a bit washed out,' said Prue.

Cleo looked across at her friend. There were dark shadows
beneath her eyes that told of troubled sleep, but other than
those, Prue looked to be in blooming health.

'I'm fine,' said Prue. 'What about you?' Come on, tell all.'

Cleo told her about the shingles, and the weeks off work. 'Not
a good idea, it's not the kind of job where you can safely take
time off, not more than a week or so at most.'

'Sounds grim,' said Prue.

'Very exciting,' said Cleo. 'You get a terrific buzz from doing
deals, keeps the adrenalin going.'

'What about Perry? You postponed the wedding, I got a card
from Gussie.'

'Postponed it *again*,' said Cleo.

'Yes, well, you do notice that when invitations arrive and then
cancellations shortly afterwards. Being abroad and pregnant and
not able to go, I did wonder.'

'Circumstances,' said Cleo.

'So when's it going to be now?'

'Oh, when I'm better,' said Cleo vaguely, shifting about on
the cushions. 'Is that coffee ready? It smells good.'

'Long day,' said Prue. 'You must be whacked, coming from
the north, and then the flight . . . Did you have to catch a train
at the crack of dawn?'

'No,' said Cleo. 'I caught the night train, I had a sleeper.'

'Lonely, catching a train at Eyot in the middle of the night.'

'Adele came to see me off. She worked late, and then we went for a meal.'

'I want to know all about everything,' said Prue, her eyes sparkling at the news of Eyot and mention of old friends. 'All about Sylvester, and Magdalena and Val. And Adele? What's she doing, working late? And why in Eyot?'

'Ah,' said Cleo. 'Now this will surprise you.'

Lovely to have a long gossip with Prue, thought Cleo sleepily. The phone had rung, and Prue was making unintelligible noises into it. Fluent Hungarian, how admirable. She herself was not a natural linguist, and felt what amounted to awe for people who could chat away in a foreign language. Particularly one as rarified as Hungarian, none of your common or garden school French here.

Prue put the phone down and sighed.

'Geza?' asked Cleo.

Prue shook her head. 'No, it wouldn't be wise. That was a silly conversation all about prices of food, it's a kind of code he's worked out, so that a friend can ring and give me news about him without any listeners-in understanding.'

Prue was quite calm, but Cleo had a flash of insight, a momentary feeling of what it must be like to be days away from giving birth to your first child with your husband absent and possibly in danger. Hardly the cosy scenario painted by the women's mags; random phrases floated into Cleo's mind.

Why your husband should be with you at the birth.

You're in control, don't let the doctor take over.

The best peak experience ever, says Jennifer, first-time mum.

Those precious first minutes when you and your partner share the wonder of a new life.

Bah, thought Cleo, getting up and going to her bag. She fished out a dress made in a printed wool in a pattern of clear greens and blues. Prue's colours. 'Adele made this for you.'

Cleo held it up, and Prue looked at it with delight. 'For me? Oh, how lovely! You wouldn't believe how dull clothes are here, and shoddy, especially maternity ones. Unless you're unbelievably rich and can shop at Klara Rothschild, and who would for baggy numbers? This is heavenly. I'll go and put it on.'

Clever Adele. Prue pirouetted as well as she could, revelling in the new dress. 'Listen, Cleo, if you can bear it, we're going out to eat. It's much nicer eating out, and then I don't have to cook. Can you bear to go out again? Or do you just want to crash out and sleep?'

Part of Cleo longed to creep into bed, but she wasn't going to give in. Here she was in Budapest, possibly only for one night, she couldn't just go to bed. She yawned widely. 'I'm fine,' she said. 'And I'd love to go out.'

'We'll go up to the castle area,' said Prue. 'Only you'll have to wrap up, it's icy at night.'

'Pretty icy in the daytime,' said Cleo.

'One day, Geza says, the Castle will come back to life, and seethe with the citizens of Budapest. Oh, and the city will be full of lights again. They all hate the dim and dreary lighting in the streets and on the bridges.'

They were huddled against the cold in the Fishermen's Bastion, overlooking the dimly lit city. The moon was up, the night clear, and Cleo could see the Danube far below, threading its silvery way through the city, dividing Buda from Pest.

'It seems a very long way from Eyot,' said Cleo.

'It is,' said Prue. 'Not just in time, or in distance, but in culture and history and everything else. We're at the centre of Europe here, you know; Eyot is really at the very edge.'

'Feels like it, too,' said Cleo. 'What's that on the left, is it an island?'

'Margaret Island,' said Prue. 'If we had time, I'd take you there, but I think we should leave as soon as possible.'

'Ah,' said Cleo, following Prue back into the street. 'Tomorrow?'

'I have to fix my exit visa, so probably the day after, if I can fix it; it's supposed to take a week. Which means that, unless I have to be in the police station all day, I can take you round a bit. It's terrible to drag you over here, and then for you not to see much of the city; I am grateful, you know.'

'I'm enjoying myself,' said Cleo. 'I needed shaking up, and

reminding that there is life outside finance and nostalgia. What with the bank and Haphazard House, one passes a fairly dream-like existence.'

Prue was planning, thinking ahead. 'If we have to wait for any reason, it would be better to be in Vienna than in Budapest. And better Cologne than Vienna, and Brussels is better still.'

'Brussels? Brussels could never be better.'

'Oh, yes, it is, and best of all is anywhere in England.'

'Very xenophobic.'

'No,' said Prue. 'It's safer for Geza and that's the only reason I'm going. And in the future, who knows, it might be much safer for our child to have been born in England. If there's going to be anywhere safe,' she added reflectively.

'Don't be so gloomy,' said Cleo.

'Not gloomy, realistic. Do you remember how small a world it was at school?'

Cleo pulled a face. 'I do indeed.'

'Small, but very calm and very safe. Hungary's a bit like that. Follow the rules, do as you're told, don't ask any questions, don't criticize powerful people, and life tick-tocks along quite nicely. You won't be robbed in the street, and you can walk in any park in the middle of the night without being in danger.'

'But?' said Cleo cynically.

'Actually, one isn't at school any more. The world isn't that small, and it isn't at all safe, certainly not when you step over the line. Do that, and you find yourself living in a world of shadows and half-truths and fear.'

'I'm not sure we didn't in the convent,' said Cleo. 'And at least there are no nuns lurking round every corner here.'

'No,' said Prue, for the first time laughing in the way she had in more carefree days. 'Just the secret police, in big boots.'

'Come on, I'm freezing,' said Cleo. 'Can we take a taxi back to your place?'

'Yes, of course. I'd be quite glad to, actually.'

'What time do we leave, if we go the day after tomorrow?'

'It depends,' said Prue. 'I've got the train times from here to Vienna, but I'm not sure about trains on from there.'

'No problem,' said Cleo. 'I've got the current Cook's time-table.'

'Good,' said Prue.

'And I must ring England tomorrow, let them know what's happening.'

'Discreetly,' said Prue.

20

Cleo slept without stirring on the sofa in the big room which had so neatly turned into a bed. She had marvelled at the cloud of white duvet which Prue hauled out from beneath the bed. Down, and at least a foot high, quite wonderful to lie under.

'Don't worry if you hear noises in the night,' said Prue.

'Noises?' said Cleo, alarmed. 'Not ghosts? Not here, surely?'

'Plenty of ghosts in Hungary if you want them,' said Prue. 'No, it's me, I don't sleep for very long at a stretch, and I tend to get cramps, so I potter around. Just ignore me. Or pretend I'm a ghost if it makes you happy. Are there ghosts at Haphazard House?'

'Very much so,' said Cleo, giving a vast yawn. 'I'll tell you about them tomorrow.'

'I hope I didn't disturb you, in the night,' said Prue as, hours later, she put out plates on the table and brought in coffee and a little jug of hot chocolate. 'I can't drink coffee first thing at present.'

Cleo felt better that morning than she had for weeks. Showered, with her dark hair gleaming and her skin glowing, she looked more like the Cleo Prue had known before, and less like a wrung-out dishcloth. Prue told her so.

Cleo didn't like that. 'Did I look very depressing yesterday?'

'You weren't depressing in yourself, but you did look quite washed out. Much better today

'That's hours and hours of blissful sleep,' said Cleo.

'Haven't you been sleeping in Eyotshire?'

Cleo thought about it. 'No, not terribly well,' she said, surprised. 'Now you come to mention it. There's a lot of noise at night in a big old house. And the voices and so on. And strange dreams. And Porthos, of course, very large in bed.'

'Porthos? What an extraordinary name. Does Perry know about Porthos?'

'It is a black mark against Perry's name that he is far from charmed by Porthos's character and beauty,' said Cleo. 'Porthos is the house cat, a delightful creature, and good company.' She helped herself to a roll and some salami. 'This all looks delicious. What are these rolls?'

'*Kifli*,' said Prue. 'And have some cheese. *Trappista*, it's called.'

'Monks cheese, then. And what's this?'

'Compote, pears, out of a jar.'

Prue ate a good breakfast, Cleo noticed.

'I make myself,' said Prue. 'Otherwise one can feel dizzy, and anyway, I'm basically hungry, it's just wondering about Geza and so on that tends to curb my appetite.'

'I can imagine. So what happens today?'

'I have to go to the district police station,' said Prue. 'Tense time, will they give me an exit visa, bearing in mind they're baying for Geza's blood.'

'Sounds unlikely, in the circumstances.'

'Ah, but Zoli Hoffman should be on duty, and he's an amateur violinist and a big Geza fan. Geza reckons he'll do me an exit visa under the counter, as it were, no questions asked, so keep your fingers crossed. It's just to go to Vienna, as far as they're concerned, which I often do, so he should be able to slip it through as nothing out of the ordinary. I hope.'

'I'll come with you,' offered Cleo.

'No way,' said Prue decidedly. 'A bad idea, to have an English visitor hovering in the background, that would make them suspicious all right. No, you want to phone England, and you do that from the central post office, I'll tell you how to get there. We can arrange to meet at various times, because this visa could take half an hour or most of the day.'

'Fall backs,' said Cleo.

'I was thinking of the Gellert,' said Prue. 'Sumptuous pastries, the best in Budapest. Oh, I meant to ask, is Flora's still going strong in Eyot?'

'Just the same,' said Cleo. 'And the coffee's as good as ever; I went there with Lily.'

'Lily! Oh, I long to see Sylvester and Lily again.'

'You will. Tell me about this coffee shop.'

'Coffee shop?' said Prue, shocked. 'Goodness, it's far grander than that. It's an institution. And a hotel, too. You can go into the hotel and see the hot baths if you want. People spend hours there, you can come and go, no one will take any notice. Mind you take your passport with you, though, and produce it when asked.'

'What, to have a cup of coffee?' Clearly, things were much worse here than Cleo had imagined.

'No, of course not. There are places where they might ask to see identification, though.'

'Such as?

'Oh, foreign currency shops. The post office, probably. They're very jumpy here just now.'

Hungarian, Cleo decided, had to be the most difficult language going. She couldn't begin to make head or tail of it. Strings of vowels and consonants, with no vaguely familiar words such as there always were in Italian or German or Scandinavian languages. And the phrases provided at the end of the guide-book, with the pronunciation indicated by means of a strange phonetic system, probably invented by the author, were hardly useful.

The factory has exceeded its production targets.

Do you have a powder for bedbugs?

Cleo didn't like the sound of that at all.

The Danube is cold at this time of year.

Hopeless.

Her encounter with the official at the post office had been rather fraught, since he didn't speak a word of English. Cleo had had to write down Sylvester's number, and, after much incomprehensible sign language, Sylvester's name. Then all kinds of details about herself, quite unnecessary, in Cleo's opinion.

'You won't be put through at once,' Prue had warned her.

'That's because they're checking up on you and on the number you're ringing. It can take anything up to two hours.'

So Cleo had gathered from the violent pointings which the clerk made to his watch, and the scrap of grubby-looking paper which was pushed through to her, with a time written in a sloping continental hand.

Cleo looked at her own watch. An hour to wait. She smiled at the clerk, although it went against the grain, sour creature, never a hint of a smile or any signs of being happy to help. He hasn't been to charm school, that's obvious, thought Cleo as she wandered out of the post office and looked about her.

She didn't feel like a coffee yet, she could do that after she'd got through to Sylvester. Two hours before the first meeting time with Prue. I'll walk to the river, she decided. Here I am, in the very centre of the Europe, as Prue so truly said; so the least I can do is go and pay my respects to the Danube.

Far away, in Midwinter, the phone rang. Lily answered it, greeting Cleo with delight before flying into the music room to find Sylvester.

'Lily,' he roared, furious at being interrupted. Lily never disturbed him when he was working, and kept everyone else at bay for him. 'Is there a fire?'

'Quick,' said Lily. 'Cleo on the phone, from Budapest.'

'Ah,' said Sylvester, laying his cello down on its side and perching his bow on top. 'Excellent.' He moved with surprising speed across the hall to the telephone.

'Cleo? How's Prue?'

It was an echoey voice which came down the line, hollow and strangely high.

'In the post office, are you?' said Sylvester. 'I know that Budapest post office, full of grim parties looking as though you wanted a direct line to MI5. Cold, is it? Yes, it would be at this time of year. Now, let me write this down. Evening train from Vienna, so into London, weather, train and acts of God permitting, the following afternoon . . . that's the day after tomorrow, I take it? Good, good. Ring me as soon as you get to England. Ring me en route, if you can. Yes, Will's installed at Haphazard, still fretting about ghostly emanations.

He should have more sense at his age; stick to his music and song-writing.'

Crackles and hisses and a general sound as of geese fly-ing across the line distracted Sylvester, and he pressed the handpiece into his ear as though that would somehow clarify the words.

'What? What's that? The man who came from King's Cross with Valdemar for the summer festival . . . the year it was so hot. Cleo, have you taken leave of your senses? No, no, go on, I'm with you now. He may be in touch? No problem. Lily or I will be within sound of the phone every hour of the day. Now, my best love to Prue, and tell her not to worry. Plenty of support here for harassed musicians, you tell her that.'

'I adore the Gellert,' said Prue, drinking her coffee gratefully. She leant back in her seat, closing her eyes for a moment and looking, Cleo thought, utterly drained. Could she really stand the journey to England?

Prue opened her eyes again. 'Pretty hairy, at the police station. This Geza fan's boss kept on appearing, so I had to pretend I'd come about a stolen bag. Anyway, there was a phone call from some party official whose dustbin had vanished, so the big cheese was off like lightning. Stamp, stamp, sign here, and here, a few more stamps, and I was out of there.'

'Good,' said Cleo. 'I spoke to Sylvester, told him when we were planning to come. He sent his love. And he's mobilizing musicianly forces in support of Geza.'

'Goodness, he wasn't too detailed on the phone, was he?'

'Trust Sylvester for that,' said Cleo. 'Very opaque. Sylvester knows a thing or two.'

'Did the telephoning take all morning?' said Prue, who had recovered sufficiently to attack a *parfé*, one of the house specialities.

'I wandered down to the river, and walked along while I was waiting,' said Cleo. 'Very cold, but worth it.'

'Hmm,' said Prue. 'The rest of the day is ours. I know, we'll do some shopping, buy presents for Lily and Sylvester and your mum.'

'And Adele,' said Cleo, liking the idea.

'And Perry,' said Prue, looking at Cleo with innocent green eyes.

'Oh, yes, of course. And Perry.'

21

'Those trees,' said Cleo. 'What are they?'

'Acacias,' said Prue. 'Stunning, in the summer. They plant them as wind breaks.'

Cleo had to take that on trust, for the view out of the train window was far from stunning; the previous day's blue skies and sharp, clear air had given way to lowering grey clouds, swept across the sky by a biting wind. The compartment they were sitting in wasn't cold; in fact, it was overheated and stuffy, and Cleo could think of lots of places where she would rather be.

Cleo had exclaimed with astonishment when she found out that it would take about six hours to cover a distance of 250 kilometres.

'About 180 miles,' said Prue helpfully. 'The trains aren't very modern, and there are always delays. All the trains seem to hang around at stations for no particular reason. You get used to it.'

'You've got used to a lot, since you married, haven't you?' said Cleo. It was a wonder to her. No one could have been less worldly-wise than Prue when she had run off with Geza on the morning of her wedding to another man. And just think of the changes to her life since then.

Becoming part of the international music circuit through Geza. That would be quite enough for most women. But then, on top of that, Prue had set up house in Budapest. She had found herself part of a large family for the first time in her life; Prue had been an orphan, brought up by an austere and joyless aunt. Geza had brothers, sisters, parents, grandparents, aunts, uncles, cousins . . . Many of them living close at hand. Then she had learnt a difficult foreign language and studied at university. There had been at least two seasons in Africa, hunting for fossil teeth and bones. Then back to life under the communists . . .

'It's amazing,' said Cleo.

Prue thought that was very funny. 'You don't do it all at once, you know. Day by day, and then at the end of a while, things have changed, and you've hardly noticed.'

Cleo didn't believe a word of it. 'Just getting married is a huge change,' she argued. 'And it wasn't as though you'd lived with a man before, you weren't used to it.'

'Living with Geza was no problem, ever,' said Prue. 'He made me laugh all the time, and we had such fun. I just wanted to be with him, and he wanted to be with me, and everything else wasn't important.'

'Your work's important.'

'Yes, of course it is, but I wouldn't want to be doing it here in Hungary if Geza weren't here.'

'You depend on Geza, then.'

'In a way. And he depends on me.'

'That's the bit I find hard to take, giving up one's independence.'

Prue looked at her friend with affection. 'You don't,' she said simply. 'You won't. I don't suppose for a moment that Perry wants a clinging wife, unable to move without him.'

'I don't know what Perry wants,' said Cleo, watching the undulating landscape slip by. Picturesque yellow-painted churches, with rounded apses and assertive spires. Clusters of houses and farm buildings. Horses in the fields. 'Except a wife, but there are times when I think almost anyone would do.'

'Just premarital frets,' said Prue wisely, arranging her bump more comfortably.

They had had the carriage to themselves until now, but the door opened and a tall, dark woman came in, murmuring a greeting in Hungarian. Very striking, thought Cleo, with that black hair caught up in a loose knot, very white skin and scarlet lips. Not as young, though, as she seemed at first, and there were little lines round her mouth and above her eyes which spoke of strain.

The new passenger settled in one of the unoccupied corners, and pulled out a magazine. Cleo, remembering her foray into the bookshop in Eyot, dug into her bag and fished out the paperbacks she had bought for Prue. 'And I picked up a couple of magazines at the airport,' she added, handing them over.

The woman in the corner looked up. 'You are English?'

Cleo nodded. The woman turned her attention to Prue. 'You are English, too?'

'Yes,' said Prue, her voice sounding slightly wary.

'You are travelling to Vienna?'

'Yes.'

'I also. You are consulting a doctor, perhaps,' said the woman, with a gesture towards Prue's bump.

Prue said nothing.

'You must be near your time,' the woman went on, measuring Prue's abdomen with an expert eye. 'Me, I have five children, I know all about it.'

Good, thought Cleo, who didn't feel at all happy at the prospect of having to deal with Prue in labour in the middle of a long train journey. Should the need arise, clearly she would have help at hand, at least between here and Vienna. She gave the woman a friendly smile.

The woman smiled back, her almost black eyes full of vitality. 'So,' she said. She rose and held out a hand to Cleo. 'I am Zsuzsa Gabor. Please call me Zsuzsa.'

'Cleo Byng.'

'Byng! So English, so typical.'

Prue was flashing warning messages at Cleo, but she forced a smile and told the woman simply that her name was Prue.

'This is better,' the woman said, sitting down again before returning to Prue's pregnancy. She was clearly determined to get to the bottom of the bump.

'Your husband isn't English, then?' she said directly. 'Or are you divorced?'

Prue blinked at her.

'You wear your wedding ring on your right hand,' Zsuzsa said.

Prue immediately folded one hand over the other, hiding the telltale ring. Zsuzsa laughed. 'I'm very nosy, yes?'

Definitely, thought Cleo.

'So why are you travelling from Budapest to Vienna, when

you should be at home, making everything ready for the baby? This isn't the time to be visiting Hungary.'

'We're on our way back to England,' said Cleo.

'And there the husband is waiting anxiously? Such a strange husband, to let his wife go across Europe without him at such a time. And in December!'

'Prue's husband is away a good deal,' said Cleo.

Zsuzsa nodded wisely. 'Then he has to be back for his baby to be born. Now, I,' she said with pride, 'have had five husbands.'

'Five?' said Cleo. Gracious, Zsuzsa wasn't exactly young, but she couldn't be more than forty-five. Five husbands seemed excessive.

Zsuzsa settled herself more comfortably in her seat. 'First, I married when I was seventeen. Very romantic, very young love. He was my childhood sweetheart, we had known each other for years. Everything was wonderful, happy parents, happy grandparents. Then there was a baby, my first son, oh, we were the ideal couple.'

'What happened?' said Cleo, fearing a tragedy.

'He had a problem.'

'Problem? What kind of problem?' Cleo was intrigued, and she could see that although Prue was leaning back with her eyes closed, she was listening hard. Drink? Sex? Neurosis? A lurid past?

'He was boring. Deeply boring. He had nothing to say which he hadn't said before. He wanted nothing new, he wanted to stay in the same job, to see the same films, to do the same thing every Saturday. He was like an old man, completely conservative, like your politicians. There was no cure for such boringness. So I left him.'

'Just like that?'

'It is easy in Hungary,' said Zsuzsa with a shrug. 'Get married, Ave Maria in the Town Hall, few months, a year or two later, round to the same Town Hall, different room, with the papers for divorce.'

'Oh,' said Cleo, struck by this novel approach to the married state. 'Who did you marry next?'

'This one was the real love of my life, you have to understand that. He was much older than me, a scientist.' She threw up her hands in an expressive gesture. 'A scientist! How could I be so stupid, to marry a hard-working scientist. I could have picked a normal one, lazy, but no. All day and all night, work, work, into the laboratories, there until two, three in the morning. He was a very clever scientist, they say he will be given a Nobel prize.'

She paused for applause.

'Nobel prize?' said Cleo obligingly. 'Very impressive.'

'Oh, yes, a great man. And sometimes he went abroad for foreign conferences, and I could go too. That was good. Then everything was fine. More or less, and he had plenty of time for making love, with good beds and good food in foreign hotels, oh, yes, very nice.'

'So you still loved him?'

'I never stopped loving him. Never.' Zsuzsa was emphatic. 'I love him to this day, even though he lives for science. However, I then found out, from my best friend, that his time was not quite always spent with the goddess science. No, there was another goddess there, in the laboratory, an assistant. Blonde, very pretty, very clever, very sexy.'

'Ah,' said Cleo.

'Gabi,' Zsuzsa spat out. 'Whore.'

'What did you do?'

'I did the most stupid thing I could do. I should have poisoned her, got her sacked, told my husband she was lesbian, anything. But no, I was still too young and not experienced enough. I challenged him. I told him, I knew everything. In a great big scene, very dramatic, very tense. I said to him, "It's me or her."' She shrugged. 'He chose her.'

Cleo could sense the drama in Zsuzsa's tale, but nonetheless, she wanted to laugh. 'Two husbands,' she said helpfully. 'Who next?'

'Next was not for long, only weeks, although very passionate. I married a sailor I met in Italy. He was a real man, such a body, muscles, wonderful shape, a wonderful lover, with dark, sexy eyes. Oh, we got sore from making love. Then he went back to his boat, and I thought, well, good, now I'm an Italian citizen, I settle down here, wait for him to come back.'

'And didn't he?'

'He came back, yes, it was his home town, where else would

he be? He came back to his poppa and momma and his pretty Italian wife and three little bambini.'

'Ouch,' said Cleo.

'So that was bigamy, huh? Not so good. And I was pregnant now, and it's not so easy to have an abortion in Italy, let me tell you.'

Cleo looked anxiously at Prue, feeling that abortion was hardly a suitable topic for one in her condition.

Prue had abandoned all pretence of sleeping, and she was listening, fascinated, to the saga of Zsuzsa's life and loves. 'Everybody has abortions in Hungary,' she told Cleo matter-of-factly. 'It's the usual method of birth control.'

Zsuzsa pounced. 'You've lived in Hungary then, to know about such things?'

'I'm a social worker,' said Prue.

Cleo was struck with admiration at her quick-wittedness; she obviously didn't want to let on that she was married to a Hungarian, lived in Budapest.

'I've studied these matters,' Prue went on airily. 'In several European countries.'

'Social worker, yes, they are always concerned with such things. Well, I go back to Hungary, but it was too late, and besides, the doctor says it is twins, and then, hey presto, there they are.'

'Hey presto?' said Prue, interested.

'Don't you believe it,' said Zsuzsa. 'I speak symbolically. Babies aren't hey presto. Babies are hard work, and a lot of pain.'

'Um,' said Prue.

'Never mind, then it's over, and you forget about it until next time.'

'I see,' said Prue. She looked Zsuzsa straight in the eye. 'How come your English is so good?'

'Because I married an Englishman.'

'Number four?'

'Yes. He was in Hungary, renting the army for a film.'

'The army?' Cleo was puzzled.

'If you make a big picture, an epic, about Waterloo, or any war with battle scenes, then it's very cheap to hire the Hungarian army. Also, all kinds of film are made on location in Hungary, and television productions, too. That was Nicky's job, to arrange all this. He directed films himself, too, but art films, and there's no money in that.'

'How did you meet him?'

'He rented me for one day. I was very short of money, and so I hired myself out with the children, very good for gypsy parts, you see. I do not actually look at all like a Rom, not a Hungarian gypsy, I can assure you, but I can look like what film directors expect a gypsy to be. I do my gypsy work, and then we go out to dinner, and·then he goes back to England, but only for a week. Then he comes back, and we are married.'

'Just like that?' asked Cleo. Here she was, fretting and brooding over marrying Perry, while this exotic Hungarian woman married anybody and everybody at the drop of a hat.

'He was so good with the twins,' said Zsuzsa reminiscently. 'My first son, he stayed with his father. That was best, because although he is so good-looking, and exceptionally clever, top of the class in mathematics every time, and also very good at football, he is nonetheless boring, like his father, and we do not get on. Nicky was such a good father to the twins, in every way. I went with him to England, and we lived in Surrey.'

'Surrey?' said Prue.

'Surrey,' repeated Cleo, looking at Zsuzsa and wondering what the inhabitants of Surrey had made of her.

'Surrey was terrible. I believe Nicky is Bohemian, living in an artistic community. Film people, painters, writers, musicians, they are friends, and they see each other, and talk a lot. But no, Nicky's friends are accountants. And the vicar, who was a very strange man. He wanted to christen the twins, to bring them into the family of God. What a bad idea, I told him. And then Nicky was upset, and Nicky's mother was upset, and then one day when I came back early from shopping, there was Nicky in bed with the vicar.'

'No!' said Cleo.

'Remember the vicar, at Mountjoy?' said Prue.

'That was Sophie, not another man. It was Daisy who . . . oh, never mind. Go on, Zsuzsa.'

Pleased with the effect she had made, Zsuzsa said that was the end of it. 'I packed my bags, zip, zip, zip, take all the money

out of the bank account, which was a nice lot, and came back
to Hungary.'

'To get divorced?' Cleo was still struck by the casual approach
to divorce in Hungary.

'Certainly not. At least, not then. I had a British passport,
which was very useful. Those were difficult times, like now. Or
I could sell it, for quite a lot of money.'

Prue was feeling hungry, and she rustled round in the bag she
had packed up with rolls, a thermos of coffee and some mineral
water. She offered a roll to Zsuzsa, who waved it aside. 'No, no,
you need to eat, you have to keep up your strength.'

Cleo was still counting. 'That was number four, then.' She
absentmindedly took a roll, and bit into it, sending a little shower
of crumbs into her lap.

'Very messy,' said Zsuzsa with disapproval.

Cleo wasn't going to be put off. 'If you didn't divorce Nicky,
how did you get to marry number five? Or was that another
spot of bigamy?'

'I was never bigamist,' said Zsuzsa, shocked. 'When I met
Laci, who is an important man, and with a good business, then
I divorced Nicky. Laci and I were very happy. Two children, one
son, one daughter, she is so pretty, so talented.'

'Were? Aren't you still married to him?'

'No, not now. He did some things that were a little bit corrupt,
and he had to leave the Party. In fact, he went to prison, although
that was politics, nothing else.'

For better, for worse, thought Cleo.

'For me, it is better not to be married to a man in this position.
It can cause some problems.'

'I bet it can,' said Cleo, awed.

The train was slowing down, and Cleo could see Prue tense
up. 'Are we coming into a station?' she asked Zsuzsa.

Zsuzsa looked at her watch and shook her head. 'The next
station is Tatabanya, and that is not yet. We are some way
from Tatabanya. Maybe there is a cow on the line, or a signal
is not right.'

Cleo stood up and peered out of the window. 'Middle of
nowhere,' she said.

Prue chewed at the corner of a nail.

'Hey, I can see soldiers,' said Cleo.

'Get back inside. At once!' said Zsuzsa.

Prue tugged at Cleo to sit down.

'I can look, can't I?' said Cleo, aggrieved. 'There are soldiers all over the place, and tanks, and armoured cars. Perhaps it's a film.'

'Perhaps it isn't,' said Prue.

Zsuzsa gave Prue a keen look. 'Prue is right, I think these soldiers are real, and when there are soldiers, it is best to keep your head down, and not look too much.'

Cleo looked at Prue, and wondered if she was going to faint. 'Are you all right?'

'Yes,' said Prue. 'Just feeling a bit sick.'

'These are troop movements, I think,' said Zsuzsa. 'The train is stopped to let them past, I do not think they are interested in the train. Or the people on it.'

'Oh, God, I hope not,' said Prue under her breath.

There was a shout outside, and a stream of Hungarian, and then some German.

'What's up?' said Cleo.

Prue and Zsuzsa were listening intently.

'Ah, silly fool,' said Zsuzsa. 'A man on the train, a German tourist I think, tries to take a photo. Very stupid. Now he loses his camera, possibly a good one, and he is in some trouble.'

Prue let out a puff of breath. 'I wish the train would move.'

The train gave a faint judder, and then began to creep forward.

'There,' said Zsuzsa. 'No need for any more worries. We are on our way.'

22

'Tatabanya,' said Zsuzsa quickly, as the train ground to a halt again. 'Shut the window, this area is very polluted.'

'It sounds delightful,' said Cleo.

'Tatabanya?' said Prue. 'It isn't, take it from me. Barrow-in-Furness, only worse.'

'You know Tatabanya?' asked Zsuzsa, keenly interested. 'You've travelled in Hungary, then?'

'I have friends here,' said Prue, diving back into her magazine.

True, thought Cleo, but evasive. I wonder why.

When the train had finally made it into Tatabanya, and then after jolts and jerks and false starts, out of it again, Cleo got the chance to ask Prue.

'Please hold my seat for me,' Zsuzsa said, getting up from her seat.

'Of course,' said Cleo.

Prue made a face at Zsuzsa's back as she went out of the compartment.

'What's she done?' asked Cleo. 'What's up? Why are you so frosty?'

'Cleo, this is Hungary, the Eastern Bloc, not the Brighton line. You have to be terribly careful who you speak to, what you say. They plant people on these trains, and they report back to the police who whip you off at the border.'

'How often?' said Cleo sceptically. 'Besides, I don't think she's a stooge. All those husbands, fascinating.'

'Made it all up, that's what's so suspicious,' hissed Prue. 'I never heard anything so improbable.'

'Nobody could make that lot up,' said Cleo. 'Sssh, she's back.'

She wasn't. Instead, three weary-looking travellers tumbled into the compartment, shell-shocked after their encounter with Tatabanya.

They were three men, one of whom, a tall man with a pained expression, made a beeline for Zsuzsa's seat.

Cleo looked at Prue, who wiggled herself into a more upright position, and said something in Hungarian. The tall man took no notice, and then the second man said in strongly accented English. 'The seat is occupied.'

'Are you English?' Cleo said directly to the tall man. 'Someone is sitting there.'

The tall man, just about to lower himself into the seat, shut his eyes and turned his head away in an exaggerated gesture of despair. The third man, shorter than the other two, who had been fussing about with bags and coats, fluttered anxiously to the tall man's aid. 'Timothy has to have a corner seat,' he said. 'And he must be facing, it's agony for him to have his back to the engine.'

'Really, to be comfortable, I should sit directly by the window,' said the tall man in pitiful tones, glancing at Prue. 'I find the corridor unnerving.'

'Isn't there space in another compartment?' said Cleo. 'Zsuzsa will be back in a moment, and she'll want her seat. So it's either in the middle on that side, and facing, or the other corner, and back to the engine.'

The man with the accent plumped himself down beside Cleo, giving her an approving look. 'Me, I sit here, very comfortable, and excellent company, and I can see that no one will fight me for this seat.'

'No,' said Prue, laughing, 'you're quite safe there.'

'Tony,' said tall Timothy, as he sat resentfully down in the wrong corner. 'My cologne, please, I can feel a terrible headache coming on.'

'I've got some aspirin,' said Cleo helpfully.

'Timothy can't take aspirin,' explained Tony. 'He has a very delicate digestion; aspirin is so harsh.'

Cleo tried to avoid Prue's eye, knowing that the resultant

laughter might offend. She turned to the man sitting placidly beside her. 'Are you French?'

'I am, yes,' he said. 'And you are English, and your friend too, who is expecting a baby.'

'Yes, we're both English.'

'And you are travelling to Vienna?'

'Yes.'

'Then I'm lucky to have such pleasant companions on the journey. I too, go to Vienna.'

'So do we,' said Tony. He was still hovering. 'Excuse me,' he went on, addressing the Frenchman. 'I would prefer to sit next to my friend, if you wouldn't mind.'

The Frenchman sprang to his feet. 'I was wrong, so it turns out,' he said to Cleo, 'but even so, I lose nothing. I sit next to one charming woman, and can look across at another.'

Prue smiled. 'You're very polite,' she said.

'No, no, it is a privilege,' he said, relaxing into his seat once more. 'Some women, when they are *enceinte*, are very unfortunate, but it suits you.'

'True,' thought Cleo. Prue was looking much better than she had before they left Budapest.

The door slid open. Zsuzsa was back. Her eyes swept round the compartment. 'Ha,' she said with approval. She nodded to Cleo and Prue. 'Thank you for keeping my seat. It's good to have company when one travels,' she added, assessing the three men with her zestful dark eyes.

Wasting your time with two of these, thought Cleo. And the third's far too young for you. Mind you, there was a distinctly predatory look in Zsuzsa's eye, and the Frenchman, although much her junior, was decidedly attractive. Women in their forties often liked younger men, Cleo told herself. Then she thought of Gussie, and wondered how she would feel if a stepfather of her own age appeared on the scene.

Gussie would never do that. Gussie was too grown up to relish the company of a younger man.

Was that why any woman liked younger men? For their conversation?

Cleo thought not.

And, since she was thinking about ages, why was Gussie and

a younger man any different from her and and older man, viz, Perry. Did Gussie mind the prospect of having a son-in-law who was her contemporary?

Cleo pushed these troublesome thoughts away into the recesses of her mind. This wasn't the time or place to think about that. Here she was, in a train in Hungary, on her way to Vienna, where she'd never been, not that they were planning to sight-see, but still . . . responsible for Prue's well-being.

And travelling in a compartment which seemed to be stuffed full of interesting people.

Cleo settled herself down to enjoy the trip.

23

The frost in Hazard had given way to tempest and downpour, and at Haphazard House the rooms rang to the sound of drips.

Mrs Grigson had run out of buckets. 'I never remember such wet,' she said with stark despair, as she wrung out another cloth and continued with her Canute-like efforts to keep the house dry.

The wind rattled all the loose windows, and the howling draughts made doors open and bang shut without reason. Even Giles and Lambert, used, as they were by now, to the ways of the house, felt jumpy.

'One's wits are shaken out of their sense,' complained Giles. 'And my lute won't tune, it sulks in the damp.'

'I don't think it's doing the telephone any good, either,' said Lambert, picking up the receiver, and hearing ominous crackles.

'That's of no account? No one's ringing up.' Giles was bored, the empty house was dull after the rush of recent visitors. And he was missing Cleo, he'd loved her liveliness which had woken the old place up after years of dullness. Adele was all right, but they had no rapport with her, and Will was simply exhausting. One night of him had been more than enough.

'How long is Cleo going to be away on her travels?'

'Not long,' said Lambert. 'One night on the train, one or two nights in Budapest, then a night on the way back. So she said.'

'That's if all goes well,' said Giles, determined to look on the dark side. 'They might be held up, highwaymen, hijackers, pirates.'

Lambert frowned. 'I think you've got your centuries mixed up again.'

'New names, old crimes. Same dangers. Then there's disease, think of all the terrible diseases those Frenchmen at court suffered from.'

'If they were the same as the ones in my day, they always claimed they caught them from the English.'

'Ha, lured by a sweet, pretty, fresh face, that taught them a lesson.'

'I didn't know you were speaking of that kind of disease in particular. And I don't see why Cleo would be in danger of that.'

'She's very free in her ways,' said Giles, morose now.

'In company with a pregnant friend?' Lambert was shocked. 'And on a long and difficult journey? Her mind will turn to the Lord, she will remember her prayers and feel remorse for her past sins.'

Giles gave a sardonic laugh. 'Not she. I expect she's enjoying every minute, Cleo takes life with gusto, she's a woman of spirit.'

'We're men of spirit,' said Lambert unkindly. 'And look at us.'

Gussie phoned Sylvester. 'Has Prue rung again?'

'No, but I didn't expect her to for a while. Do remember, Gussie, that it's tricky phoning from some of these places. It took Cleo more than an hour to get through to me from Budapest.'

'Perry's in a state.'

'Do him good,' said Sylvester brutally. 'Stir him up a bit, I never saw a man so complacent and pleased with himself.'

'Sylvester!'

'You can see it for yourself, Gussie. And, since we're on the subject, I can't think why Cleo imagines for a single moment that she wants to marry him. I'd as soon marry the plant outside my door.'

'That's a very hard judgement.'

Sylvester flexed the fingers of one hand, and switched the phone to the other one for some more useful finger-workout. He was sitting in the kitchen, with Lily darting to and fro in the background, eavesdropping furiously. 'I knew Perry was tiresome, but I didn't realize how tiresome until I met him again. All right, all right, Gussie. He may be very knowledgeable and interesting about art. He may be an excellent and attentive companion. No doubt he is considerate and pleasant in bed. All very well, but young Cleo has a zany streak, as is right and proper at her age, and she needs someone with a bit of go in him. Does Perry ever quarrel with her?'

'Perry isn't the quarrelsome sort.'

'There you are then. No pep, that's his trouble. He'd drive her mad inside a year. No, sooner than that, I'd give it six months at most. She wants someone she can have terrific rows with. Lots of noise, lots of fun. Lots of life, Gussie.'

Sylvester could hear Gussie's sigh at the other end. 'I don't know where Cleo gets it from.'

'What a ridiculous thing to say, from Val, of course. And, may I point out, it's what attracted you to Val in the first place, all those years ago.'

'It's different when you're young.'

'Well, Cleo's young. And Perry isn't. And don't give me that nonsense about a father figure. I know that's what's behind all this, and it annoys me greatly. I can tell you, when Val gets over to the other side, they're going to give him a good going over with the pitchforks before they let him loose on the fluffy clouds. He has a lot to answer for, the way he neglected those children of his.'

'Val's badgering me, too. Says I shouldn't have let Cleo go barging off to Hungary.'

'Let? What's all this let?'

'I know, but now Val's got the twins, he thinks you have control over your offspring.'

'At the twins' age you do, how old are they, five? Hardly the same for Cleo, she's been her own woman for years. Tell Val he's making a fool of himself. And that he'll learn soon enough just how much control he's got over anybody.'

'Sylvester, I have a pile of illustrations to finish, a living to earn. I don't propose to start a running argument with Val, who never listens to a word I say in any case.'

'Stop worrying. I never thought of you as a fussing mother.'

'Sylvester, I am not fussing. I am worried, however. I'm worried about Cleo, and I'm very worried about Prue, who certainly shouldn't be undertaking a long journey right now.'

'Prue will be all right. Everyone helps pregnant women, I've often noticed it.'

'Have you seen the paper today?'

'I never look at it until the evening, it would depress me for the whole day if I read it earlier.'

'The news from Hungary isn't good.'

'Ho,' said Sylvester, taking the cup of coffee offered by Lily with a nod of thanks. 'Hum. I'll let you know the minute I hear anything from Cleo or Prue. You do likewise, and meanwhile keep your nose down in those illustrations. Nothing like work for keeping the ghoulies at bay.'

He was frowning when he put down the phone. He looked at Lily.

'Yes,' she said. 'There is trouble in Hungary. Tank movements in Poland, they said on the news, and a lot of troops marching about. Mind you, I don't see that they would be much concerned about Prue.'

'No, but I dare say they'd like to get their hands on Geza. If he gets out, he won't be able to go back, you know. Not until they have a new gang in at the top, and for all one knows, a new lot would be just as bad.' He shook his head. 'Worse. Bad move of Geza's, cocking a snook at the Russians; very unwise in these troubled times.'

'Off to practise?' asked Lily, as Sylvester drained his coffee cup and made for the door.

'Off to look up a few numbers, must know someone who's abreast of the situation in Hungary.'

'What about the Foreign Office,' asked Lily. 'Doesn't your friend Norman work there?'

'I could try him,' said Sylvester. 'Although in my experience diplomats are usually the last people to know what's going on.'

'I wouldn't trouble yourself too much, in any case,' said Lily. 'They'll be here soon enough, no worse than tired after a long journey. I've made up Prue's room, and the doctor is ready to come up at any time she's needed. And she's warned them at Eyot General. Wondered about Prue's notes, but as I told her, if she had any, they'd be in Hungarian, and no use to anyone. Now, be off with you, I've got work to do, and so have you.'

The phone rang creakily in the depths of Haphazard House. Mrs Grigson put down her cup of tea and the paper and went over to the door, where an extension sat on the wall above the ancient light switch.

At the other end of the house, Lambert leapt up from the window seat; he had been surveying the windswept garden and the wild fells beyond the walls.

'Don't get excited,' said Giles, who was dusting his lute with a silk cloth. 'Double glazing salesman, I expect.'

Lambert listened attentively, his face getting longer. 'Oh, desolation,' he said, returning to his perch. 'That was Adele ringing Mrs Grigson to ask her to leave a side door on the latch. Will's coming back on her motorbike, and she's coming after evensong, getting a lift from a friend.'

'Tedious bunch,' said Giles.

'Wait till you hear the rest. Will's bringing more equipment, Adele told Mrs Grigson; infra-red cameras, trip wires, special thermometers . . .'

Giles yawned ostentatiously, tapping his mouth with two slender fingers. 'Spare me the sordid details, I beg you.'

'And the builder's coming later to have a look at the worst of the drips.'

Giles cheered up immediately. 'Oh, good,' he said. 'We can wander round with him.'

Lambert shrugged. 'Up to you, I don't find the drips of interest. It's shameful, the state this house is in.'

'I know, you've said so before,' said Giles, with another, smaller yawn. 'However, the builder can sense we're there, and he doesn't like it much. It's a good tease, and it passes the afternoon.'

'I suppose so,' said Lambert.

24

Prue had very sensibly fallen asleep, her head leaning against the headrest, her hands folded in her lap.

At the other end of the compartment, Zsuzsa was deep in conversation with the two Englishmen. Tapestries and historic textiles were the subject under discussion. Embroidered and woven, seventeenth century, Flemish, ecclesiastical. The words flickered through Cleo's brain, mingling with the Frenchman's interesting story which had dropped into her ear as the train droned across the ever-flatter landscape.

The train stopped with a sudden squeal of brakes. Zsuzsa looked out of the window. 'Ah, we're arriving at Gyor. This is where the police get on, and customs officials, to check our passports and visas and identity papers, and our luggage, and make sure we aren't smuggling state secrets in our underwear.'

Tony and Timothy looked alarmed, but the Frenchman reassured them. 'They don't bother with foreigners, unless you're on a wanted list.'

'My dear,' said Timothy languidly. 'To be on a wanted list, what an honour. Police, though, very frightening. Khaki coats and jackboots?' He gave a shudder.

'That's the army. The frontier police have grey coats with stars on the shoulders. And black boots.'

'Ooh,' said Tony, shutting his eyes for a moment, imagining such delights.

'Tony and I have been together for nine years,' Timothy announced with sudden pride. 'We travel everywhere together, I can't tell you how many places we've been to. And I must say, the communist countries are quite the worst. One can appreciate – just – the forgotten glories of a St Petersburg, but honestly, the standard of hotels and service behind the iron curtain leaves much to be desired. And the officials!' He cast his eyes heavenwards. 'Absolutely no manners, politesse of any kind is completely alien to them. It's very dispiriting.'

'Timothy finds it distressing when anyone is harsh,' said Tony. 'And these officials can be so rude. Timothy is very strongly affected by his surroundings, and he feels extremely upset when these people are so churlish.'

'As do we all,' said Zsuzsa.

Just like a married couple, those two, thought Cleo, as she spilled the contents of her shoulder bag on to her lap. Where was her passport?

Sudden panic. Prue went pale, and told Cleo to pass the bag over, it must be in there, only everything was in such a mess.

Cleo sunk her head in her hands, rubbing her eyes with her palms and trying to think. 'I had it out, on the table by the bed . . . Could I have left it there?'

'Oh, Cleo, surely not?'

'No, I'm sure I picked it up. It must be in my other bag, what a nuisance.'

The Frenchman gallantly got up to help her pull her bag down from the rack, and in the general mêlée, they didn't at first notice a young man with a long, lean, anxious face peering in at the door.

He coughed. 'I'm sorry to push in, but I gather only a few coaches go on into Austria, and mine wasn't one of them. The train is absolutely packed, but the guard says I can't stay in the corridor. I heard you speaking English, so I thought I'd ask, could I squeeze in here?'

Timothy and Tony settled themselves more firmly into their seats, and Tony firmly resisted Cleo's efforts to raise the arm rest and tuck herself further into the corner to make room for one more.

'There's no room at all, I'm afraid,' said Tony.

'You can sit here,' said Prue at exactly the same moment. Holding firmly on to Cleo's passport, which she had found in the muddle of her friend's bag, she raised her arm rest as did

Zsuzsa in the corner. The Frenchman, nothing averse, squashed
closer to Prue, and a space was swiftly made.

'Well, really,' said Tony.

'Thank you,' said the young man. 'It's very kind. It isn't too
much further from here, is it?'

'Not in kilometres, no,' said Zsuzsa. 'However, the train always
waits and waits, and officials get on and off.'

The new arrival opened the large, battered, brown leather
Gladstone bag which he had placed on his knees. He pulled out a
fat typescript, shut the bag, and sat it on the floor between his feet.

Zsuzsa was at once interested. 'You are a writer?'

The young man looked startled, but replied readily enough.
'No, well, yes, I hope so. I mean, I've written a book, and I
hope I can find a publisher for it. That's why I'm going back
to England. To get it typed out, and to send it to publishers.'

'Do you have to travel back to England for that?' asked the
Frenchman. 'Is it not possible to post it?'

The young man pushed his glasses back on to the bridge of his
nose, from which they had a habit of sliding down. 'Post? Yes,
that is, this kind of thing can get lost. And it's a lot of work.'

'Don't you have a copy,' said Prue, looking suddenly very
scholarly. 'One should also make carbon copies, I always do,
of papers and things.'

'I have a copy, but just the original, not with all my notes and
amendments on it. Besides, it's my ma's fiftieth, and I swore I'd
be there.'

'Of course, it's practically impossible to get a first novel published these days,' said Timothy, who didn't seem to like the look
of the writer.

'Unless you know someone, of course,' said Tony, in what Cleo
felt was an unnecessarily smug way. 'My uncle's a publisher.'

'So's mine,' said the young man, not looking up from his script
on which he was industriously scribbling.

Prue looked hard at him, and he gave her a quick wink before
scribbling even more furiously.

'Aha,' said Zsuzsa. 'The police. They are here. We are at
Hegyeshalom. The frontier. We stop for customs, stop to change
engines, stop because the driver wants to piss.'

Oh, the tiresomeness of it, thought Cleo. 'Why do we all have to get off the train? Are they going to search everybody's bags?'

'They may,' said Zsuzsa. 'But they are probably rather looking for stowaways. People without bags or passports, who are trying to leave the country.'

'I always thought Hungary was quite an open country,' said Cleo. 'People going into Austria to sell salami and buy fridges and so on.'

'In normal times it isn't too bad, if you've kept your nose clean, as you say, and been a good boy or girl. Not offended the Party. These days, you cough and you annoy some bureaucrat. Then nobody will let you leave the country.'

Cleo didn't like the sound of that, but she refrained from anxious glances in Prue's direction, Zsuzsa was nothing if not sharp, and she clearly scented a mystery about Prue. Prue didn't seem in the least bothered by being turned out on to the very cold platform. She tied her scarf more tightly round her neck, and sat on a bench with her hands deep in her pockets.

There was no indignation in any of these people. The realization sent a chill down Cleo's spine. Herded out of the train by brusque officials, left standing on the platform. Although one of the police had escorted Prue to the bench. Mind you, the several old biddies sitting fatly on that and the other bench would have seen to that, thought Cleo, as they nodded and becked at Prue's bulgy outline.

No protest, no resistance. Just a hope that everything would turn out to be all right, that they could climb back on board and go on with their journey.

A frowning policeman appeared at the door of one of the carriages, and shouted something at a colleague who was waiting on the platform. Out of the corner of her eye, Cleo saw Prue stiffen; what the hell was going to happen now?

'Prudence Pagan? Is there Prudence Pagan here?'

So Prue was travelling under her own name, was she?

The man advanced on Cleo, a British passport in his hand. 'You are Prudence Pagan?'

For a moment, Cleo wondered if she should answer yes. If someone was going to be in trouble, better her than Prue. Vain plan. Prue had got to her feet, and she walked, in the rolling way of pregnant women, towards the policeman. They conferred in Hungarian. The police were getting angrier and angrier, Prue, although pale, was keeping her composure.

Cleo pushed through the inquisitive throng who were gawping at Prue; glad it isn't them, she thought furiously. 'What's up?' she asked Prue.

'It seems I'm on a list,' said Prue.

'What kind of list?'

'I don't know. There's no point in asking, because they won't tell me. I don't think it's anything to do with my better half, I think it's to do with a stamp in my passport from when I went to Germany for a conference. So I'm not going to make a fuss.'

More Hungarian. More waving of arms, more snappy but quiet words from Prue.

Oh God, thought Cleo, panic creeping over her. What do I do?

At that moment there was a further outbreak of officialdom further down the platform. Another heavily coated policeman was clambering down on to the platform. This one was clutching a fat wodge of paper, which he was waving triumphantly in the air. He came panting up to the others, pushing Prue aside, talking excitedly.

That man's typescript, thought Cleo. Prue had recognized it, too, and she raised her eyebrows at Cleo. 'Now what?' hissed Cleo under cover of all the shouting.

More police arrived, holding the Gladstone bag, which they all peered into with childlike enthusiasm.

Then an angry figure came pushing his way along the platform. 'Hey, that's my book. What the hell do you think you're doing?'

'Fatal, of course, to argue,' said Zsuzsa as she took off her coat and folded it on to the rack before taking up her seat again.

'What was that name?' said Cleo, getting out a notebook. 'Angela Mitchell?'

'No,' said Prue definitely. 'Mitcham. I asked him, Ls or M at the end. I didn't catch the number, but she lives in Unthrang.'

'Isn't that in Eyotshire?' said Cleo, surprised.

'It is,' said Prue. 'So we should be able to get hold of her.'

Tony sniffed. 'A very foolish young man, to try smuggling papers out.'

Prue burst out laughing. 'He wasn't. Of course he wasn't. That's a novel, and those thick policemen can't read English. It's just that the book is a thriller, and it's called Top Secret; they recognized that, and jumped to the conclusion that he must be carrying secret papers.'

'No!' said Cleo.

'Yes.'

'So what will happen to him?'

'He has a British passport?' asked Zsuzsa.

Prue nodded. 'He's teaching at the university in Tatabanya.'

'They will take him away, and fill in a dozen or so forms, and he will ask to speak to the Consul, and they will say no, and they will lock him up for a while, and then the British Embassy will be informed that they are holding a spy, and then it will all be sorted out and he can go home.'

'With his manuscript?'

'I should think not,' said Zsuzsa. 'You told him, always the carbon copy. This was good advice.'

'Couldn't we have done more for him?' said Cleo to Prue.

'No,' said Prue. 'He'll be all right. And it meant they lost interest in me.'

Zsuzsa was watching them shrewdly. 'More important that your friend gets across the border and back to England. Prison is not a good place to have a baby, and that young man will come to no harm. That sort has friends, cousins in the embassy, he will be okay.'

Timothy had his pained expression on his face again, and he looked as though he'd been forced to travel in the company of a psychopathic killer. 'First class only, on our next little jaunt, Tony,' he said faintly to his companion. 'One hates to be caught up in any unpleasantness.'

The Frenchman made a disapproving mouth, and shrugged his shoulders in a gesture full of contempt. 'One should support one's fellow countrymen when abroad, I believe,' he said.

'That depends entirely who they are,' said Tony in a cold voice.

Cleo had been thinking. 'I meant to ring Sylvester en route,' she said to Prue. 'He wanted to know how you were. So I could tell him to get in touch with Angela Mitcham. That would save some time, she can alert the people responsible for this kind of thing in London.'

'Didn't Sylvester take a house in Unthrang, when his pipes burst?'

'He did. I bet he knows this Angela Mitcham.' Cleo sat back, relieved that she could do something for the arrested writer. 'I'll ring from Vienna.'

'From the station,' agreed Prue, hiding a yawn. 'Goodness, my back does ache.'

Cleo was concerned. Wasn't a backache one of the signs of approaching labour? Bother the guidebooks and the paperback novels. She should have bought a handbook about how to cope with sudden births while on long journeys.

Zsuzsa laughed at her consternation. 'Some days yet, I think. If you are careful,' she said to Prue. 'No shocks, everything very calm.'

Nearly getting carted off by the police probably rates as a shock, thought Cleo. Thank goodness it was nearly, though, and not actually. She gazed out of the window. What a dull scene. No hedges, just open fields.

'No fields near the border,' said Zsuzsa. 'And now we crawl along, and then we are in Austria.'

Tony gave a little sniff. Timothy had settled back in his seat, his long legs stretched out without any concern for Zsuzsa, and appeared to be fast asleep. Very neatly, though, Cleo had to admit. When she slept in trains, she knew for sure that her mouth fell open and her head lolled.

She looked at her watch. Surely not much longer now.

The train stopped, and then started again almost immediately. It stopped again, rolled back a little way, and then sat throbbing uncomfortably.

Voices wafted in from outside. A man in a boiler suit walked by, a cigarette dangling from his mouth. He shouted something to his mate further down the line, and then vanished under the train.

Cleo could see strange concrete towers in the distance.

Watchtowers. They must be at the border. Armed men would be in those towers, waiting to take a pot shot at anyone venturing across the no-man's land which ran in a barren strip along the boundary between the two countries. Oppression and freedom, thought Cleo, and then laughed at herself for being so simplistic. Different fetters, that was part of it. Nonetheless, she was heartily glad that she belonged on that side and not on this.

And Prue? Which side did she belong on? Cleo looked with affection at her friend, nose deep in one of the books, slightly wrinkled with concentration. Just the way she had looked when she was a gawky teenager at the convent, reading after lights out. Which, in the black and white world of the nuns, was accounted a sin.

Both sides, she decided, folding her arms. Citizen of the world, that was Prue. Then the train gave one of its violent jolts, a whistle screeched, and it set off towards the watchtowers.

I shan't ever forget this, Cleo told herself. I knew you crossed borders, or fled over them. I never imagined crawling, which is what the train was doing.

Signal bells pinged, the train gathered speed. There was an air of relief in the compartment. Prue gulped, and muttered a subdued Thank God.

Cleo found herself blinking, and she resolutely turned her attention to the changing view outside. Suddenly, everything was painted. Churches, houses, fences. Even the cows looked as though they'd just been through the wash.

Timothy woke up, and he and Tony started an animated discussion about Impressionists, joined by Zsuzsa and then by the Frenchman.

Cleo grinned at Prue, who was sitting with tears trickling down her face. She put out a hand and took Prue's, giving it a good squeeze. 'It'll be all right, you know. Lily says so.'

Prue nodded, her lips together, and looked out into the Austrian countryside.

25

Cleo had expected the railway station in Vienna to be built in a historical style of curly splendour. No such thing. Clean, modern, spacious, with a great glass façade, it belonged firmly in the post-war world.

'Food,' said Cleo, who was starving. 'And a phone call to Sylvester.'

'Money and tickets,' said Prue, who had consumed all the food she had brought with them.

'Nothing at all until I've at least had a cup of coffee and a bun,' said Cleo firmly.

Prue settled for that, not being averse to a little extra something herself. 'As long as we're quick.'

'It's hours before the train goes,' protested Cleo.

'Yes, but we don't have tickets or reservations. There may not be any couchettes.'

'Sleepers,' said Cleo firmly. 'Wagons-lits. Just you and me, and comfortable berths. I don't care how much it costs.'

'Okay,' said Prue. 'Phone, first. I have a call to make, to say I'm out of Hungary. You ring Sylvester.'

'Will it take hours?'

'Not from here. There's a post office in the station, and I've got some Austrian money. Enough for phone calls and coffee.'

'What time do the banks close?'

Prue looked at her watch. 'In about an hour. My bank's across the road from here.'

'Very convenient.'

'That's why. You don't have to come, you can sit and guzzle.'

'Guzzle, indeed. Where you go, I go. I'm not risking you collapsing in a heap and being carted off to hospital while i twiddle my thumbs and wonder where you are.'

'No question of heaps. Me and the prospective are going to make it back to England, no doubt about it.'

Prue looked much better after her phone call. 'Geza's all right,' she said, sliding into her seat opposite Cleo. 'Now he knows we're over the border, he's going to make his own way out.'

'How?' asked Cleo, thinking of the troops they had seen on their journey, and the tight security at the frontier. 'Isn't everywhere guarded?'

'The border's too long for that,' said Prue. 'There are places you can slip through, when you know how. And when you have the right contacts. Which Geza does.'

'Isn't it dangerous?'

'Yes,' said Prue. 'But not as dangerous as staying in Hungary is for him at present.'

Cleo looked at Prue. She may look frail, she thought, but actually, she's very tough. A survivor.

Prue sighed. 'I must say, one does lack stamina rather, and this infant is awfully violent.'

'Violent?' Cleo gazed at Prue's bump. In all of this, she had only considered Prue. The bump was somehow just a physical inconvenience. The thought of it moving, having an identity of its own, a personality, a separate existence was, Cleo had to admit, distinctly alarming.

'Hungarian genes,' said Prue, her mouth full of layers of chocolate and cream. 'Going to be a fencer, I expect. Or a double bass player, maybe. This is heaven. I think, if I had it very quickly, I could manage another one. Not much room left for one's stomach you know, so little and often is the rule. However, I need energy. Did you get through to Sylvester?'

'No, he'd gone to Eyot. His A-string broke, and then his spare as well. It doesn't matter, because Lily was there. She knows this Angela Mitcham person, and says Sylvester does, too. Lily will tell him to go over and see her as soon as he gets back. I wonder what she's like, Lily didn't seem to think Sylvester would be keen to see her again.'

'I liked him,' said Prue. 'Young Mr Mitcham. Do you realize we never discovered his first name?'

'I liked him better than Timothy and Tony.'

'Very widely travelled, those two.'

'Yes, is there anywhere they haven't been? All that talk of Egypt and India and Japan, and the Great Wall of China, and stopping over in the Maldives, and October in Boston.'

'Wonder where the money comes from.'

'Private income,' said Cleo instantly. 'And Tony deals in pictures.'

'Come on,' said Prue. 'Bank, and let them be happy with my password.'

'Password?'

'Yes. With this kind of bank account, access to the loot is only by password.'

'Can you remember it?' Cleo imagined strolling into Barclays and telling the cashier that the geese were flying westward. She'd be seen off the premises, and it certainly wouldn't release any funds.

'Yes,' said Prue. 'It's only one word. Waldhorn.'

'What horn?'

'Waldhorn. Forest horn, literally; it's the German name for French horn. Much better name, really. French horn because of my father, you know.'

Prue's father had been a notable horn player, killed at a tragically early age.

'Have you still got his horn?'

'Of course.' Prue hesitated. 'At least, I hope so. It's in our flat in Budapest. But Geza's brother lives upstairs. He's going to look after the flat for us. I'll write to him, and tell him to take care of the horn.'

The waldhorn duly opened the coffers of the bank, and Cleo and Prue went back to the station to buy tickets.

'Lucky, the man at the ticket office being a family man and concerned for your condition.'

'Lucky, me looking so plaintive and speaking such good German.'

'Lucky, him being a bit of a flirt.'

'You're outrageous, Cleo,' said Prue. 'I wouldn't be surprised to find him in our compartment tonight, the looks you were exchanging.'

'He was rather sweet, with that moustache. Perhaps I could persuade Perry to grow a moustache.' Cleo tried to picture Perry with the elegant moustache favoured by the booking clerk, but failed. Not his style, she decided regretfully.

'Don't you like the way Perry looks?' asked Prue.

'He's very good-looking,' said Cleo, with no great enthusiasm.

'Mm,' said Prue. 'You're very cagey about this Perry. I think he sounds like another Seton.'

'Heaven forbid,' said Cleo, closing the subject, but recalling with a stab of horror how close Prue had come to marrying her staid English first love. Was Perry another such? A perfect husband for someone, but not for her? Look how happy Prue was married to someone quite different. If it came to that, look how happy Seton now was with his competent Delia.

Oh, bother it, thought Cleo. To hell with the whole business, much better not to get married at all, to anyone. Look at the complications, the ties, the aggro. Better to flit from lover to lover, take life as it comes, she told herself.

Prue, rocked by the movement of the train and relieved to have got away without any hassle, slept soundly for once. It was Cleo who woke up often in the night. She dreamt she was back at Haphazard House, with the wind or who knew what tapping on the windows of her room. She could hear faint voices and music, just as she did in Hazard. The house seemed to be falling apart around her, stones slipping to the ground, ivy growing in through a crack at terrifying speed.

Enough.

The train slowed down, and then rumbled over a huge metal bridge; Cleo could tell that from the sound as they passed by the girders. She could hear voices again, but this time real ones, people on the platform of whatever station they had pulled into. Cleo yawned, rubbed her eyes and switched on the light above her bunk. Then she wriggled to the end of the bed, and pulled the taut blind aside.

Köln. Cologne. They were in Germany, of course, they must have crossed the border hours ago. Cleo looked across at other trains waiting in their platforms, windows dark as passengers slept, only the occasional glimmer of light from some fellow insomniac. Europe unrolled in the names written on the sides of the trains. München, Warszawa, Moskva, Madrid, Paris, Istanbul.

Even the towns which their train passed through in the still night hours carried a touch of romance and adventure: Linz, Nürnberg, Würzburg, Brussel, Gent, Oostende.

'You can't get excited about Brussels,' said a tousled Prue, as they sat together drinking coffee and tucking into a basket of rolls and coffee.

'Listen, when your horizons are bounded by the City of London, Brook Green and the north of England for a treat, Brussels is exciting.'

'Why are your horizons bounded by anything?'

'Three weeks' holiday a year, which you can't always take because the office is busy? Plus a day or two here and there tacked on to Christmas and Easter? Hardly scope for intrepid travel.'

'Find a different job. Or do you love it so much you can't give it up?'

'I suspect it may be giving me up,' said Cleo. 'They aren't very keen on people being away on long sick leave.'

'Not your fault.'

'No. Mind you, the longer I spend away from the office, the more I wonder if I do want to go back there.'

'If not that, then what?' said Prue, setting about the business of putting on some make-up.

'You never used to wear any make-up,' said Cleo accusingly.

'No, but I look very pale if I don't, and a bit country-bumpkin.'

'Fatal.'

Prue laughed. 'Now look what I've done.' She licked a finger and wiped away the little trail of mascara under her eye. 'Ssh. I must concentrate, or this will go all over the place.' She held the mirror away and observed her handiwork. 'There. Come on, Cleo, you haven't answered my question. What would you like to do? Get married and be a full-time wife?'

'No way,' said Cleo fervently. 'Perry's bossy enough as it is, it would be unbearable to depend on him for every penny.'

'I can see that. So, you need to find another way to earn your living. Which isn't an office job, not nine-to-five, perhaps?'

'My job isn't nine-to-five,' pointed out Cleo. 'Eight-to-eight, more like.'

'I often work twelve hours a day at the university,' said Prue. 'I don't mind.'

'It depends what you're doing, I suppose,' said Cleo. 'Immediately, what I'd like to do is save Haphazard House from being knocked down.'

'That's not a career. That's more of a mission.'

'Yes, and not very likely.'

'Besides, old houses are just that, aren't they? Old. How about something which is looking forward rather than back.'

'I just love that house. It's really got to me. You wait until you see it, then you'll understand.'

'No, I won't,' said Prue calmly. 'At least, I understand how you feel now, but I won't share your feelings; I don't respond to old houses like that. It's probably in your blood, generations of property-owning and grabbing Mountjoys. Why don't you go and study architecture and build new houses?'

'Concrete slabs,' said Cleo irritably. 'Besides, I don't want to study anything. I've studied enough. Hands on, that's what I want. Training on the job.'

'What job?'

'Oh, I haven't a clue. Don't go on at me, it's really not a problem.'

'Your life's a mess,' said Prue.

'It is not.'

'If an old friend can't see it, then who can?'

'Nobody, because it isn't.'

A polite tap on the door, and the train guard popped his head in to tell them they would soon be arriving in Ostend.

Saved, thought Cleo, cramming her possessions into her bag.

'Funny, isn't it,' said Prue, who was sitting with her feet up across three seats. 'You travel to the edge of Europe, and then you kind of drop off, and there's England.'

'You're becoming very European,' said Cleo severely. 'Talking about England as though it were some sort of offshore island.'

'Exactly what it is,' said Prue. She looked around the almost deserted saloon. 'Lucky for us it's this time of year. Plenty of room, nobody crowding us, we can move from seat to seat as the fancy takes us. Change of view any time we like.'

Change of view, indeed. Cleo looked out at the grey sea, unbroken except for swirling white tops to the waves. Impossible to say where the sea ended and the cloudy grey sky began. Winter, thought Cleo disconsolately. Draining down into the shortest day. And then the New Year, supposedly full of hope.

Full of uncertainty, in her case; quite different. A thought struck her. 'What are you going to call it?' she asked Prue. 'The baby, I mean.'

'If it's a girl, Felicia, after my mother. And Éva after Geza's mother and sister.'

'And if it's a boy?'

'My father's name was Eric, and I'm not calling any boy that these days. So probably Zoltán, after Geza's father. And James for his middle name, because he was always my favourite saint, and I reckon this one is going to travel, he can do with some extra help on the way.'

'Your life is very uncertain, too, isn't it?' went on Cleo. 'I mean, the baby will make a difference to how much you can go about with Geza, won't it? And if you can't go back to Hungary . . .'

'I don't worry about it,' said Prue. 'The future doesn't bother me. I want to know that Geza is safe, and then we can decide what to do. I expect we'll live in London, it's a good base for a violinist, and I can work at UCL. Or maybe America, they'd welcome Geza with open arms, he's very big over there.'

'Same as me,' said a man's voice. 'Hello, Cleo.'

Cleo was so surprised she simply sat and stared.

'May I join you?' He looked at Prue. 'You must be Prue. I'm glad to see you nearly home, there's quite a welcoming committee waiting for you, according to Sylvester.'

'Are you a friend of Sylvester's?' said Prue.

'I am indeed. Can I get you something from the bar? A coffee perhaps, or a tisane? And I think something stronger for Cleo, she's obviously had a shock.'

Cleo had found her tongue. 'Not a shock,' she said. 'Just sheer surprise. My mind's still abroad, I didn't expect to see anyone from Eyotshire. Prue, this is my cousin Henry. Henry the house destroyer,' she added savagely. 'A distant cousin, but family just the same. Henry Hazard, to give him his full name, and you can get me a spritzer, please, Henry, since you offered.'

26

'That was Prue,' said Sylvester to Lily. 'Safe and sound, and on her way here.'

Lily was delighted. 'If you're going into Eyot, you can buy some flowers for her room. What was all that laughter about?'

'Cleo. Apparently she and Cleo bumped into Henry on the boat. In fact, he's driving them up here, which is good of him. Only, he and Cleo argue all the time, so Prue says.'

'Argue?' Lily was intrigued. 'Argue about what?'

'Everything, according to Prue. Art, the French, German wine, currencies, music, God, the weather, the best way to get out of Waterloo. She's says it's as good as a play. Oh, and most of all they argue about Haphazard House. Cleo's fallen in love with the place, and Henry is going to have to pull it down, and that makes Cleo quite beside herself. She thinks he's callous and uncaring. Only she put it more strongly than that, Prue was saying.' He looked reflective. 'It is a shame about the house, but I suppose there's no alternative.'

'Plenty of life in that old house yet,' said Lily in her witchy way. 'Think of those long-standing residents, it's their house, too.'

'What residents?'

'The ghostly ones.'

Sylvester hooted with laughter. 'Get along with you, Lily. Now, what about baby clothes? You do realize that Prue can have very few, if any at all.'

'If I know Prue, she won't have thought about it. No doubt her in-laws will have got her a few things, but she may not have been able to bring them with her. Not to worry; there are lots of people roundabouts who've got grown-out-of baby clothes, they'll remember Prue, and they always rally round a new mum. Especially when her husband can't be with her.'

Sylvester frowned. 'I think new, for Prue,' he said with dignity. 'I could go to that French shop in Eyot.' Sylvester adored shopping, and loved buying presents for people.

'You could not. Everybody borrows baby clothes when they can; babies grow so quickly that it's not worth buying everything new. I'll make a trip into Eyot and get her the things she must have new, and no, Sylvester, you can't do that, you don't have the first idea of what's needed.'

'I shall buy the child a bear,' said Sylvester, hurt.

'You do that, and a pretty dangle to put above its cot.'

Sylvester eyed Lily. 'You're longing for this baby to arrive, aren't you?'

'I am that, and it's going to be lovely to see Prue again; time we had a bit of young life in the house.'

'I shall play my cello to him or her,' said Sylvester. 'With Geza for a father and Piers Pagan for a grandfather, it's bound to be musical. I shall go and brush up on my lullabies.'

'You do that,' said Lily. 'After you've been into Eyot and bought the flowers.'

27

'It isn't any quicker this way,' said Cleo. 'I told you it wouldn't be.'

'It isn't quicker because of that lorry blocking the road.' Henry was definite.

'If we'd gone the other way, there wouldn't have been a lorry.'

'No, but there would have been more traffic.'

'Not at all.'

In the back of the car, Prue dozed happily. She was stretched out on the back seat, having rejected the offer of the front. 'No thank you, Henry will become a dangerous driver if he's arguing with you at the back. You both sit in the front, and have a nice bicker all the way. Besides, I want to put my feet up, my ankles are aching.'

Henry had taken a great fancy to Prue. 'What a smasher,' he said. 'That hair, and those eyes.'

Cleo was pleased to hear Prue admired, but she felt Henry should be more restrained. 'She has got a husband, you know.'

'I've got a wife,' said Henry flippantly. 'But I still like compliments.'

'And do you get many?'

'Oh, I have my admirers,' said Henry annoyingly. 'Now, we need to turn off somewhere along here, by a garage.'

'No, we don't,' said Cleo instantly.

'You know London well, do you?'

'I live here, after all,' said Cleo smugly.

'And drive around a lot?'

'Of course.'

'Funny, I seem to remember you saying you didn't have a car, because there was no point driving in London.'

'No point in owning a car, is what I said. I borrow a car from a friend.'

'From Perry? Don't tell me he lets you career around London in his shiny job.'

'I do not career. And I drive someone else's car, if you really must know.' My nose will stretch, thought Cleo unrepentantly. What a handful Henry had turned out to be; how she disliked men who constantly told you what to do.

'Blast,' said Henry, stopping with a squeal of brakes. 'Missed the turning. You really are a most unhelpful passenger, you know.'

Cleo folded her arms and looked straight ahead. 'You couldn't have turned off there, because that turning had a large 'road closed' sign up across it. So you might as well get going again, and then all those other drivers will stop hooting at us.'

'I thought we'd stop at Welton.'

'Won't do for Prue,' said Cleo at once.

'And why not?'

'Disgusting ladies. Terrible. We'd better stop at Combe.'

'I can't contradict you on that one, can I,' said Henry mildly. 'Not being a frequenter of the ladies' loo at any service station.'

'Take it from me, dire.'

'The food's better at Welton.'

'Hygiene is more important to Prue.'

'Oh, no, it isn't,' came a voice from the back. 'Actually, we'll have to stop at whichever one is next, because I must have a pee. Also, I'm very hungry.'

'My point, I think,' said Henry, slowing down as he turned off on to the slip road.

Cleo was contrite. All very well her getting the better of Henry, but not at Prue's expense. 'I'll come too,' she said as Prue headed for the ladies.

That amused Prue. 'I'm not going to give birth under the hand-dryers.'

'How do you know?'

Prue survived the ladies, and tucked away a tolerable meal.

'Good,' she said. 'Now I feel thoroughly sleepy, so I'll snooze in the back while you two continue with your discussion about this and that.'

The snooze lasted until they came off the motorway and started on the slower roads which would take them towards Eyot.

'You've got hiccups,' said Cleo, turning round to peer in the back. By now it was completely dark, and she couldn't see Prue clearly, but what she could see, she wasn't sure about. 'Prue, are you all right?'

Prue gave another hiccup. 'There's nothing wrong with me, exactly,' she said. 'But are we anywhere near a hospital?'

The car gave an alarming lurch as Henry clutched the wheel. 'Eyot General,' he said. 'Must be the nearest, wouldn't you think?'

'There's a hospital on the outskirts. That's much nearer.'

'Mental hospital,' said Henry. 'Not much use for Prue.'

'If you drive this fast, we're all going to need Eyot General,' said Cleo.

'It's probably best,' said Prue. 'I'm feeling fairly strange.'

'Are you sure it isn't that cottage pie you ate?'

'No, I'm not sure, but I don't think so.'

Prue's the calmest of us three, realized Cleo, marvelling at her composure. She told her so.

'No point in getting panicky,' said Prue. 'Deep breathing is what you're supposed to do.'

'There you are, Henry, deep breaths,' said Cleo.

'I'm not having the baby,' said Henry. And then, 'Oh, bugger, rain, just what we need.'

The grey day accompanied by a chilly, damp breeze had given way to stormier skies as they drove north. Now, with a savage streak of lightning and a mighty crack of thunder, the heavens opened. Rain lashed against the windscreen, and Cleo could see the dark shapes of trees with their branches bending under the force of the wind.

'Shouldn't we stop?' she yelled at Henry, barely audible against the turmoil of the storm.

'No,' shrieked Prue from the back. 'Definitely not.'

Later, Cleo was to admit that she was glad that she hadn't been driving. Henry might have his faults – and many of them, as far as she was concerned – but he was certainly a good driver. It wasn't a quick journey, but he made it safely; Cleo felt quite sick with relief as he crawled over the speed humps and braked outside a bright light saying Emergencies.

'I presume this is the right place,' he began, but Cleo was already out of the car and racing through the swing doors.

In what seemed like seconds, people in white coats were opening the door and talking to Prue. Then she was out of the car and being wheeled away.

28 ∫

Giles and Lambert were watching *Star Trek*. This was their very favourite programme; in fact, they were fast turning into a pair of trekkie bores. There had recently been a bumper evening of shows, with several episodes one after the other until the early hours of the morning, and now they were addicted.

'Ssh,' said Giles.

'I didn't say anything,' said Lambert, affronted.

Giles zapped the screen blank. 'Will and Adele, they must be coming down,' he said.

'Unlikely,' said Lambert. 'Let's go and see.'

It was a shaken pair who flitted back to the kitchen and flicked the television on again.

'Loud as you like,' said Giles, looking as though he'd just smelt a very bad smell. 'They won't hear us, not with the racket and din they're making up there.'

'They are noisy,' agreed Lambert. 'It's wicked and sinful. May they feel repentance and make atonement.'

'What they'll feel is sore and bruised,' said Giles.

'That's not what the bed posts are intended for.'

'Unnatural,' agreed Giles, twiddling with the aerial for a better picture. 'There's a wind getting up,' he grumbled.

'According to you, whatever men and women do in bed is unnatural,' said Lambert, hitting out.

'Not at all. I don't care for women, as you know, not in that way, and the thought of bedding one is repugnant to me, I confess it readily. However, normal acts between a man and a woman are disagreeable, not unnatural. But this! Chains!' He gave an artistic shudder, and threw back the ruffle on his sleeve in a gesture of defeat. 'Terrifying. Will should be whipped.'

'He was,' said Lambert cynically. 'He clearly enjoys it.'

'Why aren't you more shocked?'

'It is a degenerate world,' said Lambert, portentous once more. 'However, such vile practices are not new. I remember one of my men, and a serving wench . . .'

'I don't want to hear,' said Giles hurriedly.

'I'm going to put Will's thermometer on the stove,' said Lambert. 'That'll throw his measurements out.'

'Did you bring it down?'

'Of course.' Lambert unearthed an air thermometer and several other items of ghost-hunting equipment from a capacious pocket, and set about laying them around the kitchen. 'Oh dear, I feel quite distracted. This is all most disturbing.'

'That's why they retired to bed so early,' said Giles, turning up the brightness on the screen.

'And why they didn't answer the phone.'

'I wonder who it was, it might have been Cleo.'

'I just hope she doesn't come back and find them up there. What a terrible shock.'

'Ssh, I want to watch.'

'I tried to ring Haphazard,' said Cleo, 'but there was no reply. I wonder where they are.'

'Gone to the cinema in Eyot, I expect,' said Sylvester soothingly. 'Or perhaps they couldn't hear the telephone. This wind is making everything rattle, and the thunder doesn't help. Now, you're staying there with Prue, are you? Then I'll just make a phone call or two, and I'll be over. Is it imminent?'

'It was, but since they got her up to the labour ward, it all went off the boil.'

'Typical,' said Sylvester. 'Full of cussedness, babies. Maximum upset and inconvenience all the way. Give Prue my love.'

Cleo had not intended to stay with Prue. Cleo's every instinct had been to cut and run, what a coward I am, she told herself, explaining to the nurse that she had to get home, she would come back in the morning, would phone up.

That was when Henry had reappeared, extremely wet, but full of bounce. He stared at Cleo. 'Go home? When your friend's about to have a baby? Have they got in touch with her mother? Or a sister?'

'Her mother died when she was little, and she's an only child.'

'Good heavens, you can't leave her.'

'The nurse seemed to think it was all right. She said Prue would be better on her own.'

'That nurse with the jutting nose and chin who was here just now? I shouldn't let her anywhere near me if I was ill or about to have a baby.'

'That's a very offensive remark. Just because she isn't dolled up like a nurse on TV, it doesn't mean she's a monster.'

'It's nothing to do with how she looks, it's the nasty, sadistic glint in her eye. Anyway, that's beside the point. The point is, Prue needs someone with her, to hold her hand.'

'You do it, then.' Cleo had dealt with her share of the minor mishaps of life, heaving drunken friends into the bathroom, sitting with a friend having a wild and grisly time on an LSD trip, even binding up a gaping wound inflicted by a barbed wire fence. Those she could cope with.

Childbirth, no, that was something else. Out of my league, thought Cleo.

'I can't possibly go in there,' said Henry. 'I met Prue for the first time this morning, remember? She doesn't want a stranger in there, she wants someone she knows, someone she can scream at if she wants to. If I suggest I go in with her, no relation, barely an acquaintance, they'll think I'm some kind of kook.'

And so you are, thought Cleo crossly.

'You should be ashamed of yourself. You don't have to be anywhere, no one's waiting for you, you haven't got an anxious hubby at home, and three squalling kids wanting to be fed. What happens if something goes wrong?'

'That's what I'm afraid of.' Cleo's voice was louder than she had intended, and it earned her a steely look from the nurse, who looked up from the desk, making clicking noises with her tongue.

Henry lowered his voice. 'Who cares what you're afraid of?

No, sorry, that's rude, but we're all afraid of almost everything, ducks. Stay here, do your duty, and you'll find you can take it.'

'Shit,' said Cleo. 'You do make me feel a louse.'

'You are a louse. So am I, so is everyone from time to time. Except that nurse, who's a full-time louse. Stop thinking about yourself, start thinking about Prue. Hop off and see how she's doing, and when she can spare you, I'll get you a coffee.' He looked around the softly lit waiting area, which was deserted.

'Strange,' said Cleo, 'isn't it? I thought labour wards were heaving with mothers-to-be, attendant fathers, fussing grannies . . .'

'Perhaps it's the wrong time of year,' said Henry. 'I spy a machine over there, guaranteed to produce a revolting brew of one kind or another.'

Cleo hesitated. She would have to go and be with Prue, there was no way to get out of it. She had visions of Henry forcibly propelling her into the labour room if she prevaricated any more. 'Sylvester's coming over.'

'Excellent. We shall entertain ourselves with a game of chess, and passers-by will take us for callous fathers-in-waiting.'

'That'll amuse Sylvester.'

'Yes, won't it? And in case you're wondering, I have a chess set here. I never travel without it and my notebook, and a paperback of Horace's poems. Armed with these, I am invincible, and can pass many otherwise tedious hours in any part of the world. In fact, I shall put in some good effort until Sylvester arrives by drawing that nurse. I can see a part for her in several of my more chilling cartoons.'

What insufferable self-sufficiency, thought Cleo. What a bundle of interference he is. 'I see,' she said.

'No, you don't. Now go.'

Cleo went.

'Thanks for staying,' said Prue, moving restlessly on her pillows. 'This is very boring, I wish it was all over.'

'Have doctors been and so forth?'

'There's one coming. He was on his way, but got beeped, and had to rush off. That nurse had a good prod round. What a bitch, she really hurt me, and when I protested, she said, that's nothing, just you wait if you want to know what pain's really like.'

Prue spoke flippantly, but Cleo could see tears glistening in her eyes. 'Oh, Prue. Henry said she was sadistic.'

'It's not that, well, not only that.' Prue wiped her eyes with her forearm. 'It's all a bit strange and improbable, having a baby. You don't know what to expect. I'm so glad you're here, one needs someone to talk to, and that hag is hardly someone you can have a chat with.'

Cleo looked round the small room, her eyes sliding over the trolley laid with instruments, and the black boxes faced with numerous dials which were lined up alongside the bed. There were some quite pretty curtains drawn across the window, keeping the unrelenting storm shut out, and matching cushions on a functional-looking chair with arms.

Cleo dragged the chair across and sat down beside Prue, who reached out and took her hand.

Her grip tightened, and she winced. 'Oof,' she said. 'Nasty.'

'Contractions?'

'Yes.'

I just can't even begin to imagine what it's like, thought Cleo.

Prue winced again, and gave a louder squeak.

'Shall I get the nurse?'

'No, don't,' said Prue. 'This baby's never going to be born if the first thing it sees is her, what a terrifying welcome to this world.'

Prue's mouth tightened again, and her fingers dug hard into Cleo's hand. Cleo got up. 'I'll get a nurse. I must.'

'No, Cleo, what I really want to do is stop my back hurting. It's agony like this lying on my back, it can't be right.'

'Look, why don't you get out of bed? Can you?'

'Brilliant idea, I'm sure it'd be better standing up.'

Cleo helped Prue slide off the bed and on to her feet. She did immediately look much better; good, thought Cleo, at least I've been of some use.

Brisk footsteps approached, and Cleo braced herself for the arrival of the sharp nurse. She'll throw me out, she was thinking, when a lively black woman came in, smiled at Cleo, and took hold of Prue's arm.

'Very sensible, love,' she said. 'Keep on your feet, none of this lying down. Now, I'm Fran, and I'm your midwife. I'll be with you all the time, all right? However long it is.'

Prue managed a smile of pure relief. 'What about the other nurse? She said there were all kind of questions she had to ask.'

'She's gone off duty, now. She told me you had no notes, is that right?'

Prue bit her lip, and there was a pause of several seconds before she could answer. 'I've got notes, but they're in Hungarian. I live there, and I only came back to England today.'

'Can I see them, love? Are they in this bag here?'

Prue nodded. 'A fat green file.'

'Do you understand Hungarian?'

Prue nodded again.

'Then we'll have a look at them, very quickly, before you have to concentrate on other things. First, have you had any problems that you know about?'

'No,' said Prue.

'Fine, so we'll see if we can make sense of any of this. You walk up and down if you want to, your friend will hold on to you. I'll just write a few things down.'

'Oh, pigs,' said Prue as she was racked by another pain. 'Can't I take something? This is hellish.'

'No problem,' said the midwife, helping Prue back towards the bed. She pressed a bell by the bed. 'We'll get you fixed up right away, happy times are just around the corner.'

29

'Happy times is right,' said Prue as she lay in a woozy state. The hospital was stirring into morning life, although it was still pitch black outside the window. 'Magic, that pethidine. I can see why doctors get hooked on it.'

Sylvester loomed over the perspex cradle beside Prue's bed. 'You'd think they'd manage something a bit better than this,' he said, giving the plastic side a disdainful tap. 'Young Felicia here is definitely going to be a musician, look at those hands.'

'She's going to play the horn,' said Prue.

'She's going to play what she wants,' said Sylvester. 'Now, I'm going to take Cleo off and get her some breakfast, and Henry will want some as well.'

'Is Henry still here?'

'Yes. He said he wouldn't come in as you're probably exhausted, but he's going to send Felicia her very first bunch of roses.'

Prue smiled.

'And I've brought her a present myself.' Sylvester opened the buttercup yellow bag which he had been carrying under one arm, and a large teddy bear of immense character slid on to Prue's bed.

'Oh, Sylvester, how heavenly.'

'Looks just like one of my great-aunts,' said Sylvester with pride. 'I took a good deal of care in choosing it, you don't want a bear with a nasty face.'

'Henry says the bear's a ringer for his great-aunt Ethel,' said Cleo.

'We'll call her Great-Aunt Griselda,' said Prue. 'Oh, thank you, Sylvester. And thank you, Cleo, for being here.'

Cleo leant down and gave Prue a warm hug. I hope you never know how nearly I wasn't, she thought. And how totally shit-scared I was, and how I never, ever want to have a baby.

Felicia gave a funny little sound, and Prue's face lit up. 'Pass her over before you go,' she said.

'Will the nurses mind?'

'To hell with the nurses. She and I and the bear have got to get acquainted, and I want to tell her all about her father.'

Sylvester overflowed with bonhomie and high spirits as he drove at speed back to Midwinter, followed by Henry at a safe distance. The door flew open as they scrunched to a stop outside the house, and there was Lily. 'How's Prue? How's the little girl?'

'Now, now, Lily,' said Sylvester, rubbing his vast hands together as he bounded into the house. 'That's stake talk. How could you possibly know it was a girl?'

'Ha,' said Lily. 'Breakfast is ready, all set in the kitchen. I'll just see to the rest of it, and then I'll be off to Eyot.'

'Why?' said Sylvester. 'We'll be going back later, take you then.'

'Prue can't have too many visitors all at once,' said Lily. 'I've got all kinds of bits and pieces that she's bound to need, and things for the baby, too. She can't stay in hospital clothes, they won't like it.'

'Take some flowers from her room here,' said Sylvester. 'I'll order some more to be sent round, but her room's a bit bare. Wish Geza were here, or that we even knew where he was, I think Prue's fretting a bit about him.'

'A Hungarian rang,' said Lily. 'Early this morning. Wouldn't give his name, but said that the parcel was leaving today.'

'Aha,' said Sylvester. 'Geza's on his way, then. Good, good.' He pulled out some chairs. 'Sit down, tuck in. Not a word to Prue, Lily, we'll wait until we hear that Geza's safely in the West. Then she'll know he's all right.'

30

Sylvester was doubtful about leaving Cleo alone in dark, deserted Haphazard House.

Cleo had no such doubts. 'I feel as though I've come home,' she said, giving a tremendous yawn. 'And I won't be alone for long, Adele will be back from Eyot soon. They won't let her stay late at the hospital; they're bound to be fussy about visitors in the evening.

'It's very lonely,' said Sylvester, following Cleo into the house. 'Although, strange to say, it doesn't feel empty.'

'No,' said Cleo, with another violent yawn. 'It's the ghosts.'

'Ghosts.'

'Don't tell me you don't believe in the Haphazard ghosts?'

'Oh, I believe in ghosts all right,' said Sylvester. 'I believe in most irrational things, I follow an irrational profession, that's my terrain. Still, I can't help feeling that Perry may be right and that it's all a hoax.'

'Not a hoax,' said Cleo, with another giant yawn. 'I think I'll leave a note for Adele, and just take myself off to bed,' said Cleo. 'I could sleep for days.'

'You're looking more like your old self, despite the long journey and all the excitement.'

'I feel better,' said Cleo, surprising herself. 'I really do, I feel like a human being again.' A thought struck her. 'Is Will going to be here tonight, I wonder?'

'No,' said Sylvester with great firmness. 'He is not. I happen to know he's involved in a concert tonight and will be in Eyot. And now you're back, he can sleep at home, no need to keep Adele company.'

'I suppose not.' Cleo regretted it, but in her present state of sleepiness, she felt she was too far gone to appreciate even Will's many fine qualities.

'I'm so glad about Geza, making it out of Hungary. How did he do it?'

'Slipped away to the border with Yugoslavia. They're Hungarian on both sides of the river there, so he was in good hands. Boat at night across the Drava. Then by car to Belgrade, and on to Switzerland. In Eyot by tomorrow evening, with any luck. To meet his new daughter, lucky man.'

'Prue will be herself again.' Cleo paused. 'She and Geza seem to have something very special going.'

'It's called marriage,' said Sylvester. 'A state full of pitfalls for the unwary, but at its best, a unique state. Achieved by very few of us.'

'Me and Perry?' said Cleo, lingering at the bottom of the stairs.

'I doubt it,' said Sylvester. 'Get you to bed, take this cat with you to keep you company,' for Porthos was winding himself round Sylvester's ankles, 'and I'll call you in the morning.'

'Night, Sylvester,' said Cleo, giving the large man a weary hug.

'A dreamless sleep and a joyful wakening,' said Sylvester, going on his way.

'He'd make a good haunter,' remarked Giles as Sylvester let himself out into the dark night. 'Good presence.'

'And lots of it,' murmured Lambert. A big man himself, he had to admire Sylvester's girth and stature.

'A musician,' said Giles, somewhat wistfully.

'So are you.'

'Limited,' said Giles with a sigh. 'Limited. Lute and voice and virginals are no match for an orchestra.'

Giles and Lambert had come across a television documentary about the history of the orchestra. Lambert had been fretted and bothered by it, and had demanded that they turn over to the football; Giles would have none of it. 'Listen to that,' he crooned. 'That's the instrument they call a violin. What a range! What a palette! I was born centuries too soon, never to have played such music.'

'That loud stuff's dreadful,' said Lambert. 'All those horns and things blasting away. What a din. What a cacophony.'

'Wagner,' said Giles reverently. 'What a genius.'

Mrs Grigson was brooding in the kitchen. 'Pot of tea just made,' she said with a gusty sigh. 'And that Adele telephoned, said she'll be back this evening.'

'Oh,' said Cleo. 'Why shouldn't she be? What time is it? Have I slept very late? Adele must have been up and off very early.'

'Never came home at all last night,' said Mrs Grigson, with sepulchral relish. 'Never made it.'

'Never made it? She didn't have an accident, did she?'

Mrs Grigson was shocked. Accidents were serious. 'No. She did telephone this morning, before you were up, a bit late, if you ask me. Said she'd been held up in Eyot, and had spent the night there.' She sniffed. 'Not very friendly, if you don't mind me saying so, leaving you all alone here, and when you've just got back from abroad. I hope you've had a good bath,' she added.

Cleo was amused. 'Yes, washed all the nasty foreign germs away,' she said, pouring herself some tea and investigating. 'In a shower, not a bath.'

'No spiders in the shower,' said Mrs Grigson unexpectedly. She became quite energetic. 'I do hate spiders; they look at you from the bottom of the bath in such a wicked way. With a shower, you can wash 'em away before they get to give you the evil eye.'

'Very true,' said Cleo, spreading butter and marmalade liberally over a thick slice of toast.

'Good to see you eating properly,' commented Mrs Grigson, as she folded a duster neatly into her basket of cleaning things. 'I like to see young people eat, before the sorrows of life get to them, and the appetite goes.'

Cleo looked at her piece of toast with new eyes as Mrs Grigson sallied forth to do battle with dust and spiders. I've done this toast without thinking, she realized. And it doesn't make me feel queasy at all. Moral: to cure shingles, go to Hungary and meet a pile of bizarre and interesting people.

She sat herself down at the table and opened the book she

had brought down with her. It was Tobias Wortle, unopened during her trip, but worth, she felt, a look. She propped it up against the marmalade pot and began to read.

'Very sluttish,' observed Sylvester as he surged into the kitchen two hours later. 'Breakfast not washed up, tea cold in the pot; come, come, Cleo, this won't do.'

Cleo looked up from her leather-bound tome with shining eyes. 'Sylvester, this is the most wonderful book.'

'Hardly straight off the bestseller lists, by the look of it,' said Sylvester, moving aside Cleo's remains and seating himself at the table. 'What is it?'

'It's all about Haphazard House. And the Hazards; goodness, what a crew. Do you suppose horrible Henry has any idea what his ancestors were like?'

'I think Henry's too taxed by his current family to worry much about the past,' said Sylvester. 'But I believe they were a colourful bunch.'

'The ones I like best are Giles and Lambert,' said Cleo. 'Giles was a poet and musician, banished by Queen Elizabeth for ogling one of her favourites.'

Sylvester thought about that. 'Male or female? The favourite.'

'Male,' said Cleo. 'Maids-in-waiting were well able to preserve their maidenly status if Giles was around. Although he did marry, his mother forced him into it. He wouldn't go near his wife, but smuggled his brother in on their wedding night. He always boasted that she never knew the difference, but I bet she did. She was called Anne, and she was one shrewd cookie. She had three children by the brother, and then, listen to this, she bumped Giles off.'

'What?' Sylvester was intrigued. 'How?'

'Poison. She was an Italian scholar, so Tobias tells us, and had picked up various useful ideas and recipes from much study in the Italian language. Probably read the diaries of Lucrezia Borgia under the bedclothes at night. Anyway, she did for Giles, who keeled over while playing the lute one evening and handed in his accounts.'

Cleo absentmindedly took a gulp of stone-cold tea, and pulled face. 'Ugh, how nasty. What exactly is a lute, Sylvester? A primitive violin which was plucked, wasn't it?'

'Really, Cleo, how can you be so ignorant.' Sylvester smoothed out the paper bag which had contained the bread, and drew a few rapid lines. 'There are many kinds of lute, in fact they come in all shapes and sizes. Take the arch-lute, for instance, a thumping great thing, which looks as though you'd need three hands to play it. What your friend Giles would have played would have looked something like this.'

He pushed the drawing across the table to Cleo.

'And what did it sound like?'

'They were playing lute music on the radio the night we came over. I commented on it.'

'No radio that I could find,' said Cleo. 'Maybe it was Giles, come back to haunt us. After all, there are definitely ghosts here. Although Will says ghosts aren't what we think they are, ghosts of actual people, but clusters of different spiritual entities which hang around in the ether.'

Giles was furious. 'Spiritual entities indeed. And how dare this rascal write all these lies about me? Who spread such falsehoods? Slanderous tongues, that's what it is!'

'You *were* poisoned,' said Lambert. 'You told me so.'

'Accidentally.'

'Oh? How accidentally?'

'The wine was meant for another.'

'Who?'

'My wife.'

'You gave *her* poison?'

'I? I am no poisoner.'

'Was.'

'Was no poisoner, then.'

'So who?'

'A groom.' Giles was sullen now.

'A groom, eh?'

Giles's voice grew warm at the memory. 'He was a pretty fellow.'

'Sin.'

'His mother was Italian, a singer. His father, the blacksmith.'

'He hanged for it, no doubt.'

'My wife was blamed, but she protested her innocence, was believed, a half-wit hanged. She married my brother.'

'Why the poison?'

Silence.

'Intended for your wife, you said.'

'Perhaps.'

'How came you to drink the wine?'

'I didn't know there was poison in it. She gave it to me, and I drank it. He had given it to her.' Pause. 'He always was a careless fellow, but such a face, such a . . .'

'That's enough, sin is sin, whatever the beauty.' Lambert reflected. 'How long have we been here together? And I never knew this. Although I might have guessed. Is that why they didn't lay you in the chapel that was here in the house, but buried you over by the lodge, and put a dog's bones in your tomb?'

'Superstition, nothing but superstition. They thought the poisoned corpse of a man would walk if buried in the house where he had been murdered.'

'They were right. Well, well, I wish I'd known this some two centuries ago.'

Giles was retreating into sulks. 'And why should you? I'd kept my secret down the years, it should have remained a secret. It's all the fault of this writer, this Wortle. A greasy clergyman, I remember him well. I gave him a nasty fright one night, I can tell you. Ha, he never returned.'

'Truth will out.'

'And,' said Giles with spirit, 'if it comes to that, you never told me, in detail, how you died. An accident, you said. An unfortunate accident.'

'And so it was, I assure you.'

'Sssh, Cleo's just getting to that bit.'

31

Cleo smoothed down the pages. 'Now listen, this is quite some time later. Giles Hazard, Sir Giles he was, died in 1606. In 1650, Haphazard House was sequestered by the Parliamentary forces. They traced a priest here, the Hazards were recusants, you know.'

'Papists,' said Sylvester in tones of deep disapproval. 'Anglicans, Evangelicals, Anglo-Catholics, can't be doing with any of them.'

Cleo knew that Sylvester held strong views on the clergy, mostly unfavourable, but she felt that taking this dislike back into history was unfair.

'The Hazards were hiding him.'

'More fool they,' said Sylvester with spirit. 'Asking for trouble, having a priest to stay.'

'It's interesting, because local historians say there must have been a priest hole, or a hidden room of some kind, and none has ever been found. Or least hadn't been when Tobias here wrote this book, and I'm sure Henry said that, despite the legend, there wasn't one.'

'If there is, it's probably full of priestly bones, and best avoided.'

'I wonder where it is,' said Cleo. 'Perry said that a house like this was sure to have one.'

'Did they find the priest?'

'No, so obviously he was tucked away in a tight little hidey-hole, not easily found, because TW here says the search party nearly tore the house down.'

'What happened to the Hazards?' Sylvester got up and prowled round the kitchen. 'No biscuits? Where do you keep the coffee?'

'On that shelf there,' said Cleo. 'Chocolate biscuits in the Jubilee tin, and I won't tell on you to Lily.'

'I should hope not,' said Sylvester with dignity, passing a biscuit to Cleo and helping himself to one before taking down the coffee.

'The Hazards were booted out, and the house and estate and all their wordly goods except a few clothes and a bible or two, were seized. That's where this Lambert comes into the story. He was given the house.'

Sylvester paused in his coffee-grinding and became a keen lawyer. 'Ha, that can't be right. You called him Lambert Hazard a while back.'

'This is very romantic. He'd fallen in love with one of the daughters of the house while clearing her and her kith and kin out. Doubtless a bit of manhandling and some flashing of unpuritanical lace might have had something to do with it. It was a bit naughty, though; Lambert was nearly forty, and the girl was only fourteen. Fifteen at her wedding.'

'Not very godly,' said Sylvester. 'Of course, that's what those Puritans were like, hypocritical down to their boxer shorts, terrible lot.'

Cleo was reading avidly. 'Goodness, she had him where she wanted. Made him change his name, bring all her family back to live in the house, even her mother, who was a menace. He had to make a will in her favour, offer protection to all kinds of friends and relations who were on Cromwell's no-no list – that can't have furthered his career. Not that it mattered,' she continued, 'because they bumped him off.'

'Who did?'

'According to Tobias, clearly a sound authority, Ma and two of her sons.'

'Why? I would have thought it a bit risky; they might have sent another Parliamentarian in to take over the house.'

'Mmm, no,' said Cleo, thinking hard. 'Lambert got thunked over the head in 1660, quite a few years later. Wasn't that when Charles came back? The Restoration, you know.'

'It was,' said Sylvester. 'I'm surprised you know that.'

'The convent was strong on history, and we spent a lot of time on the seventeenth century. All those martyrs and recusants and Covenanters.'

'So they just got fed up with Lambert and did away with him?'

'No, it says here that they found him up to a spot of this and that with a very young serving wench, and so his wife upped and at him with the candelabra. She just knocked him out, though. Then the family thought it might lead to trouble if he came round, so they polished him off. They said he'd fallen from the landing into the hall, and in those exciting times, no one was going to question it.'

'And these were Henry's forebears? Now, it seems to me that the blood is running thin in his veins, if with that in his genes, he can't get the better of Mathilda.'

'His ex?' said Cleo.

'Yes.'

'Is she very attractive?'

Sylvester rattled his fingers on the top of the coffee pot. 'Stunning,' he said, not looking at Cleo. 'Henry's an odd chap, but his girlfriends have all been a wow. No shortage of takers there, definitely not.'

'You surprise me,' said Cleo coldly. 'I find Henry extremely difficult to get along with, I can't imagine what kind of woman would put up with him. Maybe he goes for dimwits.'

'Not at all,' said Sylvester. 'Plenty of brains as well as looks. Funny, too, many of them. Henry appreciates a sense of humour in his friends. I don't know why you find him difficult; still, you probably aren't his type.'

'I should hope not,' said Cleo. 'And he's certainly not mine.'

'I can tell from that look in your eye that you're thinking about Will,' said Sylvester crossly. 'No good looking in that direction.'

'Is he gay? Is he promised to another?'

'No, but you are, and take it from me, you wouldn't suit. I wish I'd never brought him to Haphazard, it was a moment of pure folly. Plenty of other haunted houses hereabouts. He's like a leech when he's on the trail of one of his spooks, never gives up.' Sylvester looked around for cups.

'Under the shelf, in that cupboard,' said Cleo, returning to her book.

'And while we're on the subject,' said Sylvester, 'off with the old before you're on with the new. You're going to have to do something about Perry, you know.'

'Oh, never mind that,' said Cleo, flicking through some more pages. 'Those two seem to be the only ones who met grisly ends at the hands of their devoted spouses, but my goodness, the Hazards did go in for variety in their marriages. There are two bigamists, one ménage à trois, that was a Hazard who carried on with twin sisters, and joint arrangements, where each had what Wortle calls a paramour . . . And this book only goes up to the end of the Napoleonic Wars. No divorces, mind.'

'Too early,' said Sylvester. 'Wonder what the Victorian Hazards got up to.'

'Best not to enquire,' said Cleo.

Giles was full of laughter. 'I could tell her a thing or two about that lot,' he said. 'And Lambert, fancy not telling me about the serving-wench. I always wondered why you should haunt when you died in an accidental fall. I thought it was because of stealing Haphazard from the family.'

'She wasn't so very young,' said Lambert huffily. 'She came after me, honey-mouthed, looking at me from under those eyelashes, brushing against me in the passageway, bending over in my bedchamber. A limb of the devil, that's what she was.'

'What happened to her, I wonder?'

Lambert exploded. 'I know too well what happened to her, and so do you; we watched her being ogled and seduced by my brother-in-law, a fine scandal that was.'

'He married her, didn't he? And they lived together for thirty-five years in harmony and happiness?'

'That's as may be,' grumbled Lambert. 'No union founded on sin can prosper in the sight of the Lord.'

'Pipe down, Lambert,' said Giles. 'A wanton young serving-wench, oh, Lambert. I wish I'd been here then to see it.'

'It is better that you weren't,' said Lambert. 'It was a bad day when they found your grave and reburied you back in the house.'

'I'm extremely grateful to them,' said Giles. 'I was glad to get back to my house and my lute, it was very boring out there.'

32

'Gussie?'

Gussie moved the phone away from her ear. 'Yes, Val, it's me, who else would it be?'

'How do I know who you've got tucked away in that place of yours? I know nothing about your private life, thank God. Of course, it might be Perry. That's why I'm ringing you up, in fact.'

'What are you talking about? How does Perry come into it?'

'You've been going out with him.'

Gussie had to laugh. You could sneeze, and Val would get to hear of it. 'You're incredible, Val,' she said. 'Spies everywhere, snoops all over London.'

'You don't deny it, then?'

'I had dinner one evening with Perry, yes. Why not?'

'One evening? From what I hear, it was more than one evening.'

'Val, what's eating you? It's hardly the story of the moment if I go out for dinner with Perry. If you want to know, he thinks I eat very badly, and he likes to give me what he calls a proper meal.'

'He's right there, I expect you still live on chocolate and revolting heated-up pies from the supermarket, do you no good at all.'

'There you are, then.'

'That's not the point.' He paused. 'What's that slurping noise? What are you doing?'

'Swirling my brush in the water, Val.'

'Why? I'm talking to you, I want you to pay attention.'

Gussie cradled the receiver against her shoulder, and pulled out another sheet of paper. 'I am paying attention, but I have some work to finish.'

'A picture?'

'No, this is my bread and butter work. Illustrations.'

'There's another thing, I don't know why you waste your time on that. Painting's what you should concentrate on.'

'I have to live, Val. And I had an exhibition earlier this year, if you remember. I need to draw breath for a while.'

'Go abroad, somewhere warm, have a rest.'

'I'll tell the bank manager what you advise.'

'Damn it, Gussie, I'll pay.'

Gussie was so astonished she nearly fell off her stool. '*What* did you say?'

Valdemar sounded impatient. 'I said I'd pay for you to go away.'

'Just to get me away from Perry?'

'It's got nothing to do with Perry. Although I must say you're setting tongues wagging all over town, out carousing with your future son-in-law night after night.'

'Carousing! Night after night! Now look here, Val.'

There were scuffling noises down the line, and then the sound of a minor explosion before Magdalena's calm voice came through. 'Sorry, Gussie, Val is particularly intemperate just at the moment.'

'Let him kick the dog,' said Gussie. 'What's all this about Perry? What is he on about?'

'Nothing,' said Magdalena. 'You know his ways, Gussie, calm down. Val's worried about Cleo, he was horrified when she went rushing off to Hungary, says she could have got herself into serious trouble, and now he feels she's going to shut herself up in Haphazard House again, and let the whole Perry business drift.'

'Really, I don't see that it's any business of Val's.' Or yours, she thought, biting back the words.

She didn't have to. 'Or any business of mine, either, I know how you feel, Gussie. But I'm fond of Cleo, and Val is, of course, fiercely possessive and protective, however much he denies it.'

He wasn't protective or possessive when she was three or

when she was miserable at her first school, or when she was ill, or when she was at boarding school and I was away and no one came to take her out, Gussie reminded herself. He hadn't even known of her existence in those days.

'I'm sorry, Magdalena, I'm not angry with you, but Val does rather catch one on the hop. I'm worried about Cleo, too. My heart was in my mouth when she went off to Budapest like that, and I'm not at all sure how things stand between her and Perry.'

'Can't you ask him?'

'Keep-out signs up all over the place. He's just very courteous, and very firmly unwilling to discuss it.'

'Sylvester says there's no future in it at all.'

'Oh, Magdalena, I do hope he's wrong. I can't bear for Perry to be hurt. Look, I'll try to get some sense out of Cleo. I'm ringing her anyway. Geza's all right, did you hear?'

'Val said.'

Of course, Valdemar would know sooner than anyone. 'Prue's very happy, Cleo says. With the baby, and Geza safe.'

'What are they going to do? And Christmas is coming, it's a difficult time to make arrangements.'

'Geza will work something out, he's a born contriver, that man. Are you staying in London for Christmas?'

A long pause. 'We were, but Sylvester's asked us to go and stay with him. Val wants to go, he's fidgety if he doesn't get away, and of course we've let the castle for Christmas. To some very rich Swedes, which is fortunate. I hope, being northerners, they won't think anything of the cold and the draughts.'

'They all have lovely warm houses in Sweden, and saunas and so on.'

'Oh, well, it's back to basics for them, then. It'll bring out the atavistic chill, they'll revert to Viking type and have a wonderful time.'

'And a break for you, with Lily in charge.'

'I know, such heaven. What about you, Gussie?'

'I never make much of Christmas, you know. I'll work through I expect. Of course, I don't know where Cleo will be, or if she and Perry . . . There's no point worrying, they have to sort themselves out, there's nothing I can do.'

'Come to Midwinter with us. Sylvester would love to have you.'

'Possibly,' said Gussie.

She no sooner put the phone down than it rang again. 'What?' she said.

'Don't snap, Gussie, it's not the Inland Revenue here.'

'Oh, hello, Sylvester, I'm sorry. I've just had Val nagging at me, and I've got a lot of work to do.'

'I won't keep you. Just to say, would you consider coming to Midwinter for Christmas? Val and Magdalena and the twins are coming. And I feel quite sure that your headstrong daughter is planning to celebrate the festive season at Haphazard, Henry notwithstanding.'

'Um,' said Gussie, after a pause.

'Don't um at me. What is it?'

'I don't know what Perry's plans are. It could be a problem, if Cleo's going to be elusive. She might decide to spend Christmas here with me. Unlikely, I know, but who can tell?'

'Ah, yes. Perry,' said Sylvester. He rattled a pencil against his teeth. 'It goes against the grain, but I'll ask Perry, too.'

A thought struck Gussie. 'You won't have room, Sylvester. Isn't Prue coming to you, with the baby? And Geza of course.'

'Plenty of room,' said Sylvester. 'No problem at all.'

'I'll see,' said Gussie. 'Goodbye, Sylvester.' And she put the phone down, admitting to herself that she was touched that Sylvester had asked her, that Christmas in the comfort of Midwinter Hall was a great temptation, and that she would, on the whole, like to be near Cleo.

And Perry, of course.

Perry was such pleasant and civilized company.

'What cheek,' said Cleo furiously, gripping the phone so hard that her knuckles turned white. 'Listen, Mum, it's none of Val and Magdalena's business.'

'Val is your father.'

'Oh, very funny. Father is as father does. He's the last person who has any right to make remarks about anybody's marriage, or proposed marriage. When you think about what he's got up to over the years. I don't know how Magdalena puts up with him, I really don't. What a rake, and then he goes all severe about me. It is a cheek, an absolute bloody cheek.' Cleo glared moodily at the stove and kicked the chair beside her. 'And another thing, you don't need to go asking me questions. I'll sort things out with Perry for myself, thank you all very much.'

Adele poured Cleo out a drink.

'Thanks. No, just Adele passing me a drink. No, I'm not drinking too much, and I'm quite old enough to know whether I want a drink or not. I am not under stress, okay. I am in fact, very happy. I can't think of anywhere I'd rather be than Haphazard House. London? Work? Oh, Mum, I'll think about that after Christmas.'

Ping.

'You were very short with her,' said Adele.

'She was nagging.' Cleo sat up and twisted her fingers in and out of her dark fringe. 'Which is unusual; Mum never nags. She wants to know where I'm spending Christmas.'

'And where *are* you spending Christmas?' asked Adele, snapping off a thread of embroidery silk. She was working a chair cover of a brilliantly plumaged mythological bird set against an implausible background of dense green leaves and white flowers.

'Here, if I can,' said Cleo. She was staring at Adele's arm, what had she done to herself. 'You've hurt your wrist; look at those bruises.'

'It's nothing,' said Adele, pulling the sleeve of her shirt down to cover the livid marks.

'And your other wrist, too.'

'Never mind,' said Adele. 'It doesn't bother me, don't let it bother you. Here, in Haphazard House?'

'Yes,' said Cleo, still puzzled about the bruises. 'Are you going away? I could ask Mum up if you are.' I'd rather be by myself, she decided, if Mum's going to be full of concern. She pushed the unfriendly idea to the back of her mind. If she was alone, she'd probably feel dreadful, come Christmas morning.

Adele shrugged. 'Nowhere to go. Suzie's going to America with her guy, and we're closing the shop for a week or ten days. My mother's in America, she's booked herself into a health farm over Christmas, I feel sure; that's what she does every year. My father and my entirely grim stepmother will be at home in Cairo as usual. I don't feel like joining them, and they certainly don't want me.'

'Haven't you brothers? Don't I remember brothers?'

Adele rolled her embroidery up and tucked it into a gaudy bag at her feet. 'One's in China, the other's in prison.'

'Prison?'

'Yup. He's a jeweller, used to be Suzie's partner, that's how I met her. He was nabbed for handling stolen goods.'

'Was he? Handling them, I mean.'

Another pout, another shrug. 'Probably. Most do, in his line of business. He got caught, that's all. He'll be out in March, if he behaves himself. So, in the circs, I wouldn't mind staying here with you. If Henry hasn't got other plans.'

'Henry,' said Cleo darkly. 'Bother Henry.' She wandered over to the sink and picked up a tea towel, began to polish the glasses which had been left to dry on the rack. 'Marriage,' she said. 'What a wasteland. Look at them all. Your parents, mine, all those Hazards.'

'Look at Prue and Geza.'

'So far, so good,' said Cleo. 'But these Hungarians all get married and unmarried at the drop of a hat. Will it last?'

'Some do. Quite a lot do. It's worth a try, I would think. If you meet a man you've got a lot in common with. Shared interests, compatible as far as sex goes, why not?'

'Will you try?'

'Oh, yes,' said Adele, looking at her very small feet and twiddling her toes in elegant circles. 'If the terms are right.'

'You've got bruised ankles, too,' said Cleo. 'Chafed, by the look of them.'

'So I have,' said Adele, tucking her feet under the chair.

'Terms,' said Cleo. 'What terms?'

'I'm a great believer in spelling everything out,' said Adele. 'What you agree to. What you will or won't put up with. Same for him.'

'That's cold-blooded.'

'Necessary,' said Adele. 'For me, in any case.'

33

Cleo, bundled up in so many layers that she resembled the Michelin man, came round the corner of the house carrying a bowlful of scraps. She stopped abruptly, her eyes narrowing.

Just who was that in the barn?

Not Mrs Grigson; she was singing 'Happy Days' in lugubrious tones as she did battle with the boiler.

Not Arthur, either; he had arrived all too early, and was padding round the house seeing what he could do about some of the looser window panes.

Cleo put down the food she had brought out for the birds and advanced on the barn. Her breath formed little misty clouds on the frozen air; after the flurry of storms and wind and rain, winter once again had Eyotshire in her icy grip.

She might have known.

Henry.

'What are you doing here?'

Henry was hunting about in the corner of the barn among sundry old car batteries, rat-chewed wires and what must once have been a lawn mower.

'You startled me.'

'You startled me, lurking in the barn like that.'

'I was hardly lurking. And it is my barn.'

'Courtesy would suggest you told the house-sitters you were about.'

'When I arrived, you were wrapped in slumbers.'

'Mrs Grigson didn't mention seeing you.'

'Mrs Grigson keeps her own counsel, haven't you noticed?

Since you're no longer in the land of snore and zizz, you can make me some coffee.'

'I do not snore,' Cleo began indignantly, and then caught Henry's eye. Bugger him, she thought, teasing me again. She would be extremely polite and gracious. 'Coffee? Of course, you must be frozen, rummaging out here in the barn. Looking for something for the jumble sale, are you? Can I be of any help?'

'Looking for jump leads, if you must know. There's a set here somewhere, I know I saw them. Unless Mrs G has borrowed them, of course.'

'For her black bicycle? Hardly very likely. There are some jump-leads in the boot of your aunt's car,' she added. 'They're probably the ones you're looking for. Why do you need them? You must have driven here.'

'My car isn't starting properly.'

'Needs a new battery.'

'Possibly, but I shan't get one until I have to.'

What a waste of effort, fiddling round with jump leads when you could simply go and buy a new battery, thought Cleo, pushing open the kitchen door. Or maybe just mean. Mean, as well as putty in the hands of his ex-wife, and doubtless any other sizzling piece that came into his orbit.

Henry was a bit of a disaster, when you came to look at it logically.

The disaster was regarding her with considerable amusement. One has to grant him charm, Cleo acknowledged as she opened the door of the ancient fridge, so old it had rounded corners.

'Have you seen Arthur?' she asked, opening a fresh bottle of milk and plonking it on the table.

'Is he here?'

'That's why I thought you might have seen him. I'll go and find him if you like, then you can have a nice discussion about how best to tear down this house.'

Henry winced. 'A little early in the day for confrontations, don't you think?'

No, Cleo said to herself. It's confrontation all the way where you're concerned.

Porthos strolled in, stretched, showing his sharp claws and yawned, displaying his equally sharp teeth. Henry bent down to stroke him, and got a swift bite for his pains. 'Thug,' he said, sucking his hand. 'Walking wounded now, what with you and Cleo . . .'

'What was that?'

'Nothing.'

'If you don't tease him, he won't bite, will you, Porthos?'

Porthos sprang up on to Cleo's lap, gave her chin an affectionate bump, and sat bolt upright on her lap, glaring at Henry.

'Hum,' said Henry. 'I think I'll go and find Arthur.'

'Arthur?' said Mrs Grigson. She sighed heavily. 'Upstairs. In the gallery. Messing about with bits of wood, I hope he knows what he's doing. They threw him out of woodwork at school, you know. Said he was no good with his hands.'

'Ah,' said Henry, nonplussed at this bit of information.

'And if you should chance to see my feather duster,' Mrs Grigson called out after him as he climbed the stairs, 'please let me know. It's vanished; things are always disappearing in this house.'

Henry paused on his careful ascent and looked round. 'Do they reappear, Mrs Grigson?'

'Sometimes,' she admitted grudgingly. 'Sometimes they do. And sometimes they don't,' she finished, her voice swelling into a crescendo as Henry reached the landing.

'Cleo was very rude to Henry,' said Giles, flicking Mrs Grigson's feather duster over the big oak table which was placed against the wall opposite the window. 'I like this feathery affair, I've had my eye on it for some time.'

'She'll notice it's gone,' said Lambert warningly. 'She'll tell Will Wrackham, and then he'll summon the poltergeist mob, and we'll be in a parlous state.'

'That might be fun,' said Giles. 'Hurl some plates and saucepans around. Have a brawl.'

'Control yourself.'

'He's thoroughly confused by all his readings,' said Giles comfortably. 'He won't bring any other experts in. Who knows, we may never see him again.'

'With Adele staying here? He'll be back, sniffing out ghosts, sniffing out fleshly delights. I expect they'll invite him for Christmas.'

'There won't be anyone here for Christmas, it's going to be the loneliest time, I feel quite in despair about it.'

'Didn't I tell you?' said Lambert, knowing perfectly well that he hadn't. 'While you flitted out to look at the holly bush yesterday, Gussie rang Cleo.'

'You listened?'

'I did.'

'And you didn't tell me?'

'You were overflowing with the green and the red and the significance of such a crop of berries and the symbolism of new beginnings and I don't know what that I completely forgot.'

Giles turned a cold eye on him. 'Oh?'

Lambert went on hurriedly. 'I'm telling you now. It seems that Cleo wants to spend Christmas here, at Haphazard House. And I overheard Adele saying that she had nowhere to go over Christmas, so she will be here also.'

Giles was so thrilled at this news that he forgave Lambert. For the moment, at any rate, although he would store up that overheard but unreported phone call, that was naughty of Lambert. And, he suspected, quite deliberate.

'So you think Will may join them?'

'I do,' said Lambert. 'It is a sign of the times, have these young people no families to be with, at this season of the birth of our Lord?'

'Hypocrite,' said Giles. 'Your lot tried to ban Christmas, remember?'

'Sad times,' said Lambert with a shake of his head. 'Christmas is a snare for the righteous. I wonder if they'll have a yule log.'

Cleo walked gingerly up the stairs with a mug of coffee and a wedge of ginger cake for Arthur. 'Your auntie says you like lots of sugar in it, so I put in three spoonfuls.'

'That's right,' said Arthur, putting down a large hammer and taking the cup and the piece of cake from her. 'Thank you.'

'I didn't get offered any ginger cake,' said Henry.

Cleo took no notice. 'Mrs Grigson says she'll put your pie in the oven at quarter to twelve for you, Arthur.'

'Is there a pie for me?' asked Henry.

'If you brought one with you,' said Cleo. 'I shall be having some fruit and a yoghurt, if you'd like to share that.'

'Rhubarb flavour?' asked Henry, all innocence. 'To skin my teeth on?'

'Banana,' said Cleo, trying not to laugh.

Henry clattered down the stairs after her. 'Cleo,' he called. 'Don't rush off, I need to ask you something.'

'Yes?'

'About Christmas.'

Oh, hell, thought Cleo, with a lurch of her stomach. He's going to throw me out. It's back to London, office, wet pavements, cars, no Porthos . . . Perry.

'When are you planning to go back to London?'

Cleo shrugged. 'Whenever.'

'That's not very helpful.'

'Look, I said I'd house-sit, I'm house-sitting. I'm quite happy to stay here over Christmas and keep an eye on it for you, if that's convenient. After all, it'll be its last Christmas, won't it? Shame to leave it empty.'

'I'd be very glad if you'd stay,' said Henry with relief. 'And Adele, too, if she'd like to.'

'She would,' said Cleo quickly. She hadn't realized quite how much she wanted to stay on. Thank goodness Henry was going to fall in with her plans; but she mustn't seem too keen, she didn't want him to have the upper hand. 'And we thought we might ask Will, if he's at a loose end.'

Pause.

'Ah,' said Henry. 'Our wild ghost-hunter.'

'Yes,' said Cleo.

Henry shrugged. 'Up to you. Is he a particular friend of Adele's?'

'He's a friend of both of ours,' said Cleo. She wondered why Henry wasn't too keen on Will, envious of his good looks and Byronic ways, she supposed.

'Yes,' said Henry. 'Well, fine. I thought I might come over. For Christmas, I mean. If that's all right with you.'

'As you say, it's your house. While it stands.'

'Yes, it is,' agreed Henry. 'I won't get in your way,' he added politely. 'I'll stay in the new wing. With Will.'

'Er, yes, the new wing,' said Cleo, who had had vague thoughts of Will being elsewhere during the long dark nights.

'Is your fiancé coming too?'

'Fiancé?' echoed Cleo, her voice edged with scorn.

'I thought you were engaged.'

'I am, but I don't call him my fiancé.'

'I'm sorry. It seemed suitable for him, somehow.'

Touché, thought Cleo, surprised. He was goading her. 'Perry generally prefers to spend Christmas in London.'

Mass at Westminster Cathedral, friends for drinks, elegant meal in the evening. Ugh, thought Cleo, not admitting to herself that this was an entirely fictional picture; she had no real idea at all of how Perry might choose to spend Christmas.

'Then won't he expect you to join him?'

'No,' said Cleo shortly. 'I'm not well enough to take the strain of London yet.'

'You poor thing,' said Henry, forbearing to mention the little matter of the highly stressful and tiring trip to Hungary. 'I'll see to the food and drink in that case, I cook a mean bird.'

'You?' said Cleo, astonished. 'Cook?'

'One of my many accomplishments. My wife didn't care to spend much time in the kitchen, so it was cook or starve.'

Your wife sounds like a waste of space, thought Cleo.

'And you needn't look like that,' said Henry. 'My wife had – has – many other skills and attributes.'

Yes, I bet she had, thought Cleo as she went on her way downstairs. Such as scheming and digging her hands into other people's pockets. She didn't think this was what Henry was talking about.

What do I care? she said to herself, as she remembered the abandoned bird food, and went out to see to supplies for the assorted robins, thrushes, tits and blackbirds who flocked to the neglected gardens of Haphazard Hall.

34 ∫

Afterwards, Cleo accused Sylvester of cowardice.

'I came over for tea and some company, after having a dose of Henry, and look what you let me in for.'

'I didn't know they were coming.'

'You never went to see her, did you?'

'No, and you can judge for yourself why not. A phone call was quite terrifying enough, let me tell you. Angela Mitcham is not a woman to trifle with.'

'You were all set to do a bolt,' said Cleo. 'Or to hide behind the sofa.'

'With reason,' said Sylvester. 'Speaking in my own defence, that woman is a harpy, a being let loose from Pandaemonium.'

'From where?'

'From where the devils live,' said Sylvester. 'Lakes of brimstone, and the Lord of the Flies buzzing in your ear.'

'Yup,' said Cleo. 'That sounds like her spiritual home. What an incongruous pair!'

'He's only turned to the High Church as a gesture of protest.'

'I suppose so.' Cleo gave herself a quick shake. 'The way she came barging in, demanding to know who was responsible for spreading lies about the Hungarian state.'

Cleo had been totally unprepared for Angela Mitcham, and she soon found out why Sylvester, having crossed her path before, was so unenthusiastic about seeing her.

Cleo had expected something in the country lady line, so she was surprised by the long, straggly grey hair, the ill-fitting jeans and the sour complexion which went with a sour tongue. Her immediate reaction was to wonder how she had ever produced someone so seemingly human and balanced as the young man on the train from Budapest.

Her second thought was that she wasn't surprised that the son had opted for a job abroad.

'I made him go,' said Angela triumphantly. 'I knew that he would be happier by far in a socialist state, one of the workers, honoured in a truly democratic system. A country where there would be no false status accorded to anyone just because they happened to have a university degree. I told him, the proletariat are the rulers there; you intellectuals have to take your proper place in society, as servants of the state and the workers.'

What a crank, thought Cleo. What a nutter. Has she ever been to Hungary?

'I have travelled widely in Russia, as a guest of their fine cultural exchange programme. But as I said to Arnold, it's totally shaming when they come here in their turn, and they see the miseries of the capitalist state in its full horror. They all want to go to Marks and Spencer to see how a corrupt government lulls oppositions into ineffectiveness by means of consumerism.'

She whipped round and turned her guns on Sylvester. 'Have you ever been to Russia, Mr Tate.'

'Er, yes,' said Sylvester. 'I have played in Russia.'

'And don't you sense at once the enormous difference in artistic life in a country where they live according to socialist principles?'

To Sylvester's relief, as he was spared the necessity of answering what he considered a completely asinine question, and to Cleo's surprise, a tall thin Anglican priest with a face like a sheep came sidling into the room. He was introduced by a contemptuous Lily as the person she had found hanging around in the hall and supposed wanted to join the others in the sitting-room.

The door shut behind her with a definite bang.

'I thought you were going to wait in the car,' said Mrs Mitcham.

'I, um, thought I might see where you were,' he said in a gentle way.

He's rather a sweetie, thought Cleo. That's who young Arnold takes after, clearly.

'We have met,' the Rev Mitcham said courteously, extending a limp hand to Sylvester. 'But I don't think . . . ?' He looked enquiringly at Cleo.

'I'm so sorry,' said Sylvester. 'This is Cleo Byng, Mrs Mitcham.'

'Angela,' said grey locks fiercely.

'Gerald, isn't it?' said Sylvester to the Rev. 'Cleo, this is Gerald Mitcham. Cleo is a young friend who's staying at Haphazard,' he added.

Red rag to a bull; Angela leapt into action. 'That's the house owned by that perfectly dreadful man who does those appalling drawings which the stupid Americans lap up. Capitalist lackey,' she added for good measure.

I must pass that on to Henry, Cleo told herself, knowing he would find it funny.

Sylvester went on to make matters much worse. 'It's fortunate that you've come just now, because Cleo was in the train with Arnold when he was hauled off.'

'I was,' said Cleo. 'A bunch of thugs, those policemen. And thick with it.'

'That remark was a big mistake,' said Cleo later to Sylvester. 'I should have thought before I opened my mouth. Has she got shares in the Hungarian secret police or what?'

'She's just a fool,' said Sylvester.

'And fancy carrying on like that on account of your son having written a thriller.'

'Bourgeois pandering to the depraved tastes of the middle classes, wasn't that it?' said Sylvester, with a hoot of laughter.

'It was. How does she get her tongue round all the ridiculous jargon, and with a perfectly straight face?'

'They go to classes,' said Sylvester.

'However did those two ever get together?' Cleo found it incomprehensible. 'You could see from his face that he thought she was talking piffle and you could see from hers that she utterly despises him.'

'This is all quite recent,' said Sylvester. 'Gerald used to be an accountant, tripping off to his office in Eyot every morning, bringing home the bacon at the end of each month, with a bonus every March. Angela was a pillar of the community, arranger of flowers in the church, supporter of the parish litter drive, keen campaigner to keep village greens in order. The only association she was a paid-up member of was the Women's Institute.'

'So what happened?'

'An old school chum of Angela's turned up, and, just like that,' said Sylvester with a snap of his fingers, 'Angela got radicalized. Out went the discreet perm, the Eliz. Arden and the tasteful Bally pumps for special occasions. In came the natural look, the headful of highly peculiar left-wing ideology and the hatred of Gerald and all he stood for.'

'Poor Gerald.'

'Poor Gerald indeed. But he's not the sheep he unquestionably looks. He stood Angela's rantings and ravings for a while, probably thought it was a phase or hormones or something. Then it got serious. She cancelled their trip to the Austrian lakes and booked herself on an outing to Russia, and he split. Went off to a do in London, in his turn met an old friend, and the next thing was, he was enrolled at theological college.'

'Ah,' said Cleo with relish.

'Yes, and one of those ones where the ordinands call each other Rosie and Dolly.'

'Ah,' said Cleo again.

'Not, I suspect through any proclivities on Gerald's part, but just for maximum annoyance value.'

'Why hasn't she taken herself off?'

'Ha,' said Sylvester. 'No money. He holds the purse strings, and says if she tries anything funny, he'll hand all the loot over to a churchy trust.'

'Could he?'

'I doubt it, but she's not risking her creature comforts, not for any principles.'

'Poor Arnold, what a home life.'

'He's got a nice nature, that boy. Never a word of criticism of either of his parents, although it's quite obvious he thinks they're both daft. And don't you believe all that about going to Hungary because Ma fixed it up. He had his own, personal reasons.'

'What?' said Cleo, intrigued.

'He'd met a stunning girl from Tatabanya on the platform at Waterloo, and decided to see more of her.'

'And his parents stay married,' said Cleo. 'Why?'

'I've seen worse marriages,' said Sylvester, heaving himself up from the sofa. 'They probably need each other, in a strange way. It's early yet, but I think we both deserve a drink.'

'Worse marriages?' said Cleo. 'The more I see of marriage, Sylvester, the more it seems to me to be doomed.'

'And yet, you know,' said Sylvester, 'people go on doing it. And sometimes it works.'

'Huh,' said Cleo. 'Show me.'

35

'What, all of us?' said Cleo, back at Midwinter the next morning and thawing out in front of a vigorous fire in Sylvester's sitting-room after an icy drive from Haphazard House. 'The heater in the car doesn't work properly,' she said, blowing numb fingers back into life.

Sylvester rose and went to the fire, poker in hand. 'Hardly a coachload,' he said, stirring the coal and logs into even more of a blaze. 'You and Adele and Will and Henry.'

'Henry!' said Cleo crossly. 'What an annoying man. Well, that's one thing, at least he won't get to cook Christmas dinner if we're coming here.'

'Why should Henry cook Christmas dinner anywhere?' asked Prue, now out of hospital and installed blissfully at Midwinter Hall with Felicia and Geza.

'He offered.'

'Henry's a very good cook,' confirmed Sylvester.

Cleo was finding Prue's happiness hard to understand.

'Don't you mind being exiled?' she asked Geza. Not that he looked at all troubled, she thought, looking at his thin, lively face with affection. He was just the same merry, good-humoured Geza, his expressive dark eyes full of understanding. She admired his urbanity, too; he was utterly relaxed after a journey fraught with danger. No stress, no irritation at all, just courtesy and charm.

'Of course, I mind very much,' he said 'but minding will not change the situation in Hungary. I am one of the lucky ones, I can work and earn a living in the West, I can stay in England, or go to America. And then, I hope, affairs in Hungary may develop. One day, even, the whole system may collapse. Meanwhile, there is no point in fret and worry. And how can we not be happy, with such a beautiful daughter?'

Cleo envied Prue. Not that she had any desire at all to be sunk in such domesticity, not that she wanted a baby; in fact, she thought with an inward shudder, definitely not. Forget the condom-on-the-banana bit, she'd told Adele, all they need to do at school is show them what it's like having a baby; that'd stop them making whoopee without Being Prepared.

And she could appreciate the evident pleasure Prue and Geza took in each other's company. It was just so, well, settled. Established. And they seemed to enjoy life together so much.

'Could have been you and Perry,' said Lily cunningly, seeing Cleo's eyes on Prue and Geza, who were discussing a trip to Eyot, to do some Christmas shopping, ready to take the plunge and leave the sleeping Felicia under Lily's eagle eye.

'She'll sleep for hours now,' said Lily.

'Little pig,' said Prue with pride. 'Lily, what do you need?'

'You do your own shopping, I've got what I want for now, and I'll be doing a big run before Christmas.'

'Good,' said Sylvester. 'I shall help.'

'I shall do it while you're in America,' said Lily.

'Sylvester! Are you going to America?' exclaimed Prue. 'You never said, and here we are, landed on you.'

'Hardly a problem. I am indeed going to America, the day after tomorrow. I'm giving two concerts, one in New York and one in Chicago, spending a couple of days with Gabriel and then back here for Christmas.'

It sounded a tough schedule, but Cleo knew Sylvester of old; he was indestructible and thrived on trips like this. 'Big concerts?'

Sylvester nodded. '*Rococo Variations* with the New York Phil. And I'm playing with Ferenc and Gabriel in Chicago.'

'What a shame Gabriel isn't going to be here for Christmas.'

'Well, do you know, Gabriel's not awfully good at Christmas,' said Sylvester. 'He tends to get sad, which rather dampens the Christmas mood. I, on the other hand, adore Christmas. Not that I, too, wouldn't prefer Gabriel to be here, but his father is getting on and is rather frail, so Gabriel's flying to California to be with his parents.'

California. Cleo thought of oranges and sun and blue blue skies.

And pollution and fog and baking heat, whispered an evil voice in her ear.

Not at this time of year, though; but she wouldn't swap Haphazard House tingling in the frost, and the holly tree ablaze in the garden for anywhere else. Henry was right. January and February were the months that eat into your soul, time then to fly off to warm places.

Or, in her case, time to return to her stuffy London office.

Prue brought her back into the present with a bump. 'Why don't you come in to Eyot with us, Cleo?' she asked.

'Yes, please come with us,' said Geza. 'You can advise us, so many presents to buy.'

You don't need my advice, Cleo thought later as she watched Prue and Geza squabbling amicably over what to get Sylvester.

'Look,' she said suddenly. 'I've got some shopping of my own to do, and I think I may be a while. So I'll buzz off, and don't worry about giving me a lift back, I'll join up with Adele and go straight back to Haphazard.'

'Are you sure?' said Prue, sensing all was not quite well with her friend. 'Are you sure you're feeling all right?'

'Positive. Don't forget you're coming over tomorrow to see Haphazard House.'

'I look forward to this,' said Geza. 'I hear from Sylvester how historic, how haunted this house is. This is especially interesting to me, because I have Transylvanian ancestors, and we are good at hauntings and so forth.'

'Particularly so forth,' decided Cleo, as she wandered off. She had no clear idea of what she wanted or where to get it; she had just felt that Prue and Geza would rather be by themselves. And I don't feel very Christmassy, she admitted to herself. Still the aftermath of those blasted shingles, probably; the doctor had warned her that the illness could leave you depressed.

She found herself in a little square, away from the traffic. A splendid plane tree grew in the centre of the square;

it was festooned with tiny lights, already illuminated in the not very bright light of the winter's afternoon. They weren't coloured, they were just pinpoints of light shining out through the branches. The sight of them brought a prickle to the back of Cleo's eyes.

How stupid, she told herself. Shingles obviously left you feeling sentimental as well as depressed.

'Pretty, aren't they,' said Henry, sitting down beside her.

'What are you doing here?' said Cleo, uneasy and not very pleased to see anyone. She wanted to enjoy her gloom alone.

'I just came in to do a few things,' said Henry. 'Including hunt for baubles, I thought we could do with some decorations for Haphazard.'

'I was planning to bring in some branches from outside.'

'Very good, but we need some of the shinies as well, don't you agree? I planned to buy some this afternoon, before everything nice has gone. Come and help.'

Cleo was tempted. She had a sneaking liking for the gaudy side of Christmas. On the other hand, she'd end up arguing with Henry. She told him so.

'Not at all,' he said gravely. 'I'll agree in advance with everything you say.'

'Are we going to Woolies?'

'I know of somewhere better,' he said.

'Haven't you got any work to do?' asked Cleo, slightly resentful of Henry's high-handed ways.

'I do have work to do, but nothing pressing.'

'My mother always has work to do.'

'Your mother may have more ideas than me. I have to let them fester, you know, it works like that when you deal with the more grotesque side of life.'

I've never seen any of his drawings, thought Cleo as they crossed to the other side of the square. Wonder what they're like.

'Talking of work,' said Henry in a chatty way as he guided Cleo down a street which ran down towards the river, 'what are you planning to do?'

'About what?'

'Work. Your work. Your job. As in career.'

'Go back to it as soon as I'm fit.' Stupid question.

'You don't like your job.'

'Don't I?'

'No, I can tell. Distinct lack of enthusiasm and keenness about getting back to the office, I'd say. I can't see you in an office anyway. What exactly do you do when you're there, beavering away from morning till night?'

'I make money.'

'For yourself?'

'For the investment trust I work for.'

'Fascinating,' said Henry, pulling Cleo back from the road as she was about to plunge under the wheels of a squad of child cyclists. They yelled abuse at her as they went past.

'Little sods,' said Cleo.

'Perhaps your future does not lie in the field of child care or the social services,' said Henry, taking her hand as though she were a child herself and leading her across the road. 'Look right, look left, look right again.'

Cleo shook her hand free. 'All right, my job is possibly not the most fulfilling in the world. But it has a lot to offer in an imperfect world. It gives me a good buzz of adrenalin, I like the team I work with, I earn plenty of money and I have a lively life in London. Pretty good, all in all.'

'Sounds primitive,' said Henry. 'My advice to all those setting out on life is to follow your bliss,' said Henry. 'Find out the one thing you want to do more than anything else, and then do it. Only way.'

'The only thing I'd like to do right now is restore Haphazard House,' snapped Cleo.

'Ah,' said Henry. 'Not possible. Not for wanting, I assure you, just lack of cash. You could do up other houses, though. Go and train. Restoration work, conservation. It's a coming field. Now, that *would* be fascinating, if you want my opinion, which you clearly don't.'

'You're just like my mother,' said Cleo, banging angrily through the doors of The Christmas Emporium. 'Bloody artists, you're all so sure of yourselves and your beastly vocations. Sylvester's another, and Geza. You don't understand how ordinary mortals work. Oh!'

She was brought up short by the magical pageant of Christmas which lay spread out before her. From the tinkling bells above her head to the little domes with snowmen standing in a flurry of white flakes; from the trays and trays of shining and frosted balls to the yards of swaggage, it was all utterly over the top and totally delectable.

'I never knew this shop existed.'

'It doesn't,' said Henry, picking up a basket and passing it to her. He took another one for himself and scooped up a handful of baubles. 'It opens for a few fantasy weeks before the New Year and February bring their bitter taste. Come along, let's indulge ourselves.'

Cleo was aching with laughter by the time she and Henry had swept round the emporium, trying on silly hats, telling their Christmas wishes to Santa and having a ride on a rocking reindeer.

Then Henry, laden with bags, had made a sudden dive into the traffic with a wave and was gone, and Cleo was back in windswept Eyot, standing alone on the dark pavement.

Not so far from Adele's shop, she reckoned. It would be a good idea to go and make sure of the lift she had so airily told Prue and Geza that she could have. Fortunately, Adele was happy to oblige.

'Will's coming to Haphazard tonight,' she told Cleo.

Suzie shot them both a glance and pulled her welding mask down.

'He's feeling a bit forlorn,' went on Adele. 'He's hurt his hand, can't play the piano.'

'Have you seen him?'

'No, he rang me up to have a moan, so I said come over, and we'd feed him and watch the late movie.'

You can, I'll fall asleep after half an hour, reflected Cleo, grumpily aware of her present limitations.

Two hours before Adele would be ready to leave. Twenty minutes to shop for supper. Then what?

A sign standing valiantly outside a tiny shop caught her eye. 'Special today, shampoo, conditioning treatment and blow-dry with Denise.'

In I go, thought Cleo. With Will coming, it was worth making an effort, and her hair had been looking very rough. Blessed with hair that fell naturally and sleekly into a twenties bob, Cleo wasn't used to seeing it dull and strawlike.

'Have you been ill?' asked Denise, running expert fingers through it. 'Thought so, terrible condition. That and this cold weather, it really takes it out of one's hair. Going anywhere special? Hot date?'

'Just a friend coming round.'

'Not a girl friend, I'll be bound,' said Denise, plunging Cleo's hair under the spray. 'Don't worry, I'll put the shine back in this lot.'

36

'So Henry's wife takes all his money, the vixen,' said Giles, still puzzled by such a topsy-turvy state of affairs.

'It seems so,' said Lambert, who had been shocked when this simple fact had dawned on him. 'That's what Cleo told Adele. I can only take her word for it,' he added with the caution of a man who had studied law in the course of his earthly duties.

Giles was thinking hard. 'It's very strange, for a woman to live apart from her husband . . .'

'. . . in another country, moreover.'

'And to lay claim to all his wealth. It wasn't so in my day.'

'Nor mine.'

They reflected for a moment on the decline of the times and then returned to the matter in hand.

'Now, this Mathilda has lovers, but doesn't marry them.' Lambert liked to be precise.

'No, she could only marry one, in any case. One at a time, that is.'

'Divorce! What a lamentable world, where people marry and then divorce, again and again, in violation of their vows and against the will of the Lord.'

'Never mind the will of the Lord, and there's no virtue in bewailing the times. These are the times we've got to cope with, if we're to keep our house.'

'Very true. Now, the more Henry earns, the more Mathilda wants, and the more she takes.'

'He must have poor advisers,' said Giles, who hadn't spent time at a Tudor court for nothing. 'This matter has been dealt with very ill, he has had bad counsel, if you ask me.'

'Still has, from what Cleo says. She was very hot against his lawyer. Said Mathilda's lawyer chewed him up and spat him out.'

'Lawyers do,' said worldly-wise Giles.

'So if he earns less, or nothing, then Mathilda will not be best pleased.'

'If I have Mathilda's measure, she'll find herself a new, rich husband. That's what widows always did in my time. Marry a rich man, marry three or four. Divorce must work on the same principles.'

Lambert rubbed a pane of glass with his sleeve. 'Henry is an artist. He draws for his living.'

'No estates, no revenues,' said Giles. 'And him a Hazard.'

'You can't tamper with art,' said Lambert. 'God-given gifts must be honoured and respected.'

'Besides,' said cunning Giles, 'Henry needs to go on earning, otherwise how will he have money for the house?'

'Very true,' said Lambert. 'I shall get out the chessboard, and ponder.' Lambert had long since discovered the chess problems in the heavier daily papers, and he had a stack of them stored away for times when he needed to think.

Giles always took refuge in his lute, or in a book. 'I shall read, today,' he said. 'My mind plays best when I let a problem be.' He took up his book, and Lambert rattled his fingers on the table.

'I wish you would let that alone,' he said with a frown. 'Clarendon is a prejudiced, partial historian, not to be trusted.'

'He was there,' said Giles, stretching his legs along the window seat and opening the third volume of the History of the Great Rebellion. 'Which is more than I was. I've still got a lot to catch up on, all those years in the wilderness.'

'Don't think about it,' said Lambert wincing. 'It's out there waiting, right now.'

'Don't be so gloomy. I tell you, if the worst comes to the worst, we'll go visiting.'

'Worst shan't come to the worst,' said Lambert. 'The Lord will help us.'

'The Lord will have to get a move on,' said Giles, plunging into the tumultuous but simpler world of the seventeenth century.

'Ha,' said Sylvester, narrowly avoiding Henry as he heaved a load of logs into the hall. 'What's going on?'

'Atavism,' said Henry, dumping the logs and recovering his breath. 'Pure atavism. Huh, it's parky out there, I can tell you.'

'Atavism?' said Sylvester looking around him, mystified.

'Cleo,' said Henry. 'It's Cleo's fault. She has this crazy idea of decking the hall for Christmas.'

'Ah,' said Sylvester. 'I'm with you. Boughs of jolly and so on.'

'That's the one,' said Henry, rubbing his arm and flexing his hand. 'Cleo rang me up and asked if the chimney in here had been lit in living memory. How should I know, I said, but it was a rhetorical question, she'd already asked Mrs Grigson and discovered that my esteemed great-aunt used to light it up on the chilliest winter days.'

'And I suppose Cleo was asking you if she could light a fire in it once more?'

Henry gave Sylvester a very speaking look. 'Cleo? Ask?'

'I did wonder,' admitted Sylvester. 'Cleo is very possessive about this house.'

'I had noticed. No, Cleo rang me to tell me to come over and a) unearth the grate which Mrs G last saw in the barn, and b) saw up wood for logs.'

'Neat,' said Sylvester. 'You have to admire her organizational skills. Why didn't she press-gang Will into it, I wonder.'

'Has Will been here again?' Henry's voice was casual as he rolled down his shirt sleeve and did up the cuff, but Sylvester wasn't deceived.

'I believe so. More booby-traps for the ghosts, although if you ask me, he's the booby. No, I don't think she did ask Will.'

Cleo hurtled in through the front door, accompanied by an icy blast of the great outdoors. 'I did ask Will, in fact,' she said, 'but he's hurt his back.'

'How convenient,' said Henry.

'Come on, acid drop,' said Cleo. 'Let's pile up those logs over here.'

Henry bent to his appointed task, and then visibly winced. He straightened up and shook his hand in floppy circles.

'Trouble?' said Sylvester, who as a cellist was extremely careful about injuries to hands and fingers.

'Merely a bit stiff,' said Henry, picking up a log in his left hand.

Cleo looked at him with scorn, and seized an armful of logs. 'Leave them, I'll do it.'

'Cleo, Henry's hand matters. He's an artist, remember.'

Cleo wasn't used to Sylvester talking to her so sharply, and she blinked, then gave Henry a foxy stare. 'It must be from chopping wood, I don't suppose you're used to it. I'll get some arnica for you, it's in my bag.'

'Nothing like womanly sympathy,' said Henry. 'Makes you feel better at once.'

'Take the arnica, and watch that hand,' advised Sylvester. 'A minor injury can lead to all kinds of trouble.'

'This won't,' said Henry with confidence.

'It had better not,' said Cleo. 'I'm going to need a lot of help with the garlands down the stairs.'

Sylvester looked around the large and draughty hall. 'Cleo, what's this *for*? Nobody will want to stay in here a second longer than they have to.'

'You're wrong,' said Cleo. 'I'm going to make it really snug.'

'Snug!' Henry was full of disbelief. 'As soon make the nave of the Cathedral snug!'

'Cold as charity,' agreed Sylvester.

'You know nothing about it,' said Cleo with vigour, dragging what seemed to Henry and Sylvester to be most of a tree across the floor. Those curtains she had spotted in a shop just next to the hairdresser's would be ideal, she thought, mentally measuring up the doors and the single large window on the first landing. I hope Adele remembers.

'Why?' said Henry, going on strike and folding his arms. 'Why this rush of Christmas to the head?'

Cleo shrugged. 'The house needs it. Take it as an offering. I know we're going to be at Sylvester's on Christmas Day, but Christmas is more than a day, it's a season, and it's going to be celebrated at Haphazard House. Properly. My swan-song for the house,' she added, with a purposeful look at Henry.

'Your hair looks nice, Cleo,' said Sylvester quickly, moving out of the way of some pine branches which were jabbing him behind the knees. 'Had it done?'

'Yesterday.'

'For Will,' Sylvester said under his breath. 'Blast the man.'

Henry heard. He gave Sylvester a quick look, but said nothing.

Not that it had any effect, thought Cleo. Will was charming, as desperately attractive as ever, but still far more fascinated by the ghosts than by her. Noisy film it had been, too, that he and Adele had stayed up late to watch; she had woken from her dreams more than once to the sounds of distant yells and shrieks. Violent, she supposed.

'Cleo,' called Sylvester. 'Come down from Burnham Wood and tell me what Gussie would like for Christmas, I have time to do some shopping in New York. An art book, perhaps? Has she got that new biography of Miró?'

'No,' said Cleo, leaning on the banisters. 'And she'd love it. She's big on Miro.'

'And what do you want for Christmas, Cleo?' said Henry, looking up at her.

'Oh, a partridge in a pear tree, don't you think?'

'Look in at Gumbles,' advised Sylvester. 'Well, I must be off, what a hard life is that of a humble musician. Be good, see you next week, goose under my arm. Take care of that hand, Henry, you never know what that kind of thing can lead to.'

'Humble musician, indeed,' said Cleo, waving at him. 'Break a leg, Sylvester. Play beautifully, wow the American throng, and then come back for a memorable Christmas.'

'Memorable?' said Sylvester, opening the door and letting in another arctic gust. 'It might well be that, but I can tell you one thing, if the weather goes on like this, we're in for some snow.'

'Perfect,' said Cleo with delight.

'Oh, God, think of the roof,' said Henry.

By the time a frozen Adele arrived glowing-cheeked from the wind, Cleo had made considerable progress in her garland weaving.

'All the way up the stairs?' said Adele. 'Cleo, it's going to take you for ever.'

'Not at all. It's very soothing, and when I get bored, or my fingers get sore, I go and do a bit with the plasterwork.'

'Rather pointless, since it'll all be coming down.'

'I'm drawing the plaster as well. For a record.'

'I thought you couldn't draw.'

'I can *draw*,' said Cleo. 'In the way of draughtsmanship. Not like my mother, there's no inspiration, but it's fairly accurate.'

Adele flipped her curls into place, and as she tilted her head back, Cleo noticed her swollen lip. 'Adele, whatever happened?'

'I'm a bit battered generally,' said Adele. 'Came off my bike, that's all. It happens all the time; I'm quite used to it. It heals up very quickly.'

'Oh,' said Cleo doubtfully, thinking that if she were Adele and regularly ended up black and blue like that, she'd switch to the bus. 'Did you have any luck with the curtains?'

'I did. Yards and yards of red velvet, very clever of you. And I was glad to go in there, I'd never noticed that shop before, but she has some lovely old fabrics, just what I need. Will's bringing the curtains with him tomorrow. He asked if he could come back to Haphazard; he ordered some kind of sound monitor from America, and he's longing to try it.'

'No problem,' said Cleo, wondering about the easy phoning terms that Adele and Will seemed to be on.

'It's nothing,' said Adele. 'He's a dreadful gossip, you know. Loves to ring me up and tell me what's going on, especially about the scandalous goings-on at the school.'

'School?'

'The Cathedral School, where he teaches. All kinds of intrigue and mischief, I can't tell you.'

'My brother's there,' said Cleo, after a pause.

'Brother?' Adele stared. 'You're an only child. Gussie only had you, she told me that when she was here.'

'I have a prolific father. Numerous half-brothers and sisters, and those are only the ones I know about. Thomas is fourteen, he ran away from his boarding school, very sensibly, and he went to the school here this term. Sylvester teaches him the cello; I hadn't heard anything was amiss.'

'There won't be, if he's a boy and fourteen,' said Adele. 'Wrong sex, wrong age to be caught up in any of the goings-on there. He'll be fine.'

'Good lord,' said Cleo.

37

'Who's that?' said Cleo, hearing heavy footsteps in the hall below. She slid down the ladder; it must be Arthur, good, she'd found another bouncy floorboard that he could fix.

'Hi, Cleo,' said a husky voice.

'Thomas!' said Cleo, running down the stairs. 'What on earth are you doing here? How did you get here? Why aren't you at school?'

Half-brother and half-sister, both sharing the same almost black hair and brilliant blue eyes of the Mountjoys, stared at each other.

'I've finished with school,' said Thomas. 'Aren't you pleased to see me?'

'Yes,' said Cleo. 'Finished? You don't mean they've thrown you out? Or have you run away again?'

'Cleo, wake up. It's the end of term. Hymns and dull yappings from the Dean in the Cathedral, brown envelopes with reports full of wicked lies about me, bagful of dirty kit, and that's it until January.'

'Of course,' said Cleo. 'So why aren't you with Lydia, or on your way to London?' Thomas lodged with his cousin Lydia and her husband in Eyot during term time, since he had refused ever to board again.

'I will tell you all about it,' said Thomas. 'Is there anything to eat? I haven't had a mouthful since breakfast, and I'm a bit peckish.'

As Thomas ate his way through the contents of fridge and larder, he told Cleo his plans.

'I was supposed to go to London, that's what Val had fixed, he doesn't get any less bossy, does he? But London's a bit grisly just before Christmas, and then he told me that Magdalena's going to be spending a few days with a friend, taking the twins with her. Well, you know what Val's like, nag, nag; I'm not staying alone in the flat with him, I'd be bound to get up his nose in a big way.'

'So you're staying with Lydia and Alban are you, for the duration?'

'Not so. They've buzzed off to America for Christmas. I've been staying there with Lydia's ma, who's all right, but I sort of thought she'd rather have the place to herself since she's got friends coming. And as I'm spending Christmas at Midwinter, which is great, with Magdalena and everyone, and Prue's there, too, only you know about that, I thought I might as well go straight to Sylvester's. I dumped my stuff, and then Lily said she was coming over here, and so I said I'd come too, and here I am.'

'Where's Lily?'

'She stopped off at the pub, wanted to pick up some eggs and have a chat, the landlady's a friend of hers. She'll be here in a minute. I hope she's thought about lunch, because you haven't got much to eat here, have you?'

His appetite for the moment assuaged, Thomas dragged Cleo off to give him a tour of the house. He was like a large dog, tail wagging, ecstatic about everything he saw, except for the new wing, which seemed very tame in comparison with the rest. 'And look at that holly,' he said, catching sight of it through a window. 'This is the most fantastic house ever. Who is this Henry Hazard it belongs to?'

'He's a Mountjoy cousin,' said Cleo. 'And he's the pits; do you know, he's going to let this house fall down, or more likely, demolish it?'

That stopped Thomas in his tracks. 'No! He can't. Surely it's an ancient monument or whatever; he won't be allowed to.'

'It's too far gone to save, that's the opinion.'

'It's outrageous,' said Thomas. 'If he doesn't want to live here, and he must be off his rocker if he doesn't, then why doesn't he sell it to someone who does?'

'No takers,' said Cleo. 'I do admit that it would have to be a buyer with more money than sense, but if I had any money, I'd buy it like a shot.'

'And it's haunted,' said Thomas.

'Do you feel ghostly presences?'

'No, but the guy who teaches me the piano was yapping on about it, Mr Wrackham. He's a bit obsessed about ghosts. I wouldn't mind staying up and waiting for them, in fact, that's what I'll do.'

'Only you aren't sleeping here.'

'Oh, yes, I am,' said Thomas. 'You need a chap in residence, big lonely house like this. I'll stay and keep you company.'

They were engaged in a brisk argument about this when Lily flew in, bidding Thomas to pipe down and bring the box in from the car.

'Thomas has got this mad idea that he's going to stay here,' said Cleo.

'Bound to happen, the minute he set eyes on this place,' said Lily. 'Best thing for him, plenty to keep him occupied here, and it'll get him out from under my feet.'

'But Lily . . .'

'You might as well give in right away,' said Lily. 'Young Thomas is an irresistible force. He'll get his own way in the end, if only by wearing everyone down to the ground.'

'Val will be annoyed.'

'When did that worry you?'

Cleo grinned. 'No, pleasing Val doesn't figure largely in my doings. Listen, Lily, there is a big problem, have you any idea how much Thomas eats? I couldn't cope with it.'

'He's a growing lad,' said Lily. 'Needs his food. Don't worry. Have you got a freezer here?'

'There are the outhouses,' said Cleo. 'Or most of the bedrooms. I'm sure the temperature never rises above zero in them.'

'We've got a small freezer that I can manage without,' said Lily more practically. 'I'll get someone to bring it over, and I'll fill it for you. Meanwhile, I brought some food over to keep you going.'

'Oh, good,' said Cleo, more than happy to benefit from Lily's cooking.

Thomas was in his element. He took charge of the branches and swaggage with vast enthusiasm, bullied Arthur into putting up hooks and finding wire, and generally filled the hall with his loud uneven voice and crashing footsteps.

'You're growing up to be just like Val,' said Cleo.

'Do you think I'll be as tall as him?' asked Thomas, peering through an armful of foliage.

'I didn't mean physically; I meant in your authoritative nature.'

'Born to command,' said Thomas unrepentantly, and went off to the kitchen for a quick forage and an interrogation of Mrs Grigson as to where exactly a long-lost pair of antlers might be.

'Danged boy,' said Arthur, who found it much more interesting in the hall than up in his gallery. 'I never did see a lad eat so much chocolate in one go.'

Giles and Lambert were beside themselves, flitting up and down the gallery and landings, leaning over the banisters, thoroughly stirred up. 'A lively youth,' said Giles indulgently.

'Yes, a likely lad,' said Lambert, equally indulgent.

'Mountjoy through and through,' said Giles. 'There was a Thomas Mountjoy at the castle here in my day, this one is the spitting image of him. As wild a fellow as you ever met, and a most excellent swordsman. As for wenching . . .'

'The Mountjoys have always been heathens,' said Lambert primly.

Thomas came thundering up the stairs and skidded to a halt, looking directly at Giles and Lambert. 'Hello,' he said in his friendly way.

'Cleo!' he shouted down into the hall a minute later. 'Cleo, who were these two types in funny clothes up on the landing here? They just vanished, where did they go? Have you got visitors?'

'Don't be silly,' said Cleo, unfolding a large faded red velvet curtain and taking a rule out of her pocket. 'You know who's here. Arthur, Mrs Grigson and us. And Adele when she's at home, which she isn't in the daytime.'

Thomas bounced down the stairs two at a time, causing Arthur to shut his eyes and Cleo to cover her ears. 'I tell you, I just saw two blokes up there.'

'Blokes?' said Giles indignantly. 'Blokes! Gentlemen, if you please,' he hissed over the banisters.

'There you are,' said Thomas. 'One of them just said something.'

'Thomas,' said Cleo in warning tones. 'No tricks, no mischief.'

'Me?' said Thomas in hurt tones.

Mrs Grigson brought in a tray of tea. 'He saw the ghosts,' she said in her most sepulchral voice. 'The young ones often do, and the Mountjoys have the sight.'

'I'm a Mountjoy, and I haven't seen anything,' said Cleo firmly.

'Haven't you?' said Thomas shrewdly. 'I mean, you may not have seen them, but I bet you've heard things.'

'An old house like this is full of strange noises.'

'And strange sights,' said Thomas with glee. 'They looked all right. One was in doublet and hose, like I had to wear in the school play when we did *Much Ado*, blooming uncomfortable they were, too. The other one looked a bit like a soldier, sort of Oliver Cromwellish, only more cheerful.'

'Needs his eyes examining if he thinks you look cheerful,' said Giles as he and Lambert returned to base.

'Could be tricky, this,' said Lambert. 'I suppose we'll just have to stay put until he goes. It's been a long time since anyone saw us.'

'Stay put?' Giles stared at his fellow spook in amazement. 'Stay put? In this poky little place? At Christmas? With all these people about? And more coming; I overheard Cleo and Thomas making plans for Sylvester's household to come to Haphazard for Christmas Eve.'

Lambert gave a longing sigh. 'It does sound fun.'

'No,' said Giles firmly. 'I'm not staying put; I wouldn't miss any of this for the world. And stop fussing. Nobody believes what youngsters say; they never have and they never will.'

Christmas Eve had been Thomas's idea. He was more than happy to go over to Midwinter for his Christmas dinner, because he knew that Lily would provide a feast of proportions to satisfy even him. 'But Christmas Eve is the most magical part of Christmas,' he told Cleo. 'You know it is.'

'In a way, yes,' said Cleo, remembering the anticipation of childhood, when on the night before Christmas time stood still, and the world was full of secrets and promises of delights to come.

'If we can get the fire going, we can burn a huge log in here,' said Thomas. 'And there must be a table we can bring in, we can eat in here.'

'Thomas, we're going to be a crowd,' said Cleo. 'I can't cook for all of us.'

'Feeble,' said a voice apparently emanating from the centre of a large fir tree which was making its uneven way through the door. 'And I offered to cook, didn't I?'

'Oh, hello Henry, it's you,' said Cleo, as Thomas split the air with an eldritch yell of delight. 'A Christmas tree!'

Henry and the landlord of the pub laid the huge tree down on its side and emerged red-faced from their efforts. 'Yes, a Christmas tree,' said Henry. He held out a hand to Thomas. 'Henry Hazard,' he said. 'Who are you, apart from quite obviously being a Mountjoy?'

'Thomas. Are you a cousin of mine?'

'I must be, if you're related to Val.'

'He's my father,' said Thomas.

'Your father? But . . .' Henry caught the tiny shake of Cleo's head and stifled his remark. 'But I should have known, you're very like him.' He looked around the hall, his eyebrows raised. 'Good God, you are having yourselves a time.'

'I'm staying here,' said Thomas, slightly on his guard. 'Cleo said I might, instead of being at Sylvester's. To lend a hand.'

'Of course,' said Henry gravely.

Thomas put two and two together. 'If you're Henry Hazard, are you the one who owns the house?'

'I am.'

Thomas's face darkened. 'So you're the one who's planning to pull it down? I think that's a disgrace.'

'It's a pity, yes,' said Henry. 'Only because of lack of funds, though. If I had the money, then perhaps . . . But I haven't,' he finished lightly.

'Cleo told me just now that you make buckets of money, that you draw cartoon stories, very weird and creepy, and they sell in their millions in the States.'

'Something like that.'

'Then how come you aren't rolling?'

Silence, broken by a fiendish cackle from Arthur. 'Because he's got a wife, boy, let that be a lesson to you. Don't go marrying no beautiful Americans with fancy lawyers, for if you do, you'll be as poor as the day you were born.'

'Thank you, Arthur,' said Henry.

'Oh,' said Thomas, sensing a situation rather beyond his understanding. 'Does she blood-suck you?'

'You could say that, but, on the whole, if you don't mind, I prefer not to discuss it.'

'Just because she's got a fancy lawyer? Well, I think that's pathetic. If I had lots of money I'd get my own fancy lawyer, and tell hers where to get off. Why don't you ask Val, he knows all kinds of really terrifying lawyers, he'd give you the name of a real thug.'

'Out of the mouths of babes,' murmured Cleo.

'I'll be off then,' said the landlord. 'Seeing as how you've got helping hands here, Henry.'

'Thanks a lot,' said Henry. 'I'll pop in for a pint later on.'

'Looks like you might need it,' said the landlord, sliding out of the door.

'Time somebody told Henry a few basic facts,' said Giles complacently.

'It was bound to happen,' agreed Lambert. 'When do you think he'll get in touch with this Val?'

'Tonight,' said Giles.

'Fits in very well,' said Lambert.

'Careful planning and skilful groundwork, Lambert, that's the secret.'

'Teach your grandmother to suck eggs,' said Lambert rudely.

38

Among the throng of well-wishers who came backstage to see Sylvester after the concert in New York was Mathilda Hazard.

Sylvester was talking jovially to some members of the press, a glass of champagne in his hand, when he heard a whiny voice in his ear.

'Hi, Sylvester. Great concert.'

Sylvester was surprised. The Mathilda he had known in earlier days had been a low-voiced number, what had happened to her voice?

'It's stress, Sylvester. The breakdown of my marriage was so traumatic, my analyst says it's affected my vocal cords. I've told my lawyer and he's working on it; boy, does Henry have a lot to answer for.'

Sylvester didn't believe that for a moment. 'Sounds as though you've been castrated, Mathilda,' he said. 'Pity, your voice used to be very attractive. I'll tell you what, it's because you've got so bony. It isn't anorexia, is it?'

Mathilda bared her teeth in a glacial smile. 'Always a wit, Sylvester. How's Henry, do you see anything of him these days? He has a new book coming out, I hear.'

Sylvester could see her eyes glazing over with royalty lust; Henry's extreme views of daily life always went straight into the bestseller lists. He was struck by a sudden impulse, to which he immediately succumbed. 'I believe so, but of course it's likely to be his last, it's tragic.'

'Last? Tragic? Is Henry ill?'

'Not ill as in expire, no. But he's injured his hand. I think it's RSI, naturally a disaster for an artist, just as it is for a musician.

We all live in dread of it, I'm sure you know that, because it means the end of one's professional career.'

'Nonsense,' said Mathilda, but there was an uncertain note in her voice. 'Did he hurt it, have an accident?'

'No, that wouldn't be so bad. This started with a strange creeping stiffness' – true, Sylvester told himself – 'which spread gradually to his fingers.' Also true. Sylvester saw no point in mentioning the logs. None of Mathilda's business.

'Sylvester, are you kidding me?'

Sylvester looked at her with his formidably trustworthy brown eyes. Always an asset, eyes like mine, he had remarked on more than one occasion. 'Mathilda, I rarely see Henry these days. I was shocked when I did bump into him, and saw him unable to use his hand.'

'Has he seen a doctor?'

'Several,' he said.

That was quite true, Henry had remarked to him that he had recently taken a train to Manchester and found himself in a compartment full of doctors attending some conference or other. 'Gave me a nasty fright, I can tell you, hunting in packs like that. They were talking about transplants all the way, I was quite relieved to escape with my heart and kidneys intact.'

'It's going to be hard for him. The trouble's there in his other hand, as well, although to a lesser degree, which means that he doesn't have much hope of trying to relearn his skills with his left hand. God knows how he's going to earn a living, because the public's so fickle, as you know. Once there are no more new books, sales of the old ones are bound to dwindle. Ah, excuse me, Mathilda, I've just seen another old friend . . .'

Sylvester wove his way across the room to greet an astonished casual acquaintance, a violinist he had once played with in Australia, who was perplexed by Sylvester's effusiveness.

'I do apologize,' whispered Sylvester. 'Needed to get away from someone.'

'Oh, sure,' said the violinist. 'How's Gabriel?' And then, 'If it's the thin party with the ruthless cheekbones, I'm afraid she's coming after you.'

Mathilda's voice was definitely lower. 'Just before I go, Sylvester,' she cooed, 'I'd like you to say hello to Myron.'

Myron was tall and cadaverous and, he informed Sylvester, big in computers.

'Good,' said Sylvester. 'Have you known Mathilda long?'

'A while,' he said, with a crow-like grimace in Mathilda's direction. 'In fact,' he said, lowering his voice, 'I'd like to marry Mathilda. Regularize a difficult situation, if you comprehend. I'm a religious man, myself, I don't know if you're a churchgoer, but it kind of irks me not to have Mathilda in my house as my wife as well as in my bed. Her bed, mostly, because the folks round where I live don't take too kindly to lady visitors staying on.'

Sylvester gave a rumble of suppressed laughter, but Myron took it in good part.

'Do you have trouble with your digestion? I can recommend a very good antacid, many of my friends have benefited from it.'

'Thank you,' said Sylvester.

'Well, Mathilda and I are on our way out. I gather the news from her ex isn't too good on the production front, and I want to say that what's bad news for him might just be good news for me. I can't leave Mathilda to starve, she's a lady who likes to spend, and if she hasn't got those dollars coming in from England, why, I guess I can step in and fix that gold band there on her finger.'

'Myron, we're just good friends.'

'Sure, sweetheart, but you want the big bucks, you've got to sign on the dotted line. Goodbye, Mr Tate, it's been a pleasure meeting you.'

'And you, Myron,' said Sylvester, giving him such a joyful handshake that the tall man winced. 'A real pleasure, I assure you.'

39

Snow.

Great flakes of snow floating down on to an already white landscape. Snow, which had dusted the fells weeks before, had come sweeping down on valleys and villages. Snow had transformed the world in its usual astonishing way, bringing in its blinding whiteness promises of candlelight, and greenery indoors, and treble voices, and bells ringing from lonely church towers, and all the other icons of Christmas.

Thomas hurled open Cleo's door.

'Snow! Cleo, it's snowing. It must have been snowing all night. Look at the garden. And the fells!'

Yawning and stretching, Cleo wrapped herself in the blanket she kept as a dressing-gown – nothing else was warm enough – and went to the window. And once there, she just gazed and gazed, the whiteness raising her spirits even while her teeth chattered.

From another window, Giles and Lambert also looked out into the whiteness. They watched a robin hopping in and out of the holly tree, cheeping insults down at Porthos, who prowled below, his coat lightly dusted with falling snow.

Then a door opened, and Thomas and Cleo came sliding and laughing out into the snow, gathering handfuls to toss at each other.

'Ah, youth,' said Lambert.

'Phone,' said Giles. 'Will they hear it?'

Thomas's keen ears had, and the two figures vanished back into the house.

'Sylvester,' said Lambert. 'Back from America.'

'Any news of Henry's wife?'

'Why should he say anything to Cleo. No, wait, he is.'

'You saw Henry's wife?' Cleo was saying, 'I hope you strangled her, foul woman.'

'You've never met her.'

'I still know she's foul. If she weren't bleeding Henry dry, and if Henry weren't putty in her hands, as he clearly is, then he'd have plenty of money for Haphazard.'

'Even if he had all his money, would he spend it on Haphazard?'

'Of course he would,' said Cleo.

Would he? Could she be sure about that? Had Henry ever really showed much interest in the house? Perhaps it was all in her mind, and Henry really cared no more for Haphazard than he would for some unmemorable suburban villa.

After all, Adele was unmoved by the charms of the house, and Will was only interested in it for its ghostly possibilities.

'Lives there a man with heart so dead,' she said sadly.

'What?' said Sylvester. 'I can't hear you properly, really the telephone line at Haphazard is a scandal. Mathilda was incredibly thin, perhaps she'll stop eating altogether and simply fade away.'

'Did she mention Henry?'

'A few words of abuse.'

'Oh,' said Cleo.

And then, because it was nearly Christmas, and it had snowed, and a buoyant Thomas was pacing the hall, whistling his tuneless whistle, she laughed and told Sylvester not to forget they were all coming over on Christmas Eve. 'Late afternoon,' she told him. 'For tea, and then charades.'

Sylvester groaned.

'Or sardines, or murder; Thomas and I haven't decided yet.'

'You make me feel very old,' said Sylvester. 'Yes, yes, of course we're all coming. Can't wait to see what Henry's going to dish up.'

'Henry's disappeared,' said Cleo.

'Gone shopping, I expect,' said Sylvester.

'For two days?'

'Ah, possibly not, then. Just as long as he turns up in time to get busy among the pots and pans.' He paused. 'I'm expecting Val and co this afternoon, and Gussie and Perry this evening. Won't you be pleased to see Perry again?'

'No,' said Cleo, and quickly put the phone down.

Thomas was determined to light the fire. He had brought up a box of firelighters, gathered a mound of kindling, and had a stack of newspapers at the ready. He knelt on the hearth and peered up into the immense chimney.

Mrs Grigson, passing through the hall with a broomstick, pursed her lips and pulled a longer face than usual. 'That's not the way, Thomas,' she said. 'You'll never get it going like that.'

Thomas was always ready to take advice, one of his more endearing features, thought Cleo as she sat on the stairs and watched Mrs Grigson cast an ancient fire-lighting spell.

To begin with, she commanded Thomas to move the large grate to a different place within the pink brickwork of the fireplace.

'Won't that make the smoke billow out into the hall?' asked Thomas.

'If a fire's going to smoke, then smoke it will,' said Mrs Grigson gnomically. 'Fire is a living thing, you remember that. You treat fire with respect and politely, and it'll do your bidding. All those smelly lighters and paper, that's summat or nowt when you're lighting a fire like this. Of course, in bygone years, they never let the fire go out, summer or winter. Some fires burned for more than two hundred years, never once going out.'

'Wow,' said Thomas.

Mrs Grigson was lighting sheets of paper and sending them ablaze up the chimney. 'Warm it up, burn off any old soot. You keep going with that, and by the time it's good and ready, I'll be back.'

Cleo had been longing to ask what Mrs Grigson was doing with the broomstick, or possibly where she might be going on it, but she felt it might seem an impertinent enquiry.

Thomas had no such qualms.

'Sauce!' said Mrs Grigson. 'I'm going to sweep the snow off

round the side, since you ask, young man, so as I can put some food down for the birds.'

'Oh good,' said Thomas. 'When we've lit the fire, can I borrow your broom and do some sweeping? It would be fun.'

He duly lit sheet after sheet of newspaper, and sent it flying up the chimney. 'All hooey,' he remarked cheerfully to Cleo. 'There's no way this paper can warm the chimney.'

'Wait and see,' advised Cleo. 'I expect Mrs Grigson is muttering incantations out there.'

'All in the minor key,' said Thomas. 'Must be hard living with her if she's always so doomy. Has she got an old man?'

'She's married to Roy. Mrs Grigson is always having to rush off because of Roy being taken poorly. Sylvester says Roy drinks.'

'Drinks what?' said Thomas, blowing an errant scrap of flaming paper back into the fireplace. 'Blood in a chalice, laced with poison, I should imagine.'

'She is a touch melodramatic,' agreed Cleo. 'Still, they've been married for thirty years, she told me that yesterday. Very proud of it, she is.'

'Amazing,' said Thomas. 'One of the teachers at school got married, and they split up after thirty *days*.'

'How depressing.'

'When I get married, it's going to be for good,' said Thomas seriously, sitting back on his heels and carefully lighting a page three girl in a sensitive spot.

'Not following in Val's footsteps, then.'

Thomas shook his head vigorously. 'No way. What a mess he's made of his life.'

'He wouldn't say so.'

'No, but it's all a bit sordid, really, isn't it? And you know what people say, that the twins are his, not Hugo's.'

Cleo knew how fond Thomas was of Magdalena, and knew also that Thomas, for all his worldly ways, wasn't old enough to understand or forgive Magdalena's fling with her late husband's nephew, by whom she had had the twins and to whom she was now married. 'People say anything, Thomas, especially about Val.'

'If he'd married Gussie, then maybe he would have turned out quite differently.'

'He's a rake,' said Cleo. And if he'd married my mum, thought Cleo, then Thomas wouldn't be here, or the twins, not to mention one or two others. 'And no point in ifs,' she said.

'Bet he's really tough on the twins when they grow up,' said Thomas. 'In by ten, who are you going out with, no, you can't spend the night at Elfrida's house. He'll be there with a horsewhip, just you wait.'

'You're probably right,' said Cleo, much amused at the thought of a moral Val.

'Talking of horsewhips,' said Thomas, 'Mr Wrackham collects them.'

There was a roaring sound as an extra large batch of paper was despatched up the chimney.

Cleo was startled at this piece of information; what a strange thing to collect. 'Perhaps he drives horses,' she suggested.

'Perhaps he does,' said Thomas, concentrating hard on his flames. 'It's not what they say at school, though.'

'What do they say at school?'

'Oh, nothing much,' said Thomas, becoming a clam.

Cleo's mind was still on Val. 'Magdalena's been married three times, hasn't she?'

'Yup,' said Thomas.

'To a drunkard, to a lord, and to Val.'

'Hugo was great,' said Thomas swiftly. 'She was happy with him.'

'I think, in her way, she's happy with Val.'

'Huh,' said Thomas.

Mrs Grigson gloomed back into the hall, where with what was clearly a special art, she coaxed the great fire into sturdy life.

Cleo mused about marriage as she watched the glowing hearth. What a shambles most marriages were. Look at all the wedded types she'd come across just recently. In fact, a strangely large number of them, as though some guiding hand was showing her marriage in many of its myriad forms.

Warning me off Perry, she concluded. Then she jumped, as Mrs Grigson heaved her broomstick out of the door, and Thomas gave a spectacular display of mind-reading.

'You aren't ever going to marry Perry, are you?'

'Um,' was all Cleo could manage.

'Perry's okay,' said Thomas, with the careless consideration of his age, 'but he's not right for you.' He sought for reasons, which, when they came, struck Cleo with the force of revelation. 'He isn't lively enough, and he doesn't make you laugh.'

40

Giles came back to find Lambert in a pensive mood, scrutinizing his chess pieces with solemn intensity.

'Wonderful out there,' he said, dusting some imaginary snow-flakes from a velvet sleeve. 'What's up? Someone, somewhere up to some unlawful merriment? That's what usually casts you into a mood.'

Lambert sighed heavily. 'Frivolity and levity; you don't change. I'm afraid there's bad news.'

'Bad news?' Giles was at once agog. 'What bad news?'

Lambert wasn't going to squander his advantage. 'While you were out cavorting in the snow . . .'

'Amusing Porthos,' said Giles airily.

'Cavorting,' repeated Lambert, 'Cleo was telephoning Perry.'

'Ah, was she, now. To say, "Perry, greatly as I love and esteem you, our hearts do not beat as one, and we can never be wed."'

'Not in those words,' began Lambert. 'And how did you know? Were you downstairs eavesdropping?'

'I may have been,' said Giles annoyingly. 'Passing through.'

'You didn't hear what Perry had to say, though.'

'I can imagine it.'

'I shall tell you just the same. He was sorry, but not surprised, and would always hold Cleo in great affection. If she didn't find it embarrassing, he would still come north for Christmas, because he'd promised to bring Gussie, and didn't want to let her down. Had Cleo told Gussie, if not, should he break the news?'

'Ha,' said Giles. 'Good girl, high time she wriggled out of that net.'

'Faithless,' said Lambert. 'And all for lust of Will, whom we know to be a fellow of strange tastes and wicked ways.'

'Not a bit of it,' said Giles. 'Cleo lusts after Will out of habit, him being such a very fine young man, in many ways, although hardly to be trusted once the bedroom door is locked. Never mind that, Cleo's thoughts can now turn in new directions.'

Giles hummed a line or two of a bawdy ballad popular in his day, to do with a maid and her wanton ways and a country lane; Lambert, scandalized, left in a hurry without even putting his chess pieces away.

41 ∫

'You've given Perry the push?' said Thomas, delighted and intrigued. 'When did you do that? And for good, or yet another postponement.'

'Yesterday,' said Cleo. 'For good, since you ask.'

'Don't sound so dreary about it, excellent move, I'd say.'

'I feel bad about it,' said Cleo, who was overcome by mixed sensations of guilt, relief and pique that, after all, Perry hadn't seemed to mind much.

'I expect he'll marry your mum,' said Thomas carelessly.

Cleo couldn't believe her ears. 'Perry? And my mother? Oh, how absurd; what a totally ridiculous suggestion.'

'Why? They're about the same age, aren't they? Both into art, and Perry probably finds your mum a lot less trouble-some than you. Val says they've been seen around town a bit, too.'

'You're a silly boy, with an idle tongue and no sense,' said Cleo crossly. 'Mum isn't going to marry anyone. She's never wanted to, why should she think about it now?'

'P'raps she wants to settle down,' said an unrepentant Thomas.

'Besides, Perry's dull.'

'One person's dull is another person's intelligent conver-sation.'

'You, Thomas, are a pain.'

Gussie marry Perry indeed; Thomas had taken leave of his senses. Why am I so furious at the suggestion? Cleo asked herself, knowing full well why. It was fine by her if Perry buzzed off and found someone else to marry; she would expect him to do that. What she didn't care for was the idea of her mother acquiring a husband. Any husband, when it came to it, but Perry would be particularly hard to take.

Cleo shook herself into sense. As if Gussie would, she told herself stoutly.

Thomas's mind had finished with Perry, and was running on culinary tracks. 'If Coz Henry doesn't tip up fairly smartish, bearing many bags of goodies, there's going to be a starving mob here tonight. There's barely enough food in the kitchen to keep me and Porthos going for more than a day or two, I have to point out, let alone the rest of you.'

'We'll have to go to Eyot, to the shops,' said Cleo. 'What hell that'll be, on Christmas Eve.'

'Sold out of everything tasty, too,' said Thomas.

There was a sudden thud or two on the front door, and it opened slowly, the velvet curtain hung by Cleo as a draught excluder doing its job by first billowing into the hall and then wrapping itself round the incomers.

'Help,' came a muffled voice. Then there was a word in a strange language which was undoubtedly a rude oath, and the unmistakable squeal of a very young baby.

'Prue,' said Cleo, rushing to the door to disentangle Prue, Geza and Felicia.

'Oof,' said Prue. 'I wasn't quite expecting the curtain. Good heavens, what a fantastic job you've done on the hall. Look, Felicia, look at the Christmas tree. Bigger than Sylvester's,' she told Cleo. 'Hello, Thomas.'

Thomas, who was Felicia's slave, was tickling the baby's nose with his finger, an operation which she took in very good part.

'Already a flirt,' said Geza. 'There is going to be trouble with this one, she will run away with people like her mother.'

'It's lovely to see you,' said Cleo, 'but you're very early, and I have to break the bad tidings to you that there's no food, because horrible Henry hasn't turned up, as promised, to cater for the masses.'

'No problem,' said Geza, 'Henry will be here shortly, with many things to eat. We fixed it, Henry and I, that tonight we eat Hungarian, so I have come to give expert advice, and soon Sylvester will be here also, since he says he knows all about

Hungarian food. This I do not believe, but we will have a good time in the kitchen, nevertheless.'

'Typical,' said Cleo, leading the way down to the kitchen. 'Offering to cook, and then roping in all his friends.'

'Sound field work,' said Thomas, loping along behind.

Geza put two carrier bags on the table and looked around the kitchen. 'So,' he said. 'Now, there is the range, and we have to light it, this is what Henry said.'

'We do the dirty work, naturally,' said Cleo. 'While Henry is elsewhere. I haven't a clue how to light it, in any case. In fact, I doubt if it's been used these hundred years.'

Thomas was peering into one of the ovens. 'I think you're wrong, Cleo, this is all quite clean. I suppose we just light a fire in the grate and the whole thing hots up.'

'Easier said than done.' Cleo was feeling very put out by Henry's high-handed ways. 'And no Mrs Grigson to make spells until after lunch. Oh, bother Henry. And it's no use saying he'll be here; he isn't.'

'Yes, he is,' said Henry, choosing that moment to edge his way into the kitchen, burdened by two cardboard boxes and several carrier bags which dangled dangerously from his fingers.

The yule log, a great root dragged in the day before by Cleo and Thomas, smouldered and flickered in the hall. Above the door were the impressive pair of antlers which Thomas had finally unearthed, festooned with a chain of twinkling bells. Thomas could lean over and touch the top of the Christmas tree from the turn of the stairs, as he pointed out with pride, and the banisters were swagged from top to bottom with green branches intertwined with red ribbons.

Four tables of varying sizes had been pushed together and covered with the best white sheets. 'I suppose I shall be sleeping between blankets tonight,' said Henry as he passed through the hall.

'It's great,' said Thomas, surveying his handiwork with satisfaction. He cast a sideways look at Henry. 'Just as long as there's plenty to eat tonight.'

Put in his place, Henry retreated to the kitchen, followed by

Thomas, who felt it was time for a little something. There, all was chaos, with Sylvester managing the range, Geza pounding hot peppers and spicy things, and a pile of meat awaiting Henry's further attentions.

Thomas inspected these preparations with approval. 'There must be enough potatoes, though,' he said. 'And what's the pudding going to be?'

Giles and Lambert were equally busy, flitting from the bedroom in the new wing to see that Felicia was sleeping the sleep of the just, round the kitchen to enjoy the mêlée and hubbub, into the hall to dance among the greenery and then to posts at the windows to watch out for new arrivals.

'Who's this?' asked Lambert, peering over Giles's shoulder. 'Is that Perry's car?'

'No, too black, too powerful,' said Giles. 'Ho, I spy a Mountjoy.' He watched Valdemar swing himself out of the car, cast a dark look up at the house, shake his head, and go round to the passenger door to open it for Magdalena.

Twins, a boy and a girl, tumbled out from the back. They stared up at the window, and waved.

'Mountjoys, definitely,' said Giles.

'They saw us,' said Lambert.

'They would,' said Giles.

The family scattered inside the house, Magdalena to find the cooks and the twins to find the delightful pair they had spotted at the window; Valdemar went striding through the house, shouting for Cleo.

Cleo, on her way to the hall, stiffened. She looked down the stairs at her tall and formidable father. 'Before you say a word, I've given Perry the push, and there are to be no recriminations, no barking at me. Okay?'

'I know you've given Perry the push, and about time too, what a waste of everyone's time.'

'How do you know?'

'Rang Gussie, she told me. She sounded relieved, but thinks you're never going to get married.'

Cleo sat down on a handy stair. 'I'm set to wither into

spinsterish middle age, am I? And you needn't look so amused, it's not funny.'

'Plenty of men about, Cleo, and you've never had any shortage of them in your life.'

Not until recently, no, Val was right. That was fine when you were a student and had hours of happy time every day, and the promise of new joys every night. Then came reality, the busy job, the long hours. No time for dalliance, no leisure for meeting people and getting to know them, or even for more than the odd fling. And those had been far from satisfactory.

And so to Perry. Growing up time, agreeing to be part of the adult life, half of a regular couple. Nearly a paid-up member of what had, Cleo thought crossly, to be the most impossible institution mankind had created. Marriage.

'Maybe some people aren't meant to get married,' she said, standing up and walking away from her father along the landing.

'Maybe it hardly matters at your age,' said Valdemar. 'Concentrate on your job, for God's sake, make some money, enjoy life.'

'I hate that job,' said Cleo.

'Now you sound like a distressed teenager bitching about school. It's a good job, highly paid, demanding, you do it well. And you're in London, at the centre of things. Plenty going on all around you. Just what you like.'

'I don't know,' said Cleo, running her hand against the rough panelling. 'You come to a house like this, centuries old, and you wonder whether London really is the centre of life.'

'Don't be so bloody stupid.' He looked at her sharply. 'You haven't got any funny ideas about throwing up your work and coming to vegetate in Eyotshire, have you?'

'I might have, and if I do, it's entirely my own business.'

'What a waste. Good brain, excellent education, on your way to a prosperous career, what are you going to do? Be a waitress in some tourist café, hang out with the other failures who can't take the pace of London?'

'Oh, piss off,' said Cleo. 'You aren't shoving piles of money around for a living, you actually have something to show for your work at the end of the year. You've got a bank here, a shored-up cathedral there. What do I have?'

'A fat bonus.'

'Oh, rats,' said Cleo. 'I'm fed up with the whole business.'

Upon which defeatist words, there was a loud bang and a flash, and Valdemar, much startled, whirled round. 'What the hell was that? Christ, the electrics in this place must be lethal.'

'Nothing to do with the electrics,' said Cleo, laughing once she had recovered from the instant shock and had realized what the bang was. 'It's Will, the ghost hunter. One of his cute tricks, he wants to take photos of the ghosts.'

'Photos of the ghosts? I never heard such absolute nonsense in my life. Will, who's Will anyway?'

'Stop shouting. He's Will Wrackham, a friend of Sylvester's, a musician, teaches at Thomas's school among other things. He's been staying here on and off, hunting the ghosts.'

'Will Wrackham. Oh, him. I hope you haven't been up to anything with him, Cleo, that's not your scene at all.'

'Will happens to be an extremely attractive man, and . . .'

'That's not what I meant. Where is he? He'll have to clear up this mess. And, come to think of it, where's this old schoolfriend who's been staying here with you? Ada somebody.'

'Adele,' said Cleo. 'She should be here, and Will, they're spending Christmas at Haphazard; Will thinks it could be a good haunting time. They must have got held up in Eyot.'

'Hauntings,' said Valdemar scornfully. 'What does he expect? A headless monk? Bony beings in the closet? If there are ghosts here, which there probably are, then he should just leave them well alone.'

Cleo stared at Valdemar. 'Do you believe in ghosts?'

'What do you mean, believe? Old houses, and new ones, too, can have extra life, if that's the right word, hanging about the place. Yes. We've got several up at the castle. They don't bother me, and I don't bother them.'

'Oh,' said Cleo, stunned by this insight into her father; the one man she would have sworn was totally rational.

'Hey, anyone there?' Thomas's voice floated up from the hall. 'Tea time, Sylvester says, make the most of it, we won't be dining early. Lily's brought a cake, and she's made lots of little sandwiches.'

'What is this, a children's party?' said Valdemar irritably. Then there was the thunder of tiny feet; the twins, drawn from afar by the prospect of cake and sandwiches, came hurtling down from the gallery to arrive panting at Valdemar's feet.

'Come on, Pops,' said Hughie, and Helena grabbed Valdemar by the hand and tugged.

'Pops!' said Valdemar. 'Oh, very well.'

'Listen, Lily,' said Helena, her mouth stuffed with egg sandwich. 'There are two men in funny clothes up there.'

'Helena, not with your mouth full,' said Magdalena automatically. 'What men?'

'Funny types,' said Hughie. 'They're all right.'

'Cleo, who else is in the house?'

'No one,' said Cleo.

'They've met up with the ghosts, I expect,' said Henry. 'They are reputed to like children.'

'Oh, really,' said Magdalena.

'It's all right, Mummy,' said Helena. 'They're dead men, they aren't really here at all.'

'Ha,' said Sylvester.

'Someone at the door,' said Henry, winking at Cleo and going to do battle with the curtain. Will and Adele, chilled, bright-eyed and hand in hand came into the hall.

'Shut the door,' said Sylvester. 'Or the fire will smoke us all out.'

'Did you get held up in Eyot?' Cleo asked, smiling at Will.

'Sort of,' said Adele, pulling off a glove and waving her left hand in the air. 'Will and I just got married.'

Stunned silence, broken by cries of congratulations amid the clucks of surprise.

And I never suspected it, thought Cleo, shocked.

Henry materialized at her side. 'And the bride wore black and blue,' he murmured in her ear.

'What?'

'They've got a pre-nuptial contract, stating exactly what they may do to each other. Quite original, don't you think?'

He's nuts, thought Cleo, and then the light began to dawn. 'No!' she said.

'Yes,' said Henry. 'Didn't you realize? All those bruises? Screams in the night? Not my cup of tea,' he went on, 'but each to their own. SM is very fashionable these days, so I'm told. I shall put some in my next book.'

42

'Why?' Cleo asked Adele, as she sat on her bed, wrapped in the cover to keep the chill away, and watched her friend put on a pair of pretty silver safety-pin earrings.

'Why what?'

'Pain. Pain and sex.'

'Sex with pain is very, very exciting. Much better, a million times better. For me, and for Will. Have you ever tried it?'

Cleo could recall a spanking incident after a very drunken party, but the spanker had got kneed for his troubles. 'It's never appealed,' she said.

'I've always found normal sex a drag. No shooting stars, no sensations, nothing. Get a bit of the hardware going, and some rough stuff, and that's quite different. Same for Will. Can't really get it up without a bit of this and that. When he does, then no one better.'

Adele looked at Cleo's face in the mirror and laughed. 'Shocked?'

'No, perplexed,' said Cleo. 'Why did you get married?'

'Because Will and I are thunderingly in love, and can't live without one another. The usual reasons, you know. Same as everyone else; if what we choose to do in bed, with each other's agreement, is a bit different to most people, well, so be it. All marriages are weird arrangements in their own ways. I think you and Perry are fairly weird, if you don't mind my saying so.'

Adele leant forward to apply a perfect rich red bow to her lips.

'I'm not going to marry Perry,' said Cleo.

'Good for you,' said Adele. 'Hopelessly wrong for you. Why don't you marry Henry? You'd have fun with him.'

'Last person on earth I'd marry,' said Cleo with vehemence.

First Thomas, and now Adele.

'He fancies you,' Thomas had remarked as he watched Cleo count out spoons.

'Who does?'

'Cousin Henry. I like him.'

'I don't,' said Cleo, losing her place and having to start counting all over again.

'You do really,' said Thomas, skipping out of her way. 'Hey, careful with those forks.'

Now Adele was at it. Cleo got up from the bed and shook the cover off. 'You'll freeze in that dress,' she told Adele.

'You go and put your woolly underwear on,' said Adele. 'Me, I'm going to have fun. This is my wedding night, remember? Once in a lifetime.'

I bet, thought Cleo, as she jogged along the passage to her room. She could hear voices down below, Geza discussing the Tokany they were having for dinner, Valdemar talking to Sylvester about New York. And there was her mother's voice, asking where she, Cleo, was, and being told she'd gone to change, would be down in a minute.

And Perry's voice, solicitously asking Gussie what she wanted to drink.

'Creep,' said Cleo to Porthos, who had materialized beside her and was looking up at her, his magnificent tail waving from side to side. She picked him up, tickling him under the chin, and then burying her face in his long, soft fur.

'Feeling sorry for yourself?' said a voice. 'You'll sneeze if you do that.'

Henry.

'No, I'm not feeling sorry for myself, I'm just sharing Christmas wishes with Porthos. And I won't sneeze, as it happens, I'm not allergic to cats.'

'What are you allergic to?' said Henry.

Cleo didn't answer for a moment, she had just noticed how Henry's mouth crinkled at the edges when he smiled. Which he did a lot. Nice mouth, actually. Good firm lips, Cleo couldn't bear a sloppy mouth. 'What?' she said, pulling herself together, God, she must be suffering from extreme frustration if her mind had started to wander in that direction. 'Couples,' she said quickly. 'I'm allergic to couples. Listen to them down there.'

'Can't hear them,' said Henry.

It had suddenly gone very quiet. Then, on the chill air came the sound of a lute, the haunting sounds of a Burgundian carol.

'Whoever it is, or was,' said Henry, 'that's some musician.'

Porthos had slipped from Cleo's grasp and was stalking away to the stairs which led up to the gallery.

Henry put out a hand. 'Let's go and survey the holly tree from the gallery window. The moon is up, and will be streaming in; I have a yen to see it.'

'I have to change,' said Cleo.

'Later,' said Henry.

'Goodness,' said Cleo, looking at the moonlight patterned across the dusty wooden floor as it flooded in through the mullioned windows.

'There's a door at the end,' said Henry. 'Funny, I never noticed that before.'

'It's just a trick of the light,' said Cleo, following him towards the music, louder now. 'You see, unbroken panelled wall.'

Henry looked hard at the panelling.

'Nothing there,' said Cleo. 'If there had been, the searchers would have found it centuries ago.'

'Where did Porthos go?' asked Henry abruptly.

'Back along the gallery?'

'I didn't see him.'

Miaow.

'That came from the other side of the panelling,' said Henry.

'It did sound like it.'

'And there's that damned lute again. There must be a door here somewhere. A secret catch, do you think?'

'If there is, it has to be at cat level,' said Cleo.

'Very logical,' said Henry, dropping to his knees and eyeing the wood closely. 'What's so funny?'

'You. Me. Up here, scuffling round in the dust, hunting for a large cat and a ghostly lutenist. What a way to spend Christmas Eve.'

Henry got up and dusted his knees. 'It's mystifying,' he said. 'And indeed, what a way to spend Christmas Eve. However, I always think of Christmas Eve as a mad and unruly time, when the spirits of disorder come out to stalk the land, so if you don't mind, or even if you do, I shall kiss you.'

Cleo was too slow to move out of his way, and two seconds later was enjoying herself far too much to even think of moving out of his way. She leaned back against the wall, lost in a haze of unblistery sensuality but still aware of how excellently taut and trim Henry was, when there was a click, and both of them fell through the panelling to land in an untidy heap on the floor.

A candle flickered, and went out.

Henry sat up first, then got to his feet, hauling Cleo up in a very unloverlike way, she felt, as she brushed herself down.

'Priest's hole,' hissed Henry. 'We've found the priest's hole.'

'No priest in residence,' siad Cleo, with a swift look round.

'Look,' said Henry, holding her tightly by the hand. 'There's a lute, over there, on the window seat.'

Cleo inspected the oak table which was set against the wall. 'A chess set,' she said.

'And books.'

'And Porthos,' said Cleo, nearly jumping out of her skin as the cat brushed against her leg. 'And what's that beside the lute?'

'An old field telephone,' said Henry, astonished. 'That's a very modern touch, if this room's been undisturbed for decades.'

'It isn't very dusty,' Cleo pointed out. 'Look, there's Mrs Grigson's feather duster propped up in the corner over there.'

'Do you think she's been up here?'

Cleo shook her head, and moved over to the window. 'Shutters, you see. And the window built to look like one of all those running along the gallery. You'd have to do a careful count to notice.'

'And no one ever has.'

'I wonder who they are,' said Cleo.

'Those two, I should think,' said Henry.

Two pictures hung on the walls. One was a fine miniature of an Elizabethan gent, with one leg resting over the other in classic Hilliard style. It showed a bony-faced man, with dark hair. 'Tell he's an ancestor of yours,' said Cleo. 'Same crinkly hair.'

'Crinkly?'

'I rather like it,' said Cleo, flicking her fingers through it. 'And that bigger picture must date from the Civil War.'

'I know who he was,' said Henry. 'That's Lambert Hazard, who took over Haphazard House during the sequestrations, married the daughter of the house and changed his name.'

'They both came to sticky ends,' said Cleo. 'They're in a book I found in Eyot.'

Henry joined Cleo by the window, and they looked out at the holly tree, shadowy and eerie against the moonlit snow. Henry draped an arm round Cleo. 'Gather up Porthos, Cleo, we're intruding.'

'I don't think they mind.'

'No, but they will if anyone comes looking for us.'

'Cheer up, Cleo,' said Sylvester later, as he poured her a glass of fizz. 'Christmas Eve, a time for celebration.'

'I'm feeling very happy, Sylvester,' she said. 'It's just thinking, this is Haphazard's last Christmas.'

And what will become of the two upstairs, she wondered, do they face eternity in the shadows, if the house goes?

'Pooh,' said Sylvester. 'I've got some news on that front.' He raised his voice above the hubbub. 'We have to drink to two weddings,' he said, lifting his glass. 'Adele and Will, for one.'

'And?' said Magdalena, with a swift look at Gussie and Perry.

'And Mathilda, who was hitched to Myron at noon New York time.'

Henry blinked. 'What?'

'Yup. She decided that Myron's millions were more certain than your royalties, Henry.'

'Excellent,' said Valdemar. 'Best news this year. You were asking me about lawyers, Henry, and I'll give you the name of a really good one, get your affairs sorted out. And don't get married again, for Christ's sake. You're bound to be taken for a ride again if you do.'

'Oh, I don't know,' said Henry, his eyes on Cleo.